For. Ashton

Big Hugs. from Bear Cub.

Wendy Szymanski.

Sparky

The World's Most Lovable and Mischievous Bear Cub

Wendy Shymanski

iUniverse, Inc.
New York Bloomington

Sparky
The World's Most Lovable and Mischievous Bear Cub

iUniverse books may be ordered through booksellers or by contacting:

iUniverse
1663 Liberty Drive
Bloomington, IN 47403
www.iuniverse.com
1-800-Authors (1-800-288-4677)

Because of the dynamic nature of the Internet, any Web addresses or links contained in this book may have changed since publication and may no longer be valid. The views expressed in this work are solely those of the author and do not necessarily reflect the views of the publisher, and the publisher hereby disclaims any responsibility for them.

ISBN: 978-1-4401-8754-4 (sc)
ISBN: 978-1-4401-8756-8 (dj)
ISBN: 978-1-4401-8755-1 (ebk)

Library of Congress Control Number: 2009911761

Printed in the United States of America

iUniverse rev. date: 11/24/2009

For Sparky and Lucy, my two favorite bears.

For all the children of the world.
May you always share our beautiful planet with the magnificent grizzly bear.
May you always walk in peace with the spirit of the grizzly bear.

Contents

Acknowledgments

Thank you to all of the humans and animals that have given huge parts of your lives and energy to help preserve the Khutzeymateen Valley and ensure the amazing ecosystems that dwell there are safe and protected for all time.

To Dan Wakeman for his friendship and genuine love and caring for the bears.

To all the humans on the planet who recognize the importance of nature's balance as they help to preserve all species on our beautiful and fragile planet.

To Cal Pinnell for all his encouragement, patience, strength, and love.

To all the brilliant folks at iUniverse for their professional guidance and kindly encouragement.

To Canada Council for the Arts.

And most of all, to the bears and all of the other creatures of the Khutzeymateen Valley that patiently allowed my eyes to gawk at them in wonder and awe for ten seasons. I thank you for many reasons but mostly because watching you humbled me and taught me so very much about life and about myself.

Foreword

The mistakes, whether known or unknown, of those humans who came before us are taking their toll on our fragile planet and all species who dwell here. Please help to keep our Earth, the bears, and all life that is left on this beautiful unique planet alive and healthy. Please do your part so that those that cannot speak human languages will have a home, just as they have had for hundreds and thousands and millions of years. The bears and all creatures on the planet thank you.

Introduction

On the northwest shores of British Columbia, one of the last remaining natural treasures on our fragile planet lies pristine and protected as it has for a million years. This treasure is the Khutzeymateen Grizzly Bear Sanctuary. The 111,197 acres (45,000 hectares) mountainous maritime provincial park includes the Khutzeymateen Valley, river basin, estuary, and fourteen-mile (twenty-three-kilometer) long inlet that empties into the north Pacific Ocean. This remarkable harborage is home to hundreds of species of flora and fauna, including approximately sixty grizzly bears. One of these majestic grizzlies is a tiny bear cub, Sparky, in his first year of life, or as science calls first-year cubs, "cub of the year." This is the story of Sparky's adventures, experiences, and struggles as a cub of the year in the Khutzeymateen Grizzly Bear Sanctuary.

Chapter 1:
Spring Songs and Tickles

Wisps of morning fog hung in the giant ancient Sitka spruce, western hemlock, and red cedar trees of Khutzeymateen Valley. The fog draped the trees like beautiful long tresses of a mystical goddess, invisible except for the long locks that intertwined with the branches. As she playfully danced and skipped through the forest, her tresses gently lifted and fell, tickling the needles of the huge trees. Thicker strips of gray and white fog obscured the mountain peaks, breaking only momentarily to tease the peaks with a glimpse of the obscured valley.

The Khutzeymateen Inlet, with its towering peaks thrusting skyward out of the briny water, stretched like a long arm from the Pacific Ocean to the mouth of the Khutzeymateen River and estuary. A layer of mist hung above the inlet, just high enough off the water for harbor seals to poke their shiny, sleek heads with big bulbous eyes up above the water for a look. They scouted the surface for a fish breakfast and any approaching danger.

The warm breath of Princess Spring began to lovingly blow from the south, slowly melting the deep blanket of snow left by Father Winter. Gradually and with much effort, the princess convinced the old man to again lift his insulating layers and the two-meter-thick snowpack was reduced to small patches of white that dotted the thick, soft bright green moss carpeting the rainforest floor. All along the inlet shoreline the brown, red,

1

and orange colors of fall and winter were replaced by the vibrant green of sedge grass shoots. The pungent smell of skunk cabbage filled the air as the powerful plants pushed their yellow flowers up toward the sky from deep beneath the moist, spongy humus. Over a few weeks, their one- to four-foot leaves would slowly follow.

The strong aroma of skunk cabbage filled the river valley. It floated up the mountainside and entered the den where Lucy had been hibernating all winter. Her nose twitched from side to side as she woke from her deep sleep. The five hundred–pound (226-kilograms) grizzly bear stretched her legs and yawned. She opened one eye and looked around the den she had scratched out between two huge boulders in an old rockslide covered with huge hemlock and white spruce trees. Enough light filtered through the dense tree roots above her head to allow her to see her new family. In early February Lucy had given birth to her first cub. Lucy looked at her new cub and smiled as love flowed through her heart. Then she chuckled. The little male cub was sleeping on his back, propped up against a tree root with all four feet sticking up in the air. All four of his paws moved frantically, as if he were running through a large field of daisies. His nose twitched, and low *woofing* noises escaped his flapping lips.

"Oh, my little one. I can tell you will be energetic and full of mischief," she said and then laughed as he suddenly stretched his legs straight up into the air. Then, like a cartoon character with his legs still stiff, the cub flopped over onto his side and began snoring deeply and loudly.

"I can tell you will be full of fire," Lucy said as she watched as her cub's feet began to move frantically again. "You, my cub, will be called Sparky."

Lucy let Sparky sleep for a few more hours, and then she quietly began to sing a sweet happy spring bear song to wake him.

"*The breath of spring has warmed the air,*
It is time to wake from our cozy lair.
Old Man Winter's whites have left,
The palette of spring is at her best.

So come, my cub, and open your eyes,
For you will have a big surprise.
The world is yours to explore and see,
The glory of nature's majesty.

Sedge grass pokes up through the ground,
Coming to life without a sound.
Birds are fluttering in the air,
Riding the wind without a care.

So come, my cub, and open your eyes,
For you will have a big surprise.
The world is yours to explore and see,
The glory of nature's majesty.

Dragonflies dance the song of spring,
Drying the dew upon their wings.
Fish will jump to catch a fly,
Thinking that they can touch the sky.

So come, my cub, and open your eyes,
For you will have a big surprise.
The world is yours to explore and see,
The glory of nature's majesty.

Tawny deer their eyes do flash,
As they graze the shoots of grass.
Wolves will howl from dusk to dawn,
The wind of spring will carry their song.

So come, my cub, and open your eyes,
For you will have a big surprise.
The world is yours to explore and see
The glory of nature's majesty.

Now come, my cub, and open your eyes,
For you will have a big surprise.
The world is yours to explore and see,
The glory of nature's majesty. "

After she was finished the song, Sparky was still sound asleep. She patiently waited for the sleeping prince to wake, but Sparky was definitely enjoying his long winter sleep.

Lucy chuckled again to herself as Sparky continued to snore loudly. "My goodness, he is so noisy!"

She waited for a long while, and then she whispered, "Sparky. Sparky. Wake up." But the bear cub continued to madly saw the logs of the forest down. Lucy sat up and looked at him. "How am I going to wake you up?" she wondered out loud. A big mischievous grin spread across her face. Lucy giggled as she slowly and silently began to slink over to her cub. She lowered her head right beside his tummy, took a big deep bear breath, and blew as hard as she could on Sparky's exposed tiny pink bear belly.

Sparky just about went through the roof of the den from the shock of his awakening. Lucy kept on blowing as hard as she could. When Sparky realized what was going on, he burst into fits of laughter. Lucy persisted with her blowing, and he lost his breath from laughing so hard.

"Ha hee hee hoo tee he ha ... ho, Mom ... ha tee ha hee ha ... s-sttt-op. Tee hee ho ha tee hee ... ppple-eeass-ssse!" Sparky managed to plead.

Lucy was also overcome with fits of laughter. Finally she was able to say, "At last you are awake from your winter sleep. Now we can leave the den, and you can see your home for the first time."

Both bears continued to giggle, but the minute Lucy sat back on her big bear bum and turned her head away from Sparky, he jumped up and rubbed her ribs with his tiny bear paws. Sparky and Lucy rolled on the ground, laughing out of control. Lucy let her tiny cub tickle her, and they wrestled and laughed for a long time. Then finally she said, "Okay, you little tickle bug, it is time to nurse before I take you outside the den for your first look at the big old world."

Sparky stopped playing and sat down. He looked at Lucy, very concerned.

"Mom, do we have to go outside? Well … er … I'm a bit scared," he said quietly.

Lucy looked at her baby bear and nuzzled him with her long nose. "You will love exploring the world. There is so much to learn and see. I will make sure no harm comes to you. The world is there for us to enjoy. You will be fine."

"Well okay, Mom. I know I can trust you. My mom is the best!" he exclaimed. Then he snuggled on Lucy's chest and began to suckle and purr loudly like a contented kitten.

Chapter 2:
Noni the Giant

"All right, my wee one, it is time to venture out into the world and make our way down the mountain to our summer home at Mouse Creek," Lucy whispered to Sparky as he lay peacefully on her chest.

"I guess so, Mom, but can I hide behind your leg when we go out?"

"Yes, honey, and your big old mom will protect you. We just have to constantly listen for danger, like approaching male bears. Otherwise the world is ours to explore and enjoy." Lucy gently tipped Sparky onto the ground. She then stood up and waited by the den entrance. She poked her nose out into the spring air, sniffed deeply, and looked around the area. "Spring smells wonderful and there is no sign of danger. Are you ready to see Waipo, Sparky?"

"Well, I ... er ... well ... I think ... ah ... okay!" Sparky nervously said as he hid behind Lucy's leg.

"All right then, here we go."

Sparky followed at his mother's leg as she left the den. Rays of bright sunlight broke through the fog and streamed between the huge old-growth trees of the forest, surrounding the bears. The rays caught the fur on Lucy's back, and the tips glistened silver in the sunshine. She stopped, stretched, and took a long deep breath of the fresh morning air. "Oh my, it is good to be out of that stuffy old den. What do you think of your home, Sparks?"

There was no response from her cub. Lucy turned her head to see Sparky standing with his nose pressed up against her leg and his eyes shut.

"Sparky, what do you think of your home?" she gently asked.

"I am afraid to open my eyes, Mom. I am really scared."

"Oh, honey. Open your eyes and look at Waipo. The rainforest is truly beautiful, and just down the trail, there is someone very special to greet you. Open your eyes and we will go say hello."

Slowly Sparky opened one eye, then quickly opened the other, then quickly closed them again.

"It is so bright out here, Mom! It looks beautiful, but it hurts my eyes."

Lucy laughed. "Just give it a few minutes and your eyes will adjust to the light. We have been in the den all winter, so your eyes need to open slowly. Now try again, but this time do it slowly."

Sparky carefully opened his eyes. He blinked and blinked and was finally able to open them fully. At first he stood quietly, and his tiny bear head moved slowly from side to side, looking at everything surrounding them. He put his soft snout in the air and began to deeply sniff the dense humid rainforest air as his eyes took in the vibrant greens of the moss, lichen, and liverwort plants that surrounded him. Carefully he stepped onto a patch of soft moss and gently marched his feet up and down, sighing and giggling at the warm cushy wonderful feeling on his toes.

He looked at a huge six-foot (183 centimeter) wide tree trunk beside him. He started to lose his balance and slowly sat down as his eyes followed the trunk skyward until it became lost in a fog patch one hundred feet above them. Something flew out of the tree, and Sparky's head snapped to another tree where the creature landed. He watched the little brown bird zip around the tree trunk until a buzzing sound near his feet made him look down at a patch of bearberry covered with dew. A large bumble bee covered in moisture droplets and too cold to fly stumbled around on the plant's flower near Sparky's foot. Sparky playfully licked the droplets off the leaves on a huckleberry bush beside him and then nibbled at them as he listened to a *rat-a-tat-tat* noise high in one tree and a *caw-caw-caw* in another. Sunlight broke through the trees, and Sparky looked at the long rays illuminating the plants around him.

"Wow! This is really beautiful!" Sparky exclaimed.

"You just wait until all of the plants have their leaves and blossoms. Then you will really see the beauty of your home, honey. Now come on and we will follow this bear trail down to Mouse Creek, and you can meet Noni on the way," Lucy said with excitement.

"Who is Noni and what is a bear trail?" Sparky questioned.

"Well, honey, you will meet Noni shortly, and this is a bear trail," she said and pointed ahead with her nose at bear footprints perfectly etched in the moss. "For many generations our ancestors have walked through the mosses of the rainforest using the very same steps. For all bears, it is an honor to walk where our foremothers and forefathers have walked. By stepping in the same footsteps, we also leave our scent so other bears will know we have been here. It is also less destructive to the moss, and well, it just feels really good on our feet."

"Cool! Can I try walking in the steps?" he asked, his eyes lighting up.

"Of course, honey, but let Mom go first. I want to watch your first time on the bear trail."

Quickly but carefully Lucy walked a section of the trail. She stopped on the other side and turned to Sparky. "Okay, honey. Give it a try."

Proudly, Sparky put his foot in the first footprint. Then he attempted to stretch out to reach the next print. He tried every angle possible, but it was just no use. The footprints were made by much larger bears. The stride of a five hundred–pound (226-

kilogram) grizzly bear was much great than a ten–pound (4.5-kilogram) cub.

"Urg!" Sparky exclaimed. "This is so frustrating! I really want to walk in the footsteps, but they are so far apart!"

"It is all right, honey. Just walk in the ones you can reach," Lucy encouraged.

"No. I am going to walk in them all," Sparky said in a tiny determined voice. Then he began to hop from footprint to footprint like an oversized bunny rabbit.

"That's my cub!" Lucy smiled. "Great work, honey!"

"Boy … *huff, huff* … that was … *puff, puff* … hard work …" Sparky exclaimed.

"Well, sweetie, it was worth it. You have walked on your very first bear trail. Now let's continue down, and you get to meet Noni."

In a short distance Lucy said, "Here's Noni," as she walked over to the base of an enormous Sitka spruce tree. "Sparky, this is Noni, one of the keepers of the forest."

As Sparky stood at the bottom of the huge tree, he looked like a tiny pebble beside a massive mountain.

"Whoa!" he exclaimed as his eyes followed up the massive tree trunk that soared upward so high that it seemed as if it would pierce a hole in the blue sky. "Noni is huge!"

"Yes, honey. Noni is the oldest Sitka spruce in the Khutzeymateen Valley. Noni has stood watch over the valley for more than one thousand years. Noni is an extremely wise tree who has seen many changes over a very long life. For this reason, Noni commands much respect from all of the forest creatures."

"Hello, Noni," Sparky respectfully said in a tiny voice as he stood back and took in the grandeur of the amazing plant.

Much to Sparky's surprise, the massive tree suddenly began to sway from side to side.

"Mom! Noni is moving!" Sparky exclaimed nervously. "And it is not windy!"

"It is all right, honey. Noni is very happy to meet you."

"Wow! Noni, you will be one of my best friends always!" Sparky exclaimed.

Again the tree began to move, but this time in the opposite direction.

Lucy smiled. "Noni would like that very much. She will always be here for you on your journey. Now it is time to follow Mouse Creek down to the inlet so you can check out more of your new home. Oh! And on the way, I will show you my favorite bear scratch tree."

"Bear scratch tree?" Sparky questioned. "What is that?"

"It is one of the finer things in a bear's life, and you will love it, so come along, my wee one," Lucy smiled.

"Okay, Mom. See you later, Noni!" Sparky said enthusiastically and then turned and followed Lucy. "I love Waipo already. I'm looking forward to living here a long time."

Chapter 3:
Flying Fur Balls

The bears continued down the peaceful soft mossy trail. Lucy carefully placed her feet in each etched step while Sparky sprang like a bunny rabbit from one footprint to the next. Suddenly the placid silence of morning was broken by two high-pitched squeaky voices yelling in a tree above the bears.

"This is my tree for the summer!

"I saw it first!"

"You did not! I did!"

Both Sparky and Lucy stopped, looked at each other, and then looked up at a very tall Sitka spruce tree that stood majestically beside the trail.

"Who is that, Mom?" Sparky asked quietly.

Lucy smiled and shook her head. "Just wait. I will tell you in a minute," she whispered.

"You go find your own tree!"

"You just want it 'cause it gets the most cones in the fall!"

"That's why you want it!"

"I want it 'cause I saw it first!"

"How could you see the tree first? I did!"

"I'll show you who saw the tree first!"

The bears tried to follow as a whirlwind of flying fur balls zoomed up and down and all around the tree trunk.

"Get off my tree!"

"You get off *my* tree!"

The flying objects made their way down the tree until they were on the ground right in front of Lucy and Sparky. The bears watched as the area at their feet erupted into flying spruce needles, moss, twigs, and fur.

Sparky strained to see what kind of creature the flying fur ball was, but it was moving to fast.

"*Ehem,*" Lucy cleared her throat loudly. The fur ball froze instantly.

Slowly, out of the tangle of paws, tails, and legs, two tiny faces looked nervously at the bears and then relaxed. The fur ball struggled apart, and two red squirrels sat up as if nothing had happened.

"Good spring, Miss Lucy," they both squeaked.

"Hello, fellows. You could have been a morning snack if we had been different bears."

"It was his fault!"

"No, it wasn't. It was your fault for stealing my tree!"

"My tree!"

"Now, now. Tell us what you are up to and maybe we can help," Lucy said, trying to calm them down.

"We're trying to sort out homes," the fatter squirrel squeaked and pointed up at the large spruce. "This is the tree I will be in for the summer."

"Ah. No. This is *my* tree for the summer," the skinny squirrel said in a loud, squeaky voice while rolling his eyes at the bears.

"Whatever!" the chubby squirrel hissed. Then he looked at Sparky and back to Lucy. "Looks like you have a new family member, Lucy."

"Yeah," the skinny squirrel cut in. "Who's the good-lookin' cub with you, Lucy?"

Lucy stepped aside and proudly looked at her cub. "Sparky, these are the red squirrel brothers, Cliff"—Lucy's nose motioned toward the chubby squirrel and then toward the skinny one—"and Mica. They share our area of the forest."

"Hello," Sparky said shyly.

"Hey, Sparky! Fine-looking young bear you are," Mica squeaked.

"Hi, Sparky!" Cliff chirped. "You will enjoy Mouse Creek. There is lots of food here."

"Yeah, and you eat most of it!" Mica exclaimed.

"Excuse me, you skinny runt! You're so worried about staying 'lean' so you can be 'fast.'"

"I am lean because you eat everything in sight! That's why this should be my tree for the summer. So you don't blow up from eating all the cones in one day!"

"I'll show you!" Cliff growled, ready to pounce on Mica.

"Ah, excuse me … ah … squirrels," Sparky nervously said in a small voice.

Both the squirrels and Lucy looked at Sparky.

"It's just me and my mom, and if we had to choose who got the tree, I mean if we were squirrels, I think both of us would share the tree. And if I had a brother or sister, which I don't but I wish I did, I would share the tree. You are lucky to have each other."

Speechless, Mica and Cliff looked at one another.

Finally Mica said, "You know, Sparky, you are very smart for a young bear cub. Maybe we will share the tree."

"That's true," Cliff chuckled. "But I get the left half!"

"No! I do!"

"You take the right half!"

"*No*! I want the left half!"

"Okay, then you take the bottom half!"

"Oh right! Good home on the trunk! Lotsa food there!"

"Well, boys, I'm sure you will work things out. We have to continue on with our day. Come on, Sparky," Lucy said and ambled off down the trail.

"Bye, Mica. Bye, Cliff. Remember it's not the only tree in the forest," Sparky smiled and follow along behind Lucy.

"Bear ya later," Cliff squeaked. "I get the top half.

"Catch ya soon, bear friends. Yeah right, like you need the part with all the cones, you oversized lizard breath!"

"You don't eat anything anyway, so you could live on bark!"

The noise of the arguing squirrels finally faded into the chirping of spring bird voices as the bears continued to the shoreline of the inlet.

"Are all the other creatures that live on Waipo as noisy as Mica and Cliff?" Sparky asked. "Do they always fight like that?"

"Luckily most other creatures on Waipo are much quieter, except for gulls, and you will meet them very shortly on the inlet shoreline. Mica and Cliff have been fighting for three years, ever since they were born," Lucy smiled and shook her head. "I don't know why they argue. They love and protect each other, but they seem to enjoy arguing."

She stopped in her tracks. "Ah, there it is," she said. She stepped off the trail, walked over to a huge fir tree, and sniffed it dreamily.

Sparky looked at the tree. A huge patch of bark was missing off the trunk, and it looked like something had made big cuts on the rest of it. Then his mom started to rub all her paws into the ground at the same time while she sniffed the tree.

"What's wrong with that tree?" Sparky asked. "It's missing so much skin. And, Mom, what are you doing?" he giggled.

"Oh, sorry, honey, I can't help myself. This is my favorite bear tree and it smells so good that it makes me mark my territory and leave my scent. My feet just can't help themselves. They always do the bear squishy dance when I smell this tree. I guess I just have to let my bear friends know I am out of hibernation. You see, they will pass by the tree, smell my scent on the ground and on the tree, and they will know I am out and about. Come smell," Lucy encouraged Sparky.

Sparky wandered over to the tree and sniffed. "It sort of smells like a lot of different us," Sparky said as he scrunched his nose up and sneezed.

"That's right, honey, and once you get to know who smells like what, you will be able to tell who is around. Let's see, I can smell Blondie and it smells like she has cubs, and Gracie is up and around. Oh, and my great-bear aunts Bearnice and Grizelda, my mom's mom's sisters, are still around on Waipo. They are ancient." Then she sniffed deeply and said, "Your father is out of hibernation, Sparky."

"Really! My dad? Can I smell!"

"Right here." Lucy pointed with her nose.

Sparky sniffed deeply. "He smells like the other smells to me."

"As you get older and your nose becomes better at separating scents, you will be able to tell the bears apart. Okay now for the feel-good part," she said and stood on her hind legs with her back to the tree and her big pink tummy facing Sparky. Lucy leaned against the tree, reached her head back over her shoulder, and started biting at the bark. Then she vigorously rubbed her back, shoulders, and head up and down on the tree. A silly smile spread across her face, and she sighed, "Oh, this feels so good after hibernating all winter!"

"Mom! Now what are you doing?" Sparky giggled.

"Just give me a couple more rubs and then you can try."

Finally she got down on all four feet and gave a big shake. "There, that feels much better! There is nothing like a good back scratch in the spring, or anytime for that matter. You see, Sparks, we rub on trees for many reasons. The best one is it feels good, but when we rub, our scent is left so other bears know we are here. When we smell a rub tree, we can tell who else is in the area and when they passed by. We bite the tree bark to make the tree's sap run. The sap tugs on our fur and helps scratch our backs, and bits of fur stick to the sap for the other bears to smell. Also it is believed that the saps smell might also help to keep pesky bugs away from us. Now you try, Sparky," she encouraged.

"Okay!" Sparky exclaimed excitedly and scampered over to the trunk and shimmied his bum up to the trunk. "My back is to the tree. I stand up on my hind legs. Whoa! I almost fell over."

"Steady, Sparks," Lucy encouraged. "Good. Now back up and rub your back on the tree."

"Here I go," Sparky said as he slowly and cautiously started to rub his back. A big content smile spread across his face. His pace quickened, and he wiggled side to side and up and down like he was doing a funny bear belly dance. Then he rubbed his shoulders and finally got down on all fours, turned around and gave his head and ears a good long scratch. Then he plopped down on his bum and smiled at Lucy.

"Well, what do you think?" she asked.

"That felt so good!" Sparky sighed.

"Are you ready to carry on down the trail to Mouse Creek to see more of Waipo and make more friends?"

"Yes, but can we come back to the bear tree soon?"

"Not to worry, Sparky. We will come by for a good rub almost every day," she smiled and ambled off toward the inlet.

Sparky rubbed the top of his head on the tree one last time and then quickly bolted after Lucy.

Chapter 4:
Weasel-Breath Westy

For the eight summers since Lucy was born, the Mouse Creek area had been her home when she was not hibernating. She had found the perfect location for a summer den up on the bank above the creek at the top of a twenty-foot waterfall. It wasn't far from the inlet shore. The den site was under a huge Sitka spruce tree. Soil under the tree and around its massive roots had been removed by the creek during floods over many years. As the creek had changed its path, the tree base no longer flooded, but there was still a large eroded area under the tree. Over the years Lucy had dug out more soil with her five-inch claws. She had made the perfect cozy summer sleeping den under the huge old tree, and this year, Sparky would share it with her.

"Here we are. This is where we will be sleeping, Sparky," Lucy said as she cleared away leaves and pinecones from the den entrance with her front paws.

"This is the best den ever!" Sparky looked quickly inside and then pranced over to look at the waterfall. "Razoooo! This is perfect!"

"Let's go down to the mouth of the creek where it runs into the inlet so you can see the rest of our home," Lucy said and continued along the trail.

Sparky followed, but he stopped constantly to smell flowers, nibble leaves, and playfully bat at bugs flying by.

Their summer home was the large grassy area, mudflat beach, and forest that surrounded Mouse Creek—one of the many side creeks that drained into the Khutzeymateen Inlet. Towering Sitka spruce trees draped with pale green garlands of witch's hair lichen surrounded the wide, fast-running creek, which was full of large rusty red and brown boulders that looked like huge ladybugs whose spots had been washed off. The tumbling crystal-clear mountain water skipped and danced over and around the boulders until it flowed into the salty inlet. In the fall, Lucy would hop from boulder to boulder looking into the creek for salmon.

Lucy stepped out of the forest and onto the shore of the inlet and looked up at the high mountains. The sun glistened on their melting snowcaps.

"Ahhh! It is great to be out and about again!" Lucy sighed and smiled as she quickly scanned both banks of the wide inlet for movement of intruders. Then she sat down in the sedge grass that was just starting to poke up through the moist soil and looked at Sparky, who was madly tearing up and down the shore and sniffing everything in sight.

"Sparky, slow down. You have all summer to explore," Lucy laughed.

"I know, Mom, but I don't want to miss anything!" he yelled and ran over to a large stump that had long since been washed up onshore and began sniffing it with great interest.

"Good spring, Lucy! Good spring, Lucy! Good spring, Lucy," came a long loud chorus from the flock of fifty Glaucous and Mew gulls who lived in the wide area where Mouse Creek met the inlet. The combination of the mineral-rich ocean water of the inlet and the freshwater of Mouse Creek produced a high concentration of nutrients in the water and an abundance of food and sea life for all the creatures that lived in the area.

"Cute cub! Cute cub! Cute cub!" the chorus continued.

"Hello, gulls! Thanks for the compliment! Sparky, say hello to our gull friends, all fifty of them!" Lucy smiled.

Sparky momentarily stopped his exploration of the stump, looked up at all the bird faces watching his every move, and merrily said, "Hello, gull friends!" Then he went back to sniffing the bottom of the stump and the mud around it.

"Hello, Sparky! Hello, Sparky! Hello, Sparky! Hello, Sparky!" the chorus of gulls squawked.

"*Jeez*! Can't a weasel get any peace and quiet around here! Wouldya gulls hush up! The weasel's tryin' to get some shut-eye!" a voice above Sparky's head yelled over at the gulls. "Hey, kid! Whaddaya sniffin' my stump for?" the weasel grouched at Sparky.

Lucy made her way over to the stump where Sparky was sniffing. "Westy! Good spring! It's okay. The cub is with me. This is Sparky. Sparky, this is Westy the Weasel," Lucy pointed to the long skinny sharp-faced, shifty-looking rodent with her nose.

"Hi, Westy. Sorry about sniffing your stump. Everything is so new to me, and well, your stump smelled really good."

"Oh well then," Westy perked up proudly. "It's my own special scent, 'Essences of Weasel.' All the animals love it, especially the female weasels. They go crazy and—"

"Yes, well, Westy," Lucy cut in. "How was your winter?'

"Great! Lots of food, not too cold. I managed to keep my perfect self slim and trim. Well, bear friends, must run off to visit the girlfriend, Rosebud. It is that time of the year." He winked slyly. "Good to meet you, Sparky. Good to see you, Lucy. Glad to be neighbors for another summer!" he said and scampered into the forest.

"Bye, Westy," both bears called.

"He is funny!" Sparky smiled.

"Yes, he is a character, but he means well. You do have to watch him though. He can be a little weasel breath sometimes," Lucy laughed.

"Mom! That's not nice," Sparky giggled.

"Well, it is true. Weasels are always out for themselves, and we just have to be careful because he can be bossy and pushy," Lucy said cautiously.

"Okay, Mom, I will be careful." Suddenly Sparky got a funny look on his face. "Mom, what is wrong with that gull over there? It's got something stuck on its beak."

Lucy looked over at a gull sitting quietly on the shore with a half-swallowed large starfish protruding from its beak.

"Oh, it's all right, honey. He is just having breakfast. Gulls swallow starfish whole. It just takes them a while to relax their throats so the starfish goes down."

Sparky looked disgusted with the thought. "We don't have to do that, do we? It looks gross and painful."

"Starfish aren't one of the foods we eat. The gulls say it's not a problem swallowing them. It wouldn't be my choice for a snack, but I know what yours is," she said as she lay back in the grass.

"Bear milk time," Sparky said.

He bounded over to Lucy, snuggled onto her chest, and began to purr while he ate.

"After lunch we will explore the shoreline and then go back up to the den and have a nap," Lucy softly said.

Sparky just shook his head yes. He was far too busy eating to talk.

Chapter 5:
Swimming Lessons

A week after the bears came out of hibernation, Lucy sat on the wide mudflats surrounding the mouth of Mouse Creek during low tide. The mudflats stretched up the shore until they met the strip of sedge grass that decorated the inlet and separated the flats from the forest. She nibbled peacefully on fresh sedge grass shoots in the morning sun, but her ears constantly twitched from side to side as she listened for danger, such as aggressive male bears, approaching from the forest behind her. Sparky was nearby, busily investigating his new home, unaware of how vulnerable he was. To Sparky, life was just plain fun and full of exciting new treasures to sniff and territory to explore.

Lucy watched as Sparky practiced using his needle-sharp baby bear claws to negotiate the top of a large slippery drift log that had once been a towering tree. During a heavy fall rainstorm, the Khutzeymateen River had swelled into a torrent that eroded the riverbank where the tree had grown. The tree's roots had been undercut until it was uprooted by the flooding river and carried downstream to the Khutzeymateen Inlet, where it was deposited on the muddy shore of Mouse Creek.

Sparky nimbly balanced on the log and began walking its length, stopping to snuffle patches of seaweed that had become stuck on the log during high tide. Suddenly, he lost his footing on the slippery surface, and all four of his legs flew in different directions. He desperately tried to recover, but it was a lost cause. He hit the ground with an "Umph! Ouch!" Then Sparky quickly got up, shook, and began to snuffle rocks on the ground like nothing had happened.

"Yo, Sparky! Glad I wasn't under you!" Westy yelled from his stump and then continued eating mussels he had gathered that morning.

Once Lucy knew Sparky was all right, she shook her head and chuckled to herself at his not-so-graceful tumble. "You have so much to learn, my cub," she whispered to herself. She then wandered over to his side and sat looking at him.

"Sparky, I think it is time for you to know what water feels like on your body. You barely even put your toes in the water, let alone submerge your whole body. And even more importantly, you have to learn how to swim."

"But, Mom, I really don't like water. It's way too cold. My tongue doesn't even really like it!" He shivered.

"Try floating on surface, floating, surface, floating, surface, floating," a chorus came from the flock of gulls that were floating on the inlet nearby and eavesdropping on the bears' conversation.

Sparky picked up a stick and fumbled it between his paws, pretending to be very interested in its shape and smell. Then he turned his back to his mother. "I am a land mammal that loves the warm sun and playing in the grass. I am not going to swim." Then he took the stick in his teeth and shook it back and forth.

"Oh yes, you are!" Lucy said with an evil grin.

Sparky peeked over his shoulder to see his mom lunging at him. He bolted out of the way, and the chase was on around the estuary shore line. Sparky giggled and dashed as fast as he could, dodging rocks and stumps, with Lucy right on his tail.

"Mom, stop!" Sparky pleaded as Lucy steered him right for the water of the inlet. At the last second, Sparky dashed out of the way, and Lucy plunged into the water. She began splashing and playing, trying to entice Sparky to join her. He adamantly stood on the shore and refused to follow. Lucy sat on her big bear bum in the water and picked up a stick that was floating by. Gingerly she tossed it from paw to paw while she said, "Come on, Sparky. This is fun!"

Sparky immediately sat down onshore and picked up his own stick and began to mimic his mother's antics. Sarcastically he replied, "I don't have to come in the water to play with silly sticks."

Lucy dropped the stick and glared at Sparky. "That does it!" she bellowed losing her patience.

"Uh-oh," Sparky squeaked and began to again run at top speed away from the water. Lucy chased him.

They ran until both bears were out of breath. Finally Sparky sat in the grass with his back to Lucy, trying to pretend she was not there.

"Young bear, you have to learn to swim! We have had this discussion before, and you know that you will eventually have to learn to like water and swimming," Lucy said with a stern voice.

Just then Westy's face peeked over the top of the stump.

"Ah, Lucy, lighten up on the cub. That swimmin's not all it's cracked up to be. I only do it if I absolutely have to. Get all wet, fur sticks to ya, fur full of salt, kind of gross I'd say. Cut the kid some slack. If the cub doesn't wanna swim, so be it!"

"See, Mom. Westy is right," Sparky said defensively.

"That's fine to say for you, Westy, but if danger comes by, you can hide under your stump. Now don't you have an eagle to torment?" She turned back to Sparky.

"Jeez, Lucy Goosey! No need to get yer fur in a knot ball! Just tryin' to help. *Jeez!*" Westy scampered off to look for urchins washed up on the shoreline.

"Sparky, how are you going to escape if another bear chases you into the water? What if you accidentally fall in the water and have to swim to safety? We live in an environment surrounded be water," Lucy said with a kind smile. "Honey, eventually you will have to swim, and today is a good day to start learning. Now come on. Let's get started."

"Ah, Mom," Sparky whined, and then he was silent for a moment.

Lucy sat looking at his back. "Come on, honey. It is time. Let's go," she encouraged.

Sparky slumped his shoulders like he was trying to hide. Then, as if he were talking to the forest, he whispered with a shy, timid voice, "I'm scared."

"What did you say, cub?" Lucy asked patiently.

"I am scared," Sparky whispered again, and his eyes filled with tears.

"Oh, honey." Lucy wandered over to her cub and lay down, pulling Sparky gently to her side with her big paw. "It will be all right. I will make sure nothing happens to you. All bears are nervous when we have to learn how to swim. It is something that is not natural at first, but once you learn, you will love the water. Trust your big old mom. You will see."

Sparky snuggled in close to his mom. "I am still scared, Mom. Are you sure I won't drown?"

"Drown! Did someone say drown!" Cliff's voice squeaked as he screeched to a halt beside the bears from a full-speed-ahead run.

Mica was not watching and slammed right into his back end. "*Umph*! *Urg*! Whadid you stop for!" he yelled.

"Drown!" Cliff continued. "I had to save Mica from drowning one day when he fell out of a bush into the inlet. He just about drowned had it not been for my lightning reflexes and big muscles."

"Who saved who?" Mica rolled his eyes at the bears. "I was the one who hauled your tubby butt out of the inlet."

"Did not!"

"Did so!"

"I'll show you!"

And they were off again.

"Okay, my baby bear cub. I will tell you what; we will do what many bear mommies do with their cubs when the cubs are first learning how to swim. You can hold on to the fur on my neck with your teeth and claws, and I will do all the swimming. All you have to do is enjoy the ride and get used to how the water feels on your little furry body. Then when you feel comfortable, you can start kicking your legs while holding on, and eventually you will be able to let go and swim yourself. How does that sound?"

Both Sparky's and Lucy's heads whipped sideways as a blur of fur flew by.

"I saved you, twig breath!"

"*No!* I saved you, lard barge!"

"*Oh! I'll show you!*"

Sparky looked up at Lucy. "I don't know, Mom," he said apprehensively. "That still sounds dangerous. What if I lose my grip and get washed away?"

"You are worrying too much, honey," she said and stood up. "Now come on! It will be fun! And as a reward, I will take you out tonight to show you what Universe looks like at night with all her stars. What do you say?"

"Well, uh, well. Okay," Sparky finally agreed. "But if I drown, you will be sorry."

With much exuberance, Lucy playfully ran down to the water's edge. "Okay, Sparks, I will get in and you can cling to the fur on my neck." She submerged herself in the water until only her neck and head were above the surface. "Okay. Climb on, honey."

Sparky slowly began to wade into the water, picking each paw up and shaking it like a kitten trying not to get its feet wet. "It is kind of cold but not as bad as I thought it would be." He slowly entered the water a bit farther and giggled. "It feels tickly and funny on my tummy!"

Sparky's paws tightly grasped the fur on Lucy's neck. "All right, Mom. I am on," he said as he grabbed her neck fur with his teeth.

"Okay, Sparks, here we go. Hold on tight!"

Sparky could feel his little heart pounding, and every muscle in his tiny bear body was tense. His eyes were as big as the moon. Nervous "*Um! Um! Um!*" noises emitted from his mouth.

Lucy began to swim in circles laughing and saying, "Whee! Isn't this fun?"

The hot sun beat down on the bears. Gradually Sparky began to relax and enjoy the cool water seeping through his thick fur and cooling his hot skin. He began to giggle with glee as Lucy swam in tighter circles. Then he looked down into the water just in time to see a fish swim by. This made him even more excited, and he started to look for more fish and water creatures.

After five minutes, Lucy began to swim back to shore and gently tipped her cub on to the beach.

"Well, honey, what did you think of your first swim?" Lucy asked and shook the water out of her fur.

Sparky rolled around in the grass, vigorously shaking the water off of him and giggling.

"I love swimming!" he yelled and began tearing around the beach, kicking his heels up in the air. "I just love it!"

Lucy joined the fun and chased Sparky around the shoreline. They giggled and ran until they were both too tired to run any farther. Finally, Sparky flopped down in the grass, and Lucy sat beside him.

"That swimming was so cool, Mom!" Sparky said with glee. "Can we do it again tomorrow?"

"We'll see. Now it's snack time. Then we'll go up to the den for a nap, so we can see the stars tonight," she said and flopped onto her back in a patch of sedge grass.

"Oh bear!" Sparky exclaimed climbing onto Lucy's chest. He peacefully suckled and then fell into a deep sleep.

Lucy watched her tired sleeping cub as his feet madly twitched back and forth. She gently rolled him onto the ground beside her, but his feet still moved madly. Softly Lucy whispered into his ear, "You can stop swimming now, my little one."

Chapter 6:
Big Beautiful Waipo

Sparky and Lucy lay snuggled in the cozy comfort of their den. He nuzzled his head lovingly under Lucy's chin as she licked and nibbled on his ear.

"Well, honey, are you ready to go out of our den and see Waipo at night and all the stars of Universe?" Lucy asked.

"Yes, but can I ask a question first please?"

"Of course you can."

"What is Waipo? And where does that name come from?"

"I'll tell you what, let's go outside and sit under the stars, and I will answer all your questions. If we don't go out soon, it will be morning, and we will have to wait for the next clear-sky night to see them. So are you ready to go say hello to Universe at night?"

Sparky hopped to his paws. "I think so, Mom."

Lucy made her way to the den entrance, and Sparky stuck right behind her. Suddenly she stopped, and Sparky ran right into her big bear bum.

"Oomph!" Sparky exclaimed.

"Oops, are you all right?" Lucy asked. "I didn't know you were so close."

"Sorry, Mom. I guess I am a bit nervous. It is so dark, and I have never been out of the den at night. There could be monsters. I could get lost, and there are scary night creatures lurking in the forest! Those smooth skin thingies you have talked about could be hiding in the trees, ready to grab me! I don't know about this, Mom. I think maybe we should just cuddle up in here and go to sleep right now," Sparky said with much concern.

"Not to worry, Sparks. There are no monsters, and most of the smooth skins don't like to be out at night either. You are safe with me. If we are lucky, we will meet some of our night friends." Lucy smiled kindly. "Your big old mom will protect you, and we are not going to venture too far from the den. I was just going to tell you not to look up at the sky until I tell you to. I want you to be in the perfect spot to see the sky and all the stars. Okay?"

"No problem. I will stay right behind you to make sure I don't get lost in the dark and have to spend the night out all by myself. I am not going to look anywhere but at you until we stop."

"Everything is fine. Now come on. You will love the stars."

Lucy squeezed her big bum out the den entrance and waddled down the bear trail to the sedge grass on the inlet shore. Sparky followed right behind Lucy, almost stuck to her hind leg. She slowed her pace, stopped, and then sat down—almost on top of Sparky, he was so close to her.

Sparky did the same but kept his eyes looking at the ground.

"Can I look up now, Mom?" he asked.

"Yes, honey."

Slowly Sparky raised his eyes to the sky.

"Wow!" he exclaimed with amazement. "This is *so cool*! There must be a gazillion stars in the sky! I never thought Universe would look like this at night! I never thought there would be this many stars! Are you sure we are not just imagining this? Are all those stars really out there, Mom, or is it just my eyes playing tricks on me? This is so beautiful!"

"It is real, honey. This is Universe at night. As it has been for millions of years and as it will be for millions of years to come. Long after you and I and all life on Waipo have left, Universe will still continue on in all her beauty."

Suddenly Sparky stopped, frozen with fear, as a *whoo, whoo, whoooo* sound came from a tree beside them. "What was that, Mom?"

"That's Hoot the owl saying hello to us. Don't worry Hoot is a bird, and I will tell you more about him later," Lucy reassured.

"It won't attack us, will it?" Sparky said looking around.

"We are a lot bigger than Hoot, so he won't bother us," Lucy laughed. "It's all right, Sparky. Relax. I am here to protect you." Lucy lay down in the sedge and patted the ground with her paw. "Come lie beside me, Sparky, and we will look at the stars and I will answer your questions about Waipo. Then I think we should talk more about your universe and the night creatures that share your home."

"Okay, Mom!" Sparky exclaimed, eagerly snuggling with his head on her chest and looking up at the stars.

"Waipo, or Earth as other species call it, is the water planet that we live on. Our ancestors that were on Waipo when Taku, the great bear spirit, lived named our planet. In the language that was spoken then, *wai* meant 'water' and *po* meant 'planet,'" Lucy explained. "You see, honey, our planet is mostly water. Seven-tenths of the planet is covered by oceans, seas, rivers, or lakes, and three-tenths of the planet is land. Waipo is one of nine planets orbiting around the sun. The sun is one of the one hundred thousand million stars in the Milky Way Galaxy, and it is only a very tiny part of Universe that we can see right above our heads."

"Universe is huge!" Sparky said with wide eyes.

"Yes, Sparky. If you were standing on one of those stars looking out, Waipo would just be another dot in the universe. You would not see me or Noni or anything else on Waipo. Everything is just part of something else, but in some way, everything is interconnected, and what you have to understand is there are universes on universes."

"I don't understand, Mom." Sparky crinkled his nose in confusion.

"Okay. Let's take Noni. We see a very huge tree. Right?"

"Uh-huh."

"If you look closer, Noni is not just a giant tree. It is actually a universe all of its own. It is a home for plants, insects, birds, frogs, squirrels, and all sorts of other creatures," Lucy explained.

"Noni is their universe!" Sparky said suddenly.

"Right, Sparks, but in some little way, Noni might have an effect on everything else in Universe. Just a few things Noni does are help to make the air we breath, help to fertilize and aerate the soil, and provide us with shade. Noni plays a very important part in its universe called the Khutzeymateen Valley, and the Khutzeymateen Valley in its universe, and so on. And if we kept on going, Noni somewhere along the way would possibly have an effect on everything in Universe, including that star you were standing on."

"I get it! Everything needs everything else to survive."

"That's right, Sparks. Now, let's talk about your universe called the Khutzeymateen and the creatures of the night that live in it."

"My universe is the Ka-zamten." Sparky tried very hard to pronounce the name.

"Well done, honey, but let's try again. Khut."

"Khut," Sparky repeated.

"Zey-ma-teen," Lucy said slowly.

"Ze-ma-tam."

"Teen," Lucy encouraged. "Okay now all at once. Khut-zey-ma-teen."

"Khut-zey-ma-teen," Sparky said proudly. "That is my universe and home."

"Very good, Sparky!"

"Mom, what was that weird noise we heard before? I think you said it was Hoot."

"Hoot is a great horned owl. He is one of the largest nocturnal birds in this part of Waipo."

"What does *nocturnal* mean?"

31

"*Nocturnal* means creatures that sleep most of the day and are active at night. Many animals that Hoot would hunt for food, primarily rodents like mice, voles, and anything up to a smaller porcupine are nocturnal as well. "

"Good thing Westy, Mica, and Cliff aren't nocturnal," Sparky said with great concern.

"Sparky, Westy is nocturnal. He is probably out catching mice right now, but he will be all right. He is a smart little weasel breath," Lucy kidded. "He also comes out in the daylight for short periods to search for food."

"Mom! Westy is not a weasel breath!" Sparky laughed. "How can night hunters see what they are doing? I can't imagine trying to catch a mouse in the dark."

"Nocturnal animals and birds have special eyes that allow them to see well at night. Another night animal that lives here is a member of the cat family, the cougar. They are large cats that are exceptional night hunters because of their specialized eyes, sensitive whiskers, and speed."

"Ah … Mom, would these cougars be interested in eating a small bear cub?" Sparky asked apprehensively.

"Well, Sparky, cougars do not usually bother grizzly bears, but since you are a small cub, we do have to keep an eye on you."

"Oh. I think I will start to listen and look around me some more when I am playing." Sparky shivered. "Do they come out during the day?"

"Sometimes, and it is a good idea to always keep your eyes and ears alert, Sparky. There are many hazards for young animals, and that is why you will stay with Mom until you are big enough to defend yourself."

Suddenly Sparky felt something fly by his head, then again, and then back again.

"What is that, Mom?" Sparky exclaimed nervously.

"That was Skite. She is a little brown Myotis bat."

"There are a lot of birds out at night," Sparky said, looking at the air around his head.

"Skite isn't a bird, Sparky. She's a bat. They are flying mammals," Lucy explained.

Right then something landed on the large boulder next to the bears.

"I heard my name, and I thought it was your voice, Lucy. Not much gets by these big old ears," a tiny squeaky voice said cheerfully. "How's it going?"

"Hello, Skite. We are fine and happy to be out in spring. How was your hibernation?"

Sparky looked over and saw the funniest-looking little creature he had seen yet. She was cute but kind of scary at the same time. The little bat was about four inches long and covered with thick dark brown fur on its back and white fur on its tummy. The tiny bat had very big ears, beady eyes, and a slightly pug nose. Its wings were bald and boney, with hooklike appendages instead of front paws. Sparky decided that if it had been a big animal, it would have been very scary-looking.

"My hibernation was very satisfying, thank you. I see your hibernation brought you a great gift this time." Skite flashed a smile full of very sharp pointy teeth at Sparky. "And from what I can see of him, he looks very handsome. You know the old saying, 'blind as a bat' and I am that. Hello, young fella!"

"Hello, Skite. Mom and I came out to see the Khutzeymateen and Universe at night," Sparky said proudly.

"Well done, Sparky. And what do you think of it all?"

"It is pretty cool! I also think it is pretty cool that you can hunt for food at night!" Sparky said sitting up to have a better look at Skite. "How do you see your food?" he asked.

"I can hardly see you, let alone my food. We bats have the worst eyesight, but we have what is called echolocation. We use between thirty to sixty clicks or squeaks per second that bounces off our prey. Then because we can fly so quickly, up to twenty wing beats per second, we zero in on our meal and presto—dinner," Skite explained.

"Wow! You are fast, at flying and talking!" Sparky looked at the delicate membrane and bone of Skite's wings.

"Righty-o, Sparky. Some of my friends say I talk way to much, but I gotta be noisy to find food!

"Hey, Mom said some whales hunt with sound, too!" Sparky exclaimed

"Yes, whales and bats are masters of echolocation." Skite looked at Lucy. "He is not only handsome but smart, too!"

Sparky giggled shyly.

"Well, gotta fly, griz friends. A gal's gotta make a living, ya know. We'll sound you around!" Skite squeaked and she was off.

"Wow! Skite is so cool!" Sparky said as Skite flashed by them one more time then disappeared into the night. "Mom, will Skite ever come out in the daytime? I would like to see her more often."

"Sorry, Sparky, but Skite sleeps during the day."

"Why are some creatures awake during the day and some at night?"

"There are probably many reasons, but one of the main ones is that there's only so much food for all species on Waipo. In order to survive, some animals have to hunt and eat at night."

Sparky sat up and looked at Lucy.

"You are the smartest mom on Waipo!" Sparky sighed. "How do you know all this stuff?"

"Well, honey, some of the information was passed down to me from my mom and to her from her mom and so on. Much of the information was taught to all species by the great Boris the rat, who was held hostage in a laboratory for many years by the smooth skins, or humans as they call themselves. During this time he learned as much as he could to try and keep his sanity. When he finally escaped, he taught as many species what he had learned during his years of captivity. But Boris is a whole other story that I will tell you another time."

"These smooth skin things sound scary."

"Some smooth skins are bad, but most are good and kind, just like in our bear family."

"Will you tell me about smooth skins and Boris the rat tomorrow so I am not wondering about them and afraid?"

"Okay, tomorrow," Lucy agreed.

Sparky lay back beside Lucy and gazed up at the stars.

"I am so lucky to live on big beautiful Waipo. Thank you, Universe, for giving me life so I can see all there is to see," he sighed and lay quietly for a moment. Then suddenly he said, "Mom?"

"Yes, honey?"

"Do you think we could sleep out here tonight under the stars? I would really like that."

"I thought you were afraid," Lucy said.

"Not anymore. I know you and Universe and Taku and Waipo will keep me as safe as you can. I am not afraid anymore."

Chapter 7:
Boris the Rat

The early morning sun warmed Sparky and Lucy as they woke from a deep sleep. They stood, stretched, gave a big shake, and contentedly began to munch the new shoots of green sedge grass that poked up through the rich black soil near the mouth of Mouse Creek. But today the morning dew had different ideas, and it relentlessly tickled Sparky's nose.

"*Achoo!*" he sneezed and shook his head. "*Achoo!*" he sneezed again, even louder and harder.

A chorus of about fifty "Zoomtight! Zoomtight! Zoomtight! Zoomtight!" erupted from the gulls feeding on the shoreline.

"Yo, Sparky, with sneezes like that, you're gonna make all the needles and pinecones fall off *my* tree!" Cliff squeaked loudly from high in the huge spruce tree nearby.

"Good! Keep it up, Sparky! Maybe one of the pinecones will knock him out, and I can finally have *my* tree to myself!" Mica squeaked from another branch of the same spruce.

"My goodness, Sparky. What is tickling your nose?" Lucy laughed. "Those sound like the sneezes your Grampy Gimpy would make!"

"Grampy who?—*achoo*!"

The gulls erupted again. "Zoomtight, zoomtight, zoomtight …"

"Grampy Gimpy is a very large fat old bear. He is your grandpa, my dad. I think Grampy Gimpy would be impressed with your sneezes."

"Grampy Grimpy sounds funny. Will I ever meet him? Maybe I could sneeze for him—*achoo!*"

"Zoomtight, zoomtight, zoomtight ..."

"Well, Grampy Grimpy spends most of his days napping in the shade of giant trees. He is very old and doesn't like to move around much, but he always comes out for salmon season, so you could see him then."

"I hope so—*achoo!*"

"Zoomtight, zoomtight, zoomtight ..."

"I think it's the dewdrops on the ends of the grass. They are tickling my nose this morning and making me sneeze. Sorry I am making so much noise bu ... bu ... bu—*achoo!* But I can't help it ... Oh, jumpin' froghopper! I wish I could stop!!" he said and shook his little furry bear head.

"Zoomtight, zoomtight, zoomtight ..." The gulls carried on with every sneeze.

Westy's head poked out from under his tree stump nearby, and he yelled, "Jeez! Hey, Sparks! You're keepin' the old weasel awake! Could ya put a lid on the sneezin'! And will you, gulls, shut up with the zoomtight!"

"Sorry, Westy, but I can't help it—*achoo!*"

"Zoomtight, zoomtight, zoomtight, zoomtight..."

"Jeez!" Westy grouched then disappeared under the stump.

Lucy walked over to Sparky and nuzzled him lovingly with her long nose. "Oooo!" she coed. "Your fur is so nice and soft."

"Careful, Mom!" Sparky giggled. "You will knock me over!"

Lucy nuzzled even harder.

"Mom!" Sparky burst into fits of laughter. "Not my sides! That tickles!" he squealed as he rolled on the ground trying to escape Lucy's long nose.

She tickled and tickled as Sparky giggled and giggled. Then she said sweetly, "There! I think I cured your sneeze attack. Now come on, sweetie, follow me down to my favorite snooze log on the shore, and we'll rest in the sun," Lucy smiled.

"Okay, Mom!" Sparky said as he scrambled to his feet and scampered along behind her to a large log nestled in a patch of vibrant green sedge grass.

Lucy lay down in the sedge and leaned her back against the log.

"Ah," she sighed. "This is the perfect bear life."

Sparky snuggled in to her chest, and Lucy gently put her paw around her tiny cub's fuzzy body.

"I love you, Mom," Sparky sighed as he laid his head on her big furry front leg.

"I love you too, Sparky," Lucy smiled. "You are my ray of sunshine," she said and licked the top of his head.

Through the tall green sedge grass, Sparky gazed up at two small puffy white cotton ball clouds that gracefully floated across the cobalt blue sky.

"So this is how an ant sees the world," he said. "From down here the grass looks like it is twenty feet tall."

Lucy chuckled.

"Mom, what are ants for anyway?" he asked, looking at Lucy. "I mean they are so small, and they seem to always be just fidgeting around on the ground like nervous bumble bees. What purpose can they possibly have on Waipo? I always try not to step on them, but maybe I shouldn't try to avoid them because there are so many of them."

"Sparky!" Lucy exclaimed. "How would you like it if one day you were just minding your own business and a big foot came along and stepped on you!"

"I wouldn't like it, but I am so much bigger! The only difference is that I would make a bigger mess."

"Size doesn't matter. Every creature on the planet is special and has a very important purpose. Everything on Waipo works together in harmony, and that is why we are all here. If it wasn't for the ants, you and I would not be here."

Confused, Sparky scrunched his nose. "How can ants possibly affect whether or not you and I are here? They seem so small. Ants seem more like a pest on the planet. I can't stand it when they crawl on my fur!" Sparky shuddered. "It feels so gross. They drive me crazy!"

Lucy laughed. "You must realize that everything on Waipo stands together. Every creature on the planet forms the circle of life. Think of it as all living species on earth standing in a huge circle holding hands."

"Wow. That would be a huge circle! Do you mean the plants too, like Noni?" Sparky asked, and his eyes grew as big as the moon.

"Of course, Sparky. Everything on the planet stands together to make our life on Waipo strong and healthy," Lucy explained. "Now what would happen if we pulled one of the species out of the circle? Then another and another and another?"

Sparky sat back and thought deeply. "Well, two things could happen. Either we would have big holes in the circle or the circle would get smaller and smaller until it disappeared completely."

Lucy hugged Sparky. "You are my smart little bear." She smiled. "That is right. If we lose species and holes start to form, then the circle gets weaker and weaker until it eventually collapses. Or, like you said, if we lose species, the circle would get smaller and smaller and more and more unbalanced until all life disappeared. Waipo would die, and then she would have to start rebuilding again. If that happens, Waipo would never be the same as we see it now, but Waipo always wins in the end, and she would return looking much different." Lucy paused in thought then continued. "You see, Sparky, we need the numerous varieties of species on the planet to keep everything functioning as Taku intended. If we don't have trees and plants, we don't have air. If the oceans die, we will all die because they are the life force of the planet. If we don't have salmon, we will die of starvation. If the smooth skins lose all nature, they will die. And if we didn't have ants, Waipo would die quickly."

Sparky's eyes grew even bigger. "Why, Mom?"

"Well, there are approximately ten thousand trillion ants in the world."

"That's a lot! If I step on one, there are lots left!" Sparky exclaimed.

"Yes, there are many ants, but there needs to be for many reasons. Many furred, finned, and feathered ones eat them. Ants help to aerate the soil. They clean up dead things. Some help pollinate plants, plus numerous other tasks on Waipo. Ants are very important. There may be lots of ants, but there is a reason why there are a lot of them. They are a very important part of the life circle, just like everything on the planet. As for stepping on them, you shouldn't kill anything unnecessarily, Sparky. You should always respect Waipo and every species on her. If everything and everybody on the planet stepped on an ant, lots of ants would die unnecessarily. The ant population might become unbalanced, and the tasks that they perform would not get done. It could cause all sorts of problems in the world, just like if any species becomes endangered or extinct."

"Now I understand, Mom. You are so smart," Sparky sighed. "I am so glad you are my mom." He thought for a minute then asked, "How did you learn how many ants there are in the world? And who counted them anyway?"

"Well, Sparks, that's a whole other story, and not a very nice story. Do you remember last night I mentioned Boris the rat?"

"Yes, Mom. You promised to tell be about Boris today. It was so much fun sleeping under the stars!" Sparky giggled.

Lucy smiled at her cub. "Yes, it was, honey." She paused and sniffed the air deeply to make sure no intruders were approaching, then she continued. "One day a few years ago, Gertrude the pack rat gathered many of us forest creatures together to warn us all about some bad smooth skins that were conducting experiments on furred, finned, feathered, and shelled creatures. Her distant cousin, Boris the rat, was one of the furred ones they had taken hostage and were experimenting on, but he managed to escape to safety."

Sparky's eyes grew big, and he sat up and looked at Lucy. "I knew those smooth skins were trouble!" he exclaimed.

"Now, Sparks, you must realize that not all of the smooth skins are bad. The pink ones that visit us are good ones, and they help to keep our home safe," she explained.

"Why can't all smooth skins be nice to all the other beings on the Waipo?" He paused in thought. "What did the bad smooth skins do to poor Boris the rat?"

"Well, I will not tell you everything, but the bad smooth skins tested various things on Boris. They poured fluids in his eyes that made them burn. They put chemicals on his fur that made it fall out. That is all I will tell you, sweetie, because I don't want you to be afraid," Lucy sighed.

"Poor Boris!" Sparky exclaimed. "That's a big nightmare!" Sparky shivered and snuggled in closer to Lucy. "Mom, I am afraid of the smooth skins now."

"Sparky, we will have smooth skins visit us, but don't be afraid of them. They have never done anything bad to me in eight leaf droppings. Here in the Khutzeymateen, we are safe from the bad smooth skins," she reassured Sparky.

"How did Boris escape the monster smooth skins?"

"Well, one night one of the parrot hostages in the laboratory escaped and used her strong beak to pry open as many cages as she could. Some of the windows in the laboratory were open and many of the furred, finned, and feathered escaped. Boris was one of them. He couldn't see very well because of what they did to his eyes, but with the help of the others, he managed to find his way to the local park. All the animals in the park made sure he felt welcome, and to this day, he lives there. Boris began to tell his stories, both good and bad. Boris had many bad things happen to him in the laboratory, but he also learned much about all life on Waipo by listening to what the smooth skins said. Gradually the stories filtered through the animal kingdom, and soon everyone knew what some smooth skins were doing. They knew not to trust the smooth skins anymore, and they also learned much about Universe and all life on Waipo from Boris." She paused and looked at Sparky. "Just remember, my love, not all smooth skins are bad. Some do all they can to try to help all of Waipo's family. I actually feel sorry for the bad smooth skins. Universe, Waipo, and Taku will not look upon them kindly when it is time for them to leave the planet and move on to their new journey."

"Why, Mom?" Sparky asked.

"Well, Sparky, smooth skins are very intelligent, but also very silly. They know how many ants there are in the world, yet they don't know how to control their own population. With population control, they would fit in with all other life on Waipo. Instead, smooth skins use everything Waipo has to individually get ahead rather than working together, like a school of fish or a flock of birds, to make Waipo a better place for all smooth skins and all species on the planet. They use too much land to build their dens and other species lose their homes. They also create very toxic poisons that Waipo does not know what to do with, which causes species to die. Unfortunately they are unbalancing Waipo and making huge holes in the circle of life. All the fur, feather, fin, and shell know this, but we are far too advanced to be able to communicate with the smooth skins and help them. And even if we could, I don't think they would listen. They are too busy trying to make their own lives perfect, and they will do whatever it takes to accomplish that, even if they kill the planet doing it. They no longer function as a whole to keep their species flourishing together and moving forward in a healthy way." She stopped and sighed with frustration. "Oh Father Bear, what can we do? They will just have to figure things out on their own. Hopefully they will balance their own species before it is too late to save Waipo."

"Oh, those silly smooth skins. Why don't they just have one cub and one den and eat grass and just be happy and relaxed?"

Sparky sighed and stretched all four legs above him in the air and then flopped over onto Lucy's chest.

Lucy pulled Sparky in close and snuggled him in the hot afternoon sun. "Now, my sweet cub, it is time for a nap," she said gently.

Sparky gave a big yawn and stretch his legs into the air above him and relaxed. Within minutes his feet were madly flipping in midair, and he was snoring loudly, his lips flapping with each snore.

Lucy giggled and whispered, "I love you, my quiet, calm cub."

Chapter 8:
The Flying Sparky

"Mom!" Sparky exclaimed as he romped beside Lucy through the tall sedge grass on the inlet shoreline. "That was really cool seeing the stars the other night. It was also really cool going swimming. Do you think we can go swimming again? I mean, can I hold on to you and practice swimming? And, well, can we maybe watch the stars again tonight? Please!"

Lucy smiled to herself at the fact that Sparky was actually asking to go swimming. "Well, since you said please, I guess we can do both. Only this time we will go farther. We will cross the Khutzeymateen Inlet."

"What? That is a long way, Mom! I can't do that," Sparky said with apprehension. "That is way too far! I will drown for sure! I thought we could swim just offshore again." He stopped and looked across the mile-wide inlet. "I am really afraid now."

"Oh, honey. You don't have to be afraid. Your big, fat old mom floats extremely well, like a big huge whale fart bubble covered with fur. You will be just fine."

"Mom! That is so gross!" Sparky giggled uncontrollably.

Just then Lucy noticed something emerging from the inlet onto the shore.

"Look, Sparky! Daisy the blacktail deer just swam across the inlet. Over there." She pointed with her nose. "She is just climbing out of the water."

Sparky looked up and saw a pretty tawny-colored deer with huge brown eyes.

"Morning, bear friends!" she yelled over.

"Morning, Daisy." Lucy nodded. "How's the water?"

"Water's a bit cool this morning but refreshing. I'm off to find my sister, Lupine, and we are going to her favorite grass patch for breakfast. See ya!" She gave a big shake and water flew in all directions. Then with a big springy bounce, she disappeared into the forest.

"Wow! I didn't know deer swam! I guess if Daisy can swim the inlet, so can I."

"That's my cub. We will be able to stop for a rest on a sandbar halfway across. You will be safe. I promise. Now come on, let's get started," she said as she made her way to the water's edge. Sparky nervously followed close behind.

"Now remember, Sparky, hold on to my neck with your claws and teeth. Hold on tight, and we will go have some fun!"

Sparky looked across the inlet. His heart pounded with fear. *My mom will make sure I am safe. My mom will make sure I am safe,* he repeated over and over to himself as he clung to Lucy, and she began to swim.

The icy cold water tickled his tummy, and Sparky giggled with glee. Magically, his fear disappeared. "Thith ith fhun!" he tried to say while still keeping his teeth tightly clenched on Lucy's neck fur.

"It is fun, Sparks, but you must learn the ways of the water, so you will always swim safely. The inlet is affected by the tides, and the current will change because of this. I will tell you more when we are resting on the sandbar."

Lucy swam up to the sandbar in the middle of the inlet. She climbed out of the water and gently tipped Sparky off her shoulder onto the ground. He vigorously shook the water out of his fur, like a big dog after a bath. Then he rubbed and rolled in a small patch of grass that clung to the sandbar. Lucy lay back against a boulder, and Sparky climbed onto her chest and snacked on her fat, rich mother milk. When he finished, Lucy wrapped her paw around Sparky, and they basked in the sun.

"Mom, is it easier to float in the ocean water than in freshwater? When we went swimming in the inlet I felt like I could float, but when I tried to paddle around in the swimming hole in Mouse Creek, it seemed harder to stay on the surface. "

"Saltwater is much denser than freshwater because of the large amount of salt in it, so you float better. Freshwater will actually float on top of saltwater because it is less dense. That is why sometimes in the winter the surface of a calm ocean will freeze if there is a freshwater source nearby. Our inlet will freeze for quite a distance from the estuary toward the mouth of the inlet because of the Khutzeymateen River's freshwater. Large blocky chunks of ice will jam up in the estuary, and then as the weather warms, they will eventually either melt or be carried out to the ocean."

"Why are there oceans, and why is the water salty?" Sparky asked.

"There are two possibilities. One is nature at work and the other is a legend passed down from our ancestors. Which would you like to hear first?"

"The nature one."

"Well, we have oceans because Waipo had the perfect combination of hydrogen, oxygen, temperatures, and climate to make water. Shifting of the planet's plates created gaps that began to fill with water, and over millions of years, they became the oceans and seas that cover almost three quarters of Waipo. During that time minerals from the earth's surface have dissolved in the oceans and seas, making the water dense and salty. Every day water evaporates from them to form clouds and rain, but the salt does not evaporate. Rivers wash down a small amount of minerals, which also contributes to the mineral content of the ocean. It is also thought that volcanic activity over the history of Waipo has contributed to the minerals of the oceans and seas. In contrast, lakes and rivers are freshwater from rain and snow falls, or they are from glaciers melting. Although they do pick up some minerals on route to the ocean, the water does not taste salty, and it is healthy for us to drink."

"That all sounds reasonable. Now the legend," Sparky said, sitting up with interest.

Lucy cleared her throat and began. "It is said that many thousands of years ago, the great grizzly bear goddess, LaLuha, fell in love with the great polar bear god, Knaknu. Their meeting was only by chance when LaLuha became lost while searching for the huge mythical Sahou salmon that was believed to live on Waipo many centuries ago. LaLuha wandered so far north that Knaknu found her wandering aimlessly. She was lost, cold, starving, and crying. He fed her and took care of her until she regained her strength. When she was able, Knaknu helped her find her way home, but this all took many weeks, and during that time, they fell in love with each other. But because Knaknu was the mighty white bear god of the north and LaLuha was the goddess grizzly of the south, they could not stay together forever as they wished. When Knaknu kissed LaLuha good-bye, they both began to cry. LaLuha cried so hard that her salty tears formed the oceans and seas of Waipo. Knaknu cried so hard that when he left his true love and journeyed back to the cold north, his tears froze along the way and formed the glaciers and icecaps of Waipo. The salt from the frozen tears filtered into the soil beneath, and when the ice began to melt, it formed lakes and rivers. LaLuha and Knaknu loved each other very much, but they never saw each other again."

"Mom, that is so sad. Why couldn't they just live happily together? It is not fair that they had to be apart! They should have been able to stay together forever!" Sparky was obviously very upset by the story.

"Now, honey, you must realize that our polar bear cousins are different than we are. It is not possible for us to live together. We eat different food. The climate we live in is not the same. Everything about us is different."

"Where did polar bears come from, and why are they so much different than us?" Sparky asked.

"Many thousands of hibernations ago, a group of our grizzly ancestors were trapped by the advancing ice during the ice age and had to adapt into our cousins the polar bear. In order for them to survive, they had to physically change to better suit their environment. Their fur gradually became a creamy white color so they would blend in with the snow. Their claws developed an extra hook-shaped section so they could grab slippery seals. Their feet grew huge and their toes webbed for swimming. Even the pads of their feet changed, and over the years, tiny suction cups formed on them so our polar cousins do not slip on the ice when they are walking."

"Cool!" Sparky exclaimed. "Do they make a *pop*, *pop*, popping sound when they walk?" he giggled.

"No, silly willy," Lucy laughed. "But they are exceptional swimmers. You think the water is cold here. How would you like to swim in the ocean with icebergs floating around you?"

"No thank you!" Sparky said adamantly. "I will stay right here in the Khutzeymateen Valley, thank you very much! Do our cousins hibernate like we do, Mom?"

"Only mommy polar bears who are going to give birth to cubs hibernate. Otherwise, the polar bears stay awake and feed on the seals all winter. It is easier for our polar cousins to hunt on the sea ice in the winter when it is frozen. Polar bears eat more meat than we do, so their skull bones and jaws are shaped slightly differently than ours. They need heavier bones and stronger muscles to chew the meat and blubber of the seals they eat. Polar bear molar teeth are also pointier, so they are able to rip and chew seal meat—their main staple food. Grizzlies eat a combination of vegetation and meat, so our molar teeth are not as sharp and pointy. We have more flat grinding surfaces on our molars, so we can not only eat meat and salmon, but we can grind all the grass and vegetation that we need in our diet."

She paused and looked at the inlet around them. "Now it is time for you to learn about the ocean and how it affects your swimming." Lucy sat up and looked at Sparky. "Did you notice your body floating away from me?"

"Yes, Mom, I did."

"That is because the tide of the ocean was going from high to low. The water was flowing out of the river estuary, down the inlet, and back to the ocean. This happens twice a day in the Khutzeymateen. Everything in the world seems to always be moving, including the ocean.

"Why does the ocean move, Mom?"

"It has to do with the pull of gravity and where Waipo is positioned in relation to the moon and the sun. When the moon is on one side of Waipo and the sun is on the other, the tides are at their lowest. Imagine the moon and sun are having a tug of war, with Waipo being tugged. The ocean seems to stretch out between the two, and the tides stay small and low.

"When the moon and sun are on the same side of Waipo, the tides are at their highest. It is like the moon and sun are inviting the ocean to rise high and touch them while they visit on the same side of Waipo."

Sparky gave Lucy a sly grin. "No, Mom, I think you are wrong. I think someone keeps knocking the plug out of the bottom of the ocean with his big fat toe, and Mother Nature keeps putting the plug back in then turning on the rain to fill the ocean back up."

Lucy laughed. "Oh, my cub, you do have an imagination!" She gave him a frisky rub on the head with her huge paw. "Now let's get back in the water. I want you to feel the current of the tides."

Sparky latched back onto his mother's neck. As Lucy paddled hard against the strong current, Sparky felt his body being pulled from his mom. He realized that if he let go, he would be swept away. He clung tighter and practiced kicking his back legs to try and help his mom swim against the current.

After about thirty minutes, the two bears reached the other side of the inlet. Lucy stepped up onto the sandy beach and gently tipped her shoulder down to let Sparky slide off. But nothing happened.

"Come on, Sparks. We are back on dry ground."

Sparky mischievously held on tight to his mom's fur, hoping to get a free ride on her back for a while.

"Sparks, I am not going to carry you!" she warned as she again gently tipped her shoulder toward the ground, but Sparky held on relentlessly.

"You little monkey!" Lucy sighed. "Okay! You asked for it!"

"Uh-oh!" Sparky exclaimed, but it was too late.

Lucy gave a huge shake, which sent Sparky sailing not so gracefully through the air for over ten feet. Then the cub hit the ground and bounced and rolled head over tail for five more feet.

When Sparky came to a stop, he lay for a minute wondering what happened and where he was. Then he stood up and gave a big shake and looked at his mom.

"Oops! Sorry, Mom." He smiled coyly. "I was just having a bit of fun."

"I know, cubby bear," Lucy said with a big mischievous grin. "So was I! Now let's go find some nice tender grass. I am starving!"

Chapter 9:
Squiggles in My Mouth

Sheets of rain from a thick layer of gray grouchy-looking clouds that hung on the mountaintops pelted the deep green glass-smooth surface of the inlet. The water jumped in a constant frenzy as if a billion pebbles had been tossed in at once.

"Jeez!" came Westy's voice as his tiny face poked out from a knothole in his stump. He looked at the rain, shook his head in disgust, then grouchily disappeared.

Sparky sat in the sedge grass. His saturated fur clung to his tiny body, and a constant stream of water ran down his snout and drained off the end of his nose. He stood and gave a huge shake, trying to stop the moisture from touching his skin. Distracted, he sighed, nipped off some sedge grass, sat down, smacked his lips as he chewed, and sighed again. Looking up at the clouds, he noticed a big old drenched miserable-looking bald eagle sitting on top of a tall tree with its wings hanging open to the sides trying to drain the rainwater off them.

"I know what you feel like, buddy," Sparky whispered.

Lucy ripped and chewed large mouthfuls of sedge as she sat and watched her bored cub until the rain slowed.

"Sparky, since it is such a rainy day, how would you like to explore the shoreline of the inlet and try some new kinds of food?" Lucy asked with a twinkle in her eye.

"That depends on what it is, Mom," Sparky replied suspiciously. "I am very happy drinking milk and eating grass."

"Well, honey, I am sure you will love these new tastes. I can almost guarantee it," Lucy said enthusiastically, trying to encourage Sparky as much as possible.

"I don't know, Mom. It sounds like you are trying to get me to eat something that tastes bad, but you want me to eat it because it is good for me." He took a big mouthful of sedge grass, started chewing, and then lay down and looked the other direction.

"Now, Sparky, you have to learn to eat all the different foods that Taku made to keep us bears strong and healthy. Someday when you are a big bear with your own kingdom, you will have to eat well and know what to eat to stay strong and powerful."

"I don't want to be by myself, so I'm never leaving you. I'm not going to have all sorts of other male bears chasing me and trying to kill me. I'm going to stay with you forever," Sparky said in a very determined voice.

"Now, honey," Lucy sighed and sat down beside him. "Right now the world may seem like a big scary place, but when you grow to be a big bear, you will be happy to be on your own." Lucy playfully nudged Sparky with her shoulder. "You won't want your big old mom hanging around forever. There will come a time when you will want your own life. You will have your own territory of land and female bear friends to visit."

Sparky vigorously shook his head and exclaimed, "Oh yuck! No way! I don't want female bear germs! And I have Mouse Creek territory to share with you! That way we will both be safe! So I don't have to eat other kinds of food!" he said defiantly and looked away.

Lucy looked up at the sky. The rain stopped as quickly as it had started. The sun's heat began to quickly evaporate the clouds and causing steam to rise off the sedge grass and the inlet.

"Well, okay then. I guess I will have fun in the sunshine eating all the food myself," Lucy sighed. "It is really too bad because we were going to start with barnacles, then crunch a few mussels, then flip a bunch of rocks and eat the yummy rock crabs beneath them. Then we would have a treasure hunt and dig for one of my favorite foods, clams." Lucy stood up, stretched, and sighed. "Oh well. More clams for me." She turned and began to walk toward the shoreline of the inlet.

Sparky sat and thought for a moment. Suddenly he yelled, "Mom!"

Lucy stopped and nonchalantly looked at him, "Yes, son?"

"Well ... er ... well ... What do clams taste like?" he questioned and scrunched up his nose.

"Like nothing you have ever tasted before. So come on and we will dig some." She turned and continued walking.

"Oh, Mom!" Sparky whined. He sat still for a second, and then he bolted to Lucy's side.

"Where are the barnacles?" he said excitedly.

"Over here on the rocks and logs."

"They don't look very tasty. They look really hard," Sparky said as he began gnawing what looked like tiny mini volcanoes attached to a log. "I like how crunchy they are. They kind of taste like salty rocks, but they are much softer than rocks. I like the salty flavor. What are these barnacles, Mom?"

"Barnacles are tiny animals that eat itsy bitsy creatures in the ocean. Their hard shells look like pinecones with the pointy end cut off. They are related to crabs and spiders."

"Wow! They are related to spiders! Cool! Barnacles must be really small to live in some of these tiny homes." He leaned down and tried to look into a barnacle house. "Oh well. I can't see if it is home. I will have to look when the salty water covers them again and see if I can see them." He paused and looked at Lucy. "You said we would try mussels next. Where are they?" Sparky asked then looked around him. "Oh! Here they are. Look, Mom!" he said and sat down, flexing his tiny bear arms to show off his mini bear muscles.

Lucy laughed, walked over to her cub, and pushed him gently on to his side with her big long snout.

"Oh, you are a silly goose," she smiled. "Now come on, Mr. Muscle, and we will go find my favorite log. It is low tide now, and the mussels will be exposed."

Sparky and Lucy hopped over the barnacle-covered rocks until the shore changed to mud and sedge. They romped playfully in the mid-morning sun through the long sedge grass, chasing each other. Sparky kicked his back legs in the air as Lucy nipped at his bottom.

"It is so good to be on Waipo, Mom!" he yelled as he reached up and tried to grab a butterfly that stayed just out of his reach. As if wanting to join the fun, the bright orange, black, and white butterfly flitted around the cub's head. Sparky's paws flew through the air after it. Lucy stopped to watch what her son was up to. She giggled with delight as Sparky plopped down in the grass and the butterfly continued to tease him. His head jerked in all directions trying to keep the busy butterfly in sight. Finally the butterfly landed on the end of Sparky's nose and moved its wings slowly up and down. As Sparky tried to see the butterfly, his eyes crossed and he lost his balance. He tumbled over, and the butterfly flitted off to a large patch of lupine.

Lucy burst out into fits of laughter and ran to her cub, gently jostling him and tickling his ribs with her paws. Sparky giggled and giggled while trying to fight his mom off. Lucy grabbed Sparky with both her paws and cuddled him to her chest.

"Oh, I love you, son," she smiled and rolled back and forth on her back, holding Sparky.

"I love you too, Mom!" Sparky giggled and cuddled his mom even harder.

Lucy finally set Sparky down and began to run again. "Come on, Sparks! Let's go eat mussels!" she cried and ran down to the water's edge where a huge drift tree lay. It was covered with hundreds of black mussel shells.

"Wow! That is pretty cool, Mom. Look at the gazillions of mussels on that log!" Sparky said as he climbed up on the log. "I can climb on the log really easy with all these rough pointy lumpy mussel thingies!"

"Sparky! You are climbing all over our dinner!" Lucy joked.

"Oops!" Sparky grinned. "Do you want me to get down? This is fun."

"No, honey, you are having too much fun. Since you are way up there, try one of the mussels on top of the log," Lucy encouraged.

"Okay!"

Sparky grabbed a large mussel with his teeth and tugged with all his might. He pulled and pulled and tried really hard to tear the mussel loose, but it was firmly attached to the log. "Wow!" he fretted. "Those things are really glued to the log."

"That is a big mussel you are trying to pull off. Tug even harder, sweetie, and it will free from the log. Come on! Use those big muscles you showed me earlier. Come on, honey! You can do it!" Lucy encouraged.

"Okay, Mom!" Sparky said with much determination. He grabbed the mussel in his mouth and braced his little body by widening his mini bear leg stance and digging his needle-sharp claws into the log. Then with all the strength he could find inside himself, he tugged on the stubborn mussel.

"Urg! Grr!" he grunted as he pulled and pulled.

Suddenly the shellfish foot let go of the log. In a split second, Sparky was airborne, flying off the top of the log with the mussel in his mouth.

"Umph!" he grunted as he bounced off of Lucy's back, and then, "Oof!" as he landed on the ground in a heap. "Pwaff," Sparky spit the mussel on to the ground. "Sorry about that, Mom. Those mussels are really on there good. I hope I didn't hurt you." He vigorously shook to get the sand and mud out of his fur.

"No, son, I am fine. Are you all right?" she asked after she stopped laughing. Lucy shook her coat to fluff it back up. "I must say, you are a dangerous mussel picker to be around!"

"I got the mussel!" Sparky said proudly.

"Good cub! Now pick it up and crunch it in your teeth to get at the yummy mussel inside the shell. You can spit out the larger shells, but the small thinner shells you can chew up with the mussel and swallow."

"Are you kidding, Mom? It looks kind of yucky and hard, and well, it smells funny!" Sparky protested as he wrinkled up his nose and looked at his mom.

"Trust me, son. Thousands of bears eating thousands of mussels can't be wrong. Now try the mussel. And besides that, you put so much effort into getting it. Now you have to try it!"

"I guess so," Sparky said apprehensively. He picked up the large mussel in his teeth, closed his eyes, and with a grimace, crunched down on the shellfish. Suddenly Sparky's eyes opened wide. "Whoa! Thyth ith raleey goot!" he tried to say as he devoured the mussel. He swallowed the bits, and with a satisfied smile, he sat down. "*Burp!*"

"Sparky! What do you say?" Lucy smiled.

"Oops. Excuse me, Mom. That was really, really yummy," he said with a satisfied grin. "Can I get another one?"

"Of course, honey. The tree is covered with them. Help yourself," Lucy encouraged.

Sparky began to climb to the top of the log where he'd gotten the first mussel.

"Where are you going, Sparks?" Lucy questioned. "There are tons of mussels down here!"

"I know, Mom, but I am sure the best ones are at the top!" he said over his shoulder as he scampered higher.

"All right, but save some room for the rest of the treats."

"'Kay, Mom!" Sparky yelled down from the top.

While Sparky ate mussels, Lucy sat beside the log and surveyed her domain for intruders. She sniffed the air deeply and listened intently in all directions. Then she looked all around her. Cotton puff clouds floated in the deep blue sky above them. Bright afternoon sunlight glistened on the shimmering new green leaves of the aspen and alder trees that mingled in with huge conifers and decorated the mountainsides. All the trees in the wide valley danced and swayed in perfect time to the buffeting song of the northwest wind. High on the rocky peaks, Father Winter's last snow was melting quickly in the heat of the midday sun. The water tumbled in streams and freefalling waterfalls to the inlet far below, but the low tide had pulled the water out into the inlet, exposing large areas of gray-green mudflats that the snow meltwater had to cut channels through in order to reach its destination.

Lucy sat and enjoyed the sun's warmth for some time. Then she looked up to see what Sparky was doing. The corners of her happy bear mouth turned up into a huge smile as she saw the tiny cub almost upside down, holding gingerly onto a large branch while tugging with all his might at the mussels and then blissfully munching them.

"Sparky!" Lucy had to raise her voice to get his attention off the mussels.

Sparky stopped crunching and looked at Lucy upside down with a silly contented grin. "Yeth, muom?" he tried to say with a mouthful of mussels.

"Come down and we will go flip rocks and look for rock crabs," Lucy encouraged.

"Okay, Mom, just one more mussel and I will be right down," he said and then began to tug and pulled off a huge muscle. Crunching the shellfish all the way down, Sparky dug his long needle-sharp claws between the mussels into the slippery wood and skillfully negotiated the log until he was at Lucy's side. "Yummy!" he smiled and bounced around his mother with all four feet coming off the ground at the same time. "Those things are so good! Let's go! If the crabs are as good as the mussels, I can hardly wait to try them."

"They are much better, Sparky. Come on. Follow me down to the beach to my favorite rock patch, and we will flip rocks and look for crabs!" Lucy said excitedly and began to trot down the mudflats of the inlet shoreline toward a stretch of rocks exposed by the low ocean.

Sparky ran playfully after her. He stopped briefly to stand on his hind legs and swat at a bee buzzing around his nose. As they ran through a patch of particularly soft mushy mud, Sparky giggled and slowed down to play in the gooey muck.

"Ohhh!" he said blissfully. "This feels so good. So gushy and squishy between my toes!" Then he giggled with glee as he ran around in circles in the mud. A spray of muck flew out from under him as he skidded around in reckless circles, sliding sideways. "Yahoo!" he howled. Then he ran as fast as he could and skidded on all fours. "Wee!" he squealed. Sparky looked up and saw Lucy had carried on ahead of him. "Wait for me, Mom!" he yelled and scampered after her. His feet squished into the mud, leaving perfect tiny bear paw prints behind him.

Sparky's feet were covered with a thick coating of mud that made him look as though he were wearing two pairs of rubber boots—one pair on his front feet and one pair on his hind feet. The fur on his sides and back was also caked in mud. Speckles of muck had sprayed all over his face, which made him look like he had big freckles all over his nose. He stopped suddenly and looked cross-eyed at a large piece of mud that had flicked up on his long snout. He shook his head to remove it and continued running down the shoreline after his mother.

Lucy heard Sparky's voice and turned to see where her son had gotten to. When she saw him, she burst out into laughter.

"Jumpin' jellyfish! Sparky! What a mess you are! You look like you got attacked by the mud monster from the ooey-gooey swamp! After we eat clams, it is bath time for you at the river!"

"Oh bear! I get to swim! Yippee!"

They ran together down the beach and arrived at a large flat area covered with rocks.

"Where's the crabs, Mom?" Sparky said excitedly.

"Well, Mr. Mud Cake! We start flipping the rocks and look for the tasty crabs underneath them. Here! Watch me!"

Lucy skillfully took her paw and hooked her five-inch toenails under the edge of a very large rock and flipped it over. About sixteen small rock crabs scurried out from under the rock, and Lucy quickly slurped them into her mouth and crunched them up and swallowed them down.

"Wow!" Sparky exclaimed. "You have to be really fast!"

"Yes, Sparks. It may take time, but you will catch the crabs. Now go ahead and give it a try."

Sparky looked at a rock beside him. He put his paw ready over the top of it and extended his claws over the edge. He looked at his mother and, with great determination, said, "Okay, Mom, I am ready." Then as fast as his paw could go, he quickly flipped the rock. Ten rock crabs bolted in all directions trying to get to the safety of surrounding rocks. Sparky frantically raced after them all, but he did not catch one.

"Oh frog fart!' he groaned and sat down looking very dejected. "I missed them all."

Lucy laughed. "It is okay, cubby. The little fellows are fast. The first time I tried, it took me about ten rocks before I got one crab. The key is to focus on one crab at first, not all of them. Now keep trying, Sparks. You will be successful if you just keep on trying."

"Did it really take you that long to learn, Mom?" Sparky asked.

"Yes, it did. Taku made the crabs move quickly so bears would not eat them all at once. Now try again and pick one crab to catch."

Again Sparky readied his paw over a rock and then quickly flipped it over. He grabbed a crab in his front teeth and sucked it into his mouth. He closed his eyes, and his face contorted as if he had just sucked on a very sour lemon. Then he forcefully spit the crab back on the mud with a *pahpht*! sound.

Lucy looked at her cub with great concern. "What is the matter, honey?"

Slowly Sparky opened his eyes and relaxed his face. Finally he blurted out. "That crab felt really yucky in my mouth, Mom! It was squiggly and squirming all over the inside of my mouth! I really don't think I can eat crabs, Mom! They are gross feeling!"

Lucy laughed. "Oh, Sparks!" she exclaimed. "All bears feel that way when they first try eating crabs. You have to crunch them up really quickly and not let them move around in your mouth. They taste so good that once you eat your first one, you will forget about the movement and just want more. Now try again."

"Oh yuck! Can't we just move on to clams?" Sparky pleaded.

"No!" Lucy insisted in a stern voice. "Now try again!"

Sparky looked at her longingly.

"Please, Mom!" he begged.

"Go on. Try again!" she insisted.

"Oh, Mom! You will be sorry when I get sick all over the place!" Sparky scowled as he readied himself over a rock. "I really don't want to do this," he said in one last attempt to not feel the crab in his mouth.

"Sorry, buddy. No luck. Now flip the rock and eat the crab," Lucy insisted.

Sparky rolled his eyes. "Okaaay!" he whined.

Quickly he flipped the rock and grabbed a crab in his mouth. He fell backward with the same sour lemon face as before, and this time, he plugged his nose with his paws as he crunched madly. Suddenly he began to slowly untie his contorted tiny bear body and sat up munching peacefully.

Lucy stopped her fits of laughter long enough to ask, "Well, what do you think, young bear?"

"Wow! Those squiggly critters are great! They still feel gross and yucky squirming in my mouth, but they are really yummy!" Then he poised his paw over another rock, flipped it, and grabbed and crunched another crab. Quickly he moved to another rock and did the same.

"That's my cub!" Lucy encouraged. "You are the best crab grabber I have ever seen!"

"Thanks, Mom! It is easy!"

Lucy began to feast on the crabs herself and occasionally glanced at her son to watch his antics. Suddenly she caught sight of a large male bear that stepped out onto the mudflat shoreline on the other side of the inlet. "Sparky! Stand still for a moment!" she quickly whispered.

Sparky knew her tone of voice meant possible trouble, so he froze. The male was moving quickly toward the estuary and did not see Lucy and Sparky. She waited until he was out of sight then said, "Okay, Sparky, the male bear is gone."

"What male bear?" Sparky gasped as he remained frozen.

"The one on the other side of the inlet across from us."

"The other side of the inlet? He couldn't see us from over there, could he?" Sparky squinted his eyes as he checked the direction Lucy was still watching.

"Well, honey, I could see him, so he could see us. Most adult bears are very perceptive to movement, so he may not see a bear shape, but he would see something moving, and he might have come over to investigate. And if the wind was blowing in his direction, he could have smelled us. We just always have to be cautious and aware of our surroundings," Lucy explained.

"Did you see who it was, Mom?" Sparky asked.

"I could not make the bear out from this distance, but it was a very big bear that moved and walked like Scarface. Whoever it was, he's heading into the estuary. We'll have to keep a good watch out over the next few days until he moves on out of the area. We don't want any surprises or trouble," she said with concern as she continued to look in the direction the huge bear had traveled.

"I think I better start looking around more often for danger. I didn't even see him. Life on Waipo is kind of scary with all the male bears just popping out of nowhere," he said nervously. "Can I move now, Mom?"

"Yes, you can move, and it is a good idea to be more aware of your surroundings. For now I am here to protect you, but you will have to learn to keep an eye open at all times for danger. The main goal for this green time is to make sure you make it through safely to leaf-dropping season. When you are safe in the den hibernating, we will have gotten you through your most vulnerable time of life."

Sparky looked at Lucy. "Have you ever had a fight with a male bear, Mom?"

Lucy snuggled Sparky closer. "Well, honey, this is probably a good time to tell you my story about male bears. It is not a nice story, but you have to learn about the dangers of being a bear some time, so I will tell you the story.

"It sounds scary, Mom. Are you sure you I am old enough?" Sparky said nervously.

"Yes, Sparky, I will have to tell you some time. Now come sit close." She pawed the ground beside her, and Sparky cuddled in. "It happened just after I had come out of hibernation in my second spring. My mom and two brothers and I were on an adventure down to the next creek toward the ocean. We had stopped for a break when a large aggressive male bear came charging out of the forest and attacked us. My mom was trying to protect us cubs and herself, but I was the only one to survive."

"That's really horrible and scary! I am really afraid now! We better keep looking for male bears!" Sparky exclaimed and looked around nervously.

"Right now we are fine," Lucy reassured. "I always listen and watch for danger, Sparky, but it is good that you do too."

"I will start, Mom," he sat and thought for a moment. "Were you as small as I am when it happened?"

"I was in my second flower bloom, but I was still very small, so I was very lonely and scared. For a week, I hid in a cave, afraid to move. Finally I got so thirsty and hungry I had to eat, so

I came back here to Mouse Creek where I had lived with my family. I knew I had to start a life of my own or I too would die. Every day I sat and ate grass all alone. I dreamed about my family and wished I could play with my brothers and snuggle my mom. I was very lonely. Every day I wished for a friend to keep me company. I missed my family so much."

Sparky hugged Lucy. "You will never have to be alone again, Mom. You have me."

"I know and I love you for that." Lucy licked Sparky's head and continued. "Then one day as I ate grass, I got very sleepy. I lay down in the grass, and just as I was falling asleep, I again wished for a friend. When I woke up, my wish had come true. There in the water was that funny-looking round-shaped hollow log that the 'tall one'—the male that always comes to see me—calls a boat, or Zodiac, and the log was full of smooth skins. At first I was scared, just like you are, but they did not show aggression, and they did not try to grab me when I got close, so I decided that Taku had sent them to be my friends."

"Well, I guess the smooth skins are all right, but I still don't trust them. And I am really going to watch for male bears." Sparky took a deep breath and sighed. "It seems like everyone is trying to eat me or kill me, and all I want to do is have a long happy fun life on Waipo."

"You can have fun on Waipo, but you must always be aware of your surroundings. We will try to make sure we are both safe, but just in case, I want you to learn as much as possible and that starts with crabs. Now where were we? Oh yes, you had mastered rock flipping and crab nabbing, so off you go. Let's continue on. You are doing so well."

Sparky flipped and munched his way down the beach, trying to remember to constantly look around and on the opposite shoreline for danger. Soon he came to a very large rock.

"Wow! I bet there is a million crabs under this rock!" he exclaimed.

Focusing all his attention on the rock, he placed his paw over top of it and quickly tugged up on the edge. Nothing happened. So Sparky put two paws on the edge of the rock and tugged with all his might. Still nothing happened. Determined to flip the huge rock, he climbed on top of it and put his claws under its edge and readied himself. With all his might, he tugged and pulled and grunted and groaned until his little bear eyes bugged out of his head. He jumped up and down on the rock and then tugged and pulled again. Suddenly he lost his grip and flew backward, landing in a heap on the ground, puffing from exhaustion.

Lucy, who had seen Sparky's eagerness, hurried to his side. She did not want him to get discouraged, so she eagerly said, "I bet there is enough crabs under this rock to feed us both. Come on, Sparks. We will both grab this side and flip the rock together."

Sparky enthusiastically jumped to his feet and positioned himself beside his mom.

"Okay, honey," Lucy smiled. "I will say 'mussel, clam, crab,' and when I say 'crab,' we will tug on the rock and flip it over. Okay?

"Okay, Mom!" Sparky said excitedly.

"Ready? Mussel! Clam! *Crab!*"

When they pulled the rock, it flipped easily, and about fifty crabs ran from under it. Lucy and Sparky frantically licked the crabs off the ground, and Sparky giggled the whole time. With bulging cheeks like a pair of fat squirrels with too many nuts in their mouths, they both sat down and began to munch the crabs. Sparky closed his eyes, chewed, swallowed, and took a deep breath. "Boy, those were so good, Mom, but I am getting full and very sleepy."

"Well, sweetie, we still have to go on a clam treasure hunt. We will walk to the river and clean the mud off your fur first. By the time you walk and swim, you will be ready for a clam snack before we have an afternoon nap."

"Okay, Mom," Sparky said, and with a bloated belly, he tottered along behind his mother to the edge of the Khutzeymateen River.

The hot summer sun beat down on Sparky's back, and he yawned so wide that all his teeth showed.

"Look!" Lucy said as she watched him. "It's a huge canyon with teeth! You yawned so wide, you swallowed your head!"

"Mom!" Sparky giggled. "I am really sleepy! Can we have a nap for a bit before we swim and dig for clams?" he pleaded with sleepy eyes.

"Well, piggly wiggly, you have been such a good cub today, I will agree to a nap first. After all, you will no doubt get mucky digging clams, so we might as well do the entire clean-up job later." She looked at Sparky as his eyelids hung heavily over his eyes. "Come on, sleepyhead. Quickly into the sedge grass and snuggle in beside me here for a nap."

Sparky flopped down against Lucy's chest and was asleep before his little body hit the ground. His wee mouth hung open, and tiny bear snores came out from between his small bear teeth. Lucy looked at the mud freckles on her cub's adorable, peaceful face. She smiled to herself and said, "Oh, I do love you, my little one." Then she gently licked his nose, lay her paw protectively over him, closed her eyes, and fell into a deep sleep in the warm spring sun.

Chapter 10:
The Magic of Feathers and Fur

Sparky woke from his afternoon nap and opened one eye. He snuggled in closer to Lucy, who was still sound asleep with her paw protectively over Sparky's back. Quietly he listened to the sounds of the forest. In the cedar tree above him, a choir of chickadees sang a variety of pitches. "*Chick-a-dee-dee-dee, chick-a-dee-dee-dee-dee*," they merrily sang as they flitted from branch to branch, picking at bugs and seeds. In the distance one hermit thrush called to another with a shrill high-pitch whistle.

Taking care not to wake Lucy, Sparky wiggled out from under her paw and sat up. He could see a proud set of harlequin duck parents swimming with their family of four. The male made high-pitched nasally squeaking sounds, trying to keep his family together as they scurried around the edge of the inlet in search of food.

"I wish I could speak bird," Sparky whispered. "Then I could understand what all my forest friends were saying."

Suddenly Sparky heard a humming sound coming from behind him. Frantically, he look around and listened intently as it got closer and closer.

"That sounds like a pretty big bee!" he whispered nervously.

Then a streak came toward him, and the humming became very loud. The streak momentarily stopped right in front of Sparky's nose and hovered effortlessly. Cross-eyed, Sparky tried to focus on the iridescent green hummingbird with a very long sharp beak. It was looking him right in the eye. As if to say hello, the tiny bird made a buzzing squeaky sound and then darted off to a nearby patch of bright red Indian paintbrush flowers. With its long beak, the bird began to drink the nectar of each flower.

"Wow!" Sparky whispered, trying not to wake his mom, who was snoring with giant peaceful rumbles. "That was so cool! Can hummers ever fly fast!"

Sparky heard a noise high in a hemlock tree near the water's edge. "*Pee-pee-pee-pee-pee.*" He looked up and saw a bald eagle regally surveying its territory. Suddenly the large raptor dove headfirst toward the inlet water. To become more aerodynamic and streamlined, the eagle tucked its wings close to its body, which made him travel at amazing speed. At the last minute, he extended his feet out in front of him, and no sooner did the eagle's feet hit the water than they emerged with a very large fish. The eagle struggled to lift the extra weight of the fish out of the water and into the air. He flapped his wings hard and with much effort slowly flew the tasty treat back up to the nest where two noisy hungry eaglets waited impatiently for their lunch.

"Wow!" Sparky whispered. "That fish was bigger than me! I wish he had dropped that fish in the grass beside me! Mom keeps telling me how yummy fish are to eat. I guess I will have to wait until fall when all those, hmmm … What did mom call them? Hmmm … oh yeah, simon. No, that's not right … somon … er …"

Sparky held his head with his paws.

"Hmmm … oh yeah! Salmon!" he exclaimed. "When the salmon start to swim up the rivers to lay their families. That is when I will taste fish!" Sparky thought for a moment about the fish. He wondered what they looked like, how they would taste, where they came from, and why bears ate them. He wondered if it was actually fair to eat the fish if they were coming to lay their families. "I wish Mom would wake up so I could ask her."

Sparky felt Lucy's paw slide by his back as she stirred from a deep sleep. He turned to see his mom stretching her long bear legs out straight to the side. All of her pointy yellowed teeth and her big fat pink tongue showed during a huge yawn. She snorted a couple of times, rolled onto her back, and rubbed her back into the ground for a scratch. Then she opened one eye and smiled at him. Before she could open her other eye, Sparky began to ask her all about salmon.

Westy's head suddenly popped up over a large mossy patch on top of his stump where he had been snoozing on his back in the sun.

"Salmon! Was I dreamin'? Did someone say salmon? Did I hear that magical word *salmon*?" he asked enthusiastically.

"No, no, sorry, Westy. False alarm. Sparky is just asking questions about salmon," Lucy explained sleepily.

"*Ah jeez!*" he grouched disappointedly and his head disappeared.

Sparky again asked his questions about salmon.

Lucy yawned and stretched then said, "Oh, my starfish Sparky, how come you have so many questions all of a sudden?" she yawned again. "Let me wake up a bit more, and I will answer all your questions about salmon."

"Did someone say salmon! Is green time over already?" Mica and Cliff excitedly chimed as they scurried down their spruce tree and bolted across the shore to Sparky and Lucy.

"Sorry, Mica and Cliff. Sparky is just asking about salmon. It is not time for the leaves to fall yet," Lucy explained.

"Oh phew! I thought I had to start collecting cones for the winter and stashing them away in my secret place so intruders," Cliff said as he looked at Mica, "won't steal them."

"Who caught who stealing cones out of whose stash last snow?" Mica scowled defensively at Cliff. "And like there will be any cones left in the entire forest by leaf-dropping time! You will have eaten them *all* and added them *all* to your fat collection!"

"I'll show you!" And they were off.

"But, Mom!" Sparky continued with concern. "Is it really fair to be eating the salmon if they are coming to have their families? Won't they become, what's that word you told me the other day? Hmmm ... axpinked?"

Lucy could tell her cub was very worried about the salmon.

"Now calm down, my love. That word is *extinct*, and no, the salmon will not become extinct from bears and other animals eating them. There are hundreds of thousands of salmon, and they lay millions of eggs every year. Many thousands of salmon hatch each year to replace the ones we eat. You see, son, the great bear spirit Taku has everything very well balanced in nature. The salmon are food for many creatures including whales, seals, sea lions, eagles, gulls, rodents, wolves, and bears. Many animals depend on the salmon for food, and that is why Taku made so many salmon. Even though we all eat salmon, there are still many left to lay eggs so the salmon will continue on forever. Taku balances everything so all can survive. It is only when too many salmon are taken in large quantities or if the salmon are disrupted in some way that their survival would be a problem."

Sparky thought for a moment then asked, "Mom what is an egg? I know you told me my bird friends come from eggs and their mommies have to sit on the eggs so they hatch. Do fish have to sit on their eggs to hatch them?"

"Yes, birds do lay eggs and patiently sit on them until they hatch, but salmon do not. The female salmon use their tails to dig their nest, or red as they are also called, in the bottom of the rivers and creeks in the sand or pea gravel. They lay their eggs, the male fertilizes them, and then the male covers them back up with his tail. Both parents then swim away. With their life cycle completed, they then die. Fish do not sit on the nest like birds do."

"But what is a salmon egg?" Sparky persisted. "Or any egg for that matter?"

"A salmon egg is yummy! A salmon egg is yummy! A salmon egg is yummy!" all fifty gulls began to squawk at once.

"Thank you, gulls, but I don't think that is what Sparky meant," Lucy said to the gulls and then turned back to Sparky. "You have much to learn about life and nature, my little one. An egg is what all life comes from. You came from an egg," Lucy explained patiently.

"I hatched! " Sparky exclaimed in shock. "Did you sit on me for a long time 'til I was done enough to be a baby bear!"

Lucy laughed and laughed and held her cub close.

"Oh, my wee little one, you are such a blessing to me." She managed to stop laughing at her son's innocence. "No, you were not hatched. You were born."

"Did I come out like I look now?" Sparky pointed and looked at his tummy and paws.

"No, no, no. You only weighed one pound, and you were almost bald. You only had a little bit of very fine gray hair in spots on your body. You also could not see because it took three weeks for your eyes to open."

"Yuck! No fur! I must have been all pink and funny-looking!" Sparky wrinkled up his nose. "I am glad I could not see myself! I must have looked really ugly! Yuck!"

Lucy hugged Sparky close. "From the day you were born, you were beautiful, and I have loved you very much. Hair or no hair."

Sparky giggled. "Thanks, Mom. I know you have always loved me. How big am I now?"

"You are about twelve pounds (5.4 kilograms). When we came out of the den, you were ten pounds (4.5 kilograms)."

"How big will I get, Mom?" Sparky questioned.

"Well that depends on a few things, like how much salmon you eat, how much rest you get, and if you take after your ancestors. Your great-grandfather Pojah was a giant bear that weighed 1,300 pounds (590 kilograms). He was king of the forest for twenty years. Every bear in our territory respected him, and few challenged his intelligence, power, and strength. So you could grow to be as big as Pojah."

"Wow! I could get that big?" Sparky looked at his tiny bear body, and then he looked up at his mom. "I better start growing faster if I want to be that big!"

Lucy laughed. "You will have time enough to grow, my wee one. And yes, you could get that big. We are the largest and strongest mammals on our landmass. We are also one of the strongest mammals on Waipo. Your father, Buffalo, is also a very large strong bear, and he weighs 1,000 pounds (454 kilograms). He is now king of our forest."

"Will I ever meet him, Mom?"

"No, Sparks. He is to busy watching his kingdom. He is not a very patient bear, and he, like most older male bears, does not take kindly to young male bears. Male grizzly bears are very territorial. There is only so much land for us to live on, and they will fight other male intruders to the death to keep their homes. Male grizzly bears also try to make as many of their own baby bears as they can to keep their line of offspring alive. Males will try to kill bear cubs that they come across in the forest. They will even kill their own offspring from previous years. That is one of the many reasons it is very important for you to stay close to your big old mom at all times," she explained.

Sparky's eyes popped open wide with fear. "I knew other bears would kill me, but even my own dad? I don't ever want to run into any male grizzly bears! Ever! And I am never leaving my mom! Ever!"

"Not to worry, Sparky. I will do everything I can to protect you, and by the time you are on your own, you will be big enough and have all the bear knowledge you need to say alive. It is best for us to both stay away from all male bears. You will understand how male bears are as you grow older. Now come on. Let's munch on some grass before we go dig for clams," she said enthusiastically.

At the thought of clams, Sparky jumped to his feet, but before he ran to the beach, he scanned the shoreline and all around him for danger.

"Oh boy!" Sparky exclaimed. "I get to eat clams. Can we skip the grass and go right to clams? I know I will love clams!"

Lucy smiled and said, "Grass first, young bear."

Chapter 11:
Cats and Dogs

"The sun is beginning to hide behind the mountain, Sparky. It's time to make our way back to Mouse Creek and into our den for the night."

"Okay, mom." Sparky romped beside Lucy as they sauntered along a bear trail beside the inlet.

The sky turned a pale yellow-blue color as the last clouds of the day glowed golden in the sky. Gradually the colors turned to peach and orange, and the spaces between the tall spruce trees along the bear trail grew darker and darker.

"Are we almost there?" Sparky said nervously. "It's getting pretty dark, and I wish we were safe in our den."

"Not much farther," Lucy reassured her cub. "Stick close, honey, and we will be there soon."

Suddenly the bears heard a loud thud on the ground close behind them followed by an ear-piercing "*Raaarrr!*"

Lucy spun around like a leaf in a tornado, and Sparky bolted between her front legs just as quickly.

"Not funny, Calvyn!" Lucy yelled at a cougar standing aggressively on the trail in front of the bears. The cat's ears were slicked back, and its tail twitched confidently from side to side.

"Hello, Lucy, darrrling! What, no sense of humorrr tonight? I thought it would be a purrrfect night to drrrop out of my trrree and say hello. And purrrhaps get lucky and grab the little appetizerrr underneath you."

Sparky hid farther under Lucy's tummy. He shivered so hard with fear that his little bear teeth knocked together.

"Nice try, Calvyn," Lucy said impatiently, "but you will have to eat me first, and we both know that is not going to happen. Now don't you have to go sharpen your claws on a tree or something? We have to get back to our den." She put her hackles up and stood as tall as she could and began to pop her teeth irritably.

Calvyn's aggressive stance suddenly deflated, and he turned slightly sideways to try to look bigger.

"Well, no need to be rrrude, Lucy." Calvyn sulked.

"Calvyn, you just jumped out of a tree and scared the tails off us. Then you threatened to eat my cub. I am not happy to see you now, so have a good night. We have to be on our way. Now beat it!" Lucy warned.

"Oh *rrraaarrr* yourself!" Calvyn snarled, his face scrunched up like a dried apple and all his sharp pointed teeth glistening in the remaining light of evening. "Grrrouchy bearrr! No sense of humorrr!" he exclaimed and bounded off into the deep shadows of the forest.

"Oh, he is annoying!" Lucy said and nuzzled Sparky gently. "Are you all right?"

"That cougar was the scariest yet!" Sparky shuddered.

"I will protect you, Sparky. Here, walk ahead of me until we get back to the den."

"Good idea, Mom."

The bears briskly walked the remaining short distance to their den and quickly slipped inside to safety as the sky turned a deep red color and the wolves began to howl.

"Mom, that cougar was really horrible," Sparky stuttered. "He was mean to scare us like that."

"Calvyn is all talk, Sparky. He likes to sneak up on creatures that he cannot compete with because it makes him feel tough.

He won't bother you once you are my size or bigger. Until then I will protect you," she reassured her cub.

"Mom, what is that noise?" Sparky asked with great concern.

"That's the local wolf pack out on an evening hunt," Lucy explained.

"I am glad we are safe in our den," Sparky sighed and snuggled closer to Lucy. "What are wolves? Do they eat us too?"

"Wolves are a member of the canine or dog family. They don't usually bother us bears. Sometimes a lone wolf out scouting for prey will get bored and will try to play with us for a while. And in the fall, the wolves can get pretty cocky and say nasty things when they stay thin and us bears get a little pudgy, but generally, we all keep to ourselves. They do their dog thing, and we do our bear thing. Now, it has been a long day, so off to sleep we go."

Sparky looked at Lucy and sweetly said, "I am really glad you are my mom." He cuddled in beside her. "Good night, Mom."

Lucy licked Sparky's head and put her paw protectively over him. "Sweet dreams, my special little cub."

Chapter 12:
Nibbly Bits

As the bears ambled down the bear trail that ran alongside Mouse Creek from their den site to the inlet shoreline, Sparky followed close behind Lucy and mimicked her every move. When Lucy stopped to sniff a salmonberry flower alongside of the trail, Sparky sniffed the same flower. He watched Lucy out of the corner of his eye as she put her front paws against a tree, gave a big stretch, raked her claws down the tree, and continued on the trail. Sparky put his front feet on the same tree—lower to the ground—stretched, and raked his claws along the tree trunk. Lucy walked up to a balsam fir and stood on her hind legs with her back against the tree. With a look of great pleasure on her face, she wriggled her body back and forth and up and down, scratching on the bark and sticky sap of the tree. Then she plopped back on all fours and snuffled her nose along the moss between the bear steps, scenting for intruders during the night.

Sparky waddled over to the fir, stood on his hind legs, and wriggled and jiggled his tiny back along the rough sticky bark. Then he rubbed the top of his head on the tree, dropped on all fours, put his nose to the moss, and snuffled his way along the footprints. They finally came out on the sedge grass beside the inlet and began to eat it. The grass was now taller than Sparky.

"Mom, how come we eat sedge grass?" Sparky asked as he made a big effort to find the newest shoot and nibble bits off the tender tops of the younger sedge grass.

"Our bodies need the moisture from the sedge grass, especially in the spring when we have not had any water all winter. It is also good roughage to get our tummies working again after not eating during hibernation. We also need all the nutrients that the sedge grass produces. There are many minerals from the ocean that collect in the sedge and the plants' chlorophyll that absorbs light through photosynthesis is very healthy for us. Sedge grass is also good food to hold us over until the berries ripen and the tubers and plant roots are ready to dig, and the very best thing is when the salmon come in the fall to spawn. Then we eat like the bear gods."

"Well, these nibbly bits are really good," Sparky said and smacked his lips.

Lucy looked up at her cub and smiled. The green chlorophyll in the sedge had stained his tiny soft muzzle around his mouth and turned his tongue a bright green color.

"I am glad you like the sedge because it is one of our staple foods. When you grow up to be my size, you will eat up to eighty pounds of sedge grass a day," Lucy explained.

"Wow! That's a lot of grass!" Sparky exclaimed.

"Yes, it is, but we need to eat that much to get all the nutrients we need."

"Mom!" he suddenly said.

"Yes, Sparky?" she said between mouthfuls.

"What is frot ... er ... froto ... er ... frotosinasis?" he asked inquisitively.

"That is photosynthesis, son. It is the way plants make food," Lucy patiently explained. "Plants contain chlorophyll; it gives them their green color. Chlorophyll absorbs energy from sunlight, which allows the plant to change carbon dioxide and water into food. This process forms glucose, a type of sugar that travels through the plants vascular system in a liquid called sap, or you could say the plants' blood. Sunlight allows the process to occur. In fact, if you think about it, plants actually eat light, Sparky."

"Wow! That is so cool!" Sparky said with amazement. "Plants are pretty smart if they can eat light! I wish we could eat light. Can you imagine how much more playtime we would have if we did not have to find food and eat it! We could just play all the time! And my jaw would never get tired from all the chewing we do, and my teeth would last forever!"

Lucy laughed at her son's imagination. "Well, honey, that is true, but unfortunately, we have to eat, and there is no way around it."

"Mom. Does Noni eat light?" Sparky asked sweetly.

"Yes, Sparks. Most all plants on the planet eat light, Noni included. Even the ocean plants. And do you know what else?"

"No, what?"

"Plants give off the oxygen that we breathe, and they absorb carbon dioxide, our waste product from breathing. Plants not only supply us with essential nutrients we need to eat, but they also create the oxygen we need to breathe. "

"Wow! Noni is even more important to me now! Noni helps me survive. I will always try to protect Noni," Sparky sighed and sat down. He looked at the top of the spruce that reached over one hundred feet into the sky.

"Yes, Sparky. Without Noni, all her friends, and all of the ocean plants, where most of the planet's oxygen is produced, our water planet Waipo, would be much different. Without plants and particularly trees, we would not have oxygen to breathe, and we would not be able to stay alive. Without healthy forests, there might not be enough oxygen for us to breathe, and we would not survive. The great bear spirit Taku and all the other animal spirits that created Waipo thought of everything. Everything on Waipo is in perfect balance." She looked at Sparky as he munched more grass. "And without all these tender shoots of sedge grass, we would have a hard time surviving. You see, Sparky, we must eat large quantities of sedge grass to get enough nutrients. Herbivores are able to get all the nutrients they need from eating plants. Omnivores need a variety of foods including vegetation."

Sparky contemplated all his mother's words of wisdom as he ripped off a huge mouthful of sedge, chewed for a few minutes, swallowed, and then asked, "Mom?"

"Yes, Sparky?" Lucy said patiently.

"What are ... er ... herbvorss and ... er ... omvores?"

"Good question. Sorry, I should have explained that further. In the animal world, there are basically three different groups—herbivores, carnivores, and omnivores. The herbivores include animals like deer, mountain goats, elk, moose, and sheep. Do you remember Daisy Deer you saw swimming across the inlet?"

"Yes," Sparky said. "She can't just eat grass and plants and be able to swim across the inlet!"

"Yes, Sparky. That is all Daisy eats. Herbivores eat only vegetable matter, grasses, and other plants. Now do you remember Calvyn, the cocky cougar we had the run in with on the trail along the inlet? Remember he jumped out of a tall tree right behind you. Luckily I was close, or you would have been his bedtime snack."

"Oh yeah! The cat that wanted to eat me!" Sparky shivered. "I didn't like him too much. He gave me the wormies in my tummy. I hope I will never see him again. I don't want to be his snack! I'm getting the feeling lots of animals would kill and eat me, at least until I am big enough to protect myself."

"Unfortunately that's true, Sparky, but that's why your mom is here to protect you until you are big enough to defend yourself." Lucy nuzzled Sparky reassuringly and then continued. "Calvyn the cougar wanted to eat you because he is a carnivore. They eat meat, mostly the herbivores, but they will try to eat other animals, as we found out. Their diet is very low in vegetation."

"Well, I really don't want to be a food group in anybody's diet!" Sparky exclaimed.

"Not to worry, my cub. We'll not let any harm come to you," she said and put her big paw around him and pulled him in close to her. "Mom will take good care of you, honey."

Sparky snuggled in close beside her.

"Now, in the middle of herbivores and carnivores are the omnivores, who eat both vegetable matter and meat. Each group has a much different shaped skull and teeth. Also the muscle structure of the skull in each group is very different. Herbivores have a long jaw with more delicate muscles because they do not need to chew tough meat or hard bones. Most of their teeth have flat grinding surfaces and are located at the back of the jaw where most of the jaw strength is focused."

"Hey! I remember Daisy had a long nose!" Sparky said.

"Very good, Sparks, that is right. Carnivores have a shorter well-muscled skull and jaw for maximum strength to rip and chew meat. Their jaw is full of very sharp, pointy jagged teeth good for breaking down the meat they survive on."

"Like that pudgy-faced, mean-looking Calvyn. I remember his mouth full of really sharp teeth when he made that horrible snarling sound right at us." Sparky cringed.

"Honey, Calvyn was just trying to be a pushy cat. We will make sure he does not sneak up on us again. The other animal type is omnivore. They are a combination of both. Like the carnivores, they have a heavily muscled skull with a midrange jaw. The jaw is full of a combination of teeth shapes and sizes good for processing all of the different kinds of food omnivores eat. They have grass-ripping teeth in the front. Their meat-grinding teeth at the back are not as jagged as the carnivores, but not as flat surfaced as the herbivores. They also have sharp long canine incisor teeth and other similar teeth midjaw, which are used for killing and ripping flesh." She paused for a moment and looked at her cub. "Do you know which group we are in, Sparky?"

Sparky thought for a second then sat up and looked at Lucy. "We are omnivores because we eat both plants and meat!" Sparky said smartly.

"Very good, son! Yes, we are omnivores because we eat a variety of foods, both plant and animal. Sedge grass and other plants are our main food when we come out of hibernation, up until the time of year when the sun is at its highest and hottest. Then when the sun begins to sleep more each night, and the sedge is at its tallest and toughest and falls over on the ground, and the leaves are starting to think about turning yellow, we eat berries and roots. The berries give us lots of vitamins, and the roots help to kill off parasites in our bodies before we hibernate. When the leaves are yellow, we love to eat salmon. The combination of the roots killing parasites and the salmon oil making our tummies slippery so anything living in them will slide out easily makes us healthy for our hibernation. We don't want anything eating the fat stores we need to survive the winter, or we may not live through hibernation. And of course any opportunity to eat red meat is a big treat for us. Nothing beats a yummy fat seal or two or a mountain goat or even a plump little mouse treat."

Sparky thought about everything his mom had just told him. Then he said, "Mom?"

"Yes, Sparky?"

"What are berries?"

Lucy playfully smacked her lips and said, "Oh yummy! They are the super delicious sweet fruit that Taku puts on some of the bushes in the forest when the leaves on the trees turn yellow. My favorite is salmon berries. Oh, Sparks! You will love the berries. They are *so* sweet and juicy!" She sat down on her big furry back end and closed her eyes. "I am dreaming about them, and I can taste them right now." She licked and smacked her lips again.

"Stop it, Mom!" Sparky giggled. "You are making me so hungry! Those berry things sound really good!"

He thought again and then said, "Mom?"

"Yes, son?" Lucy again said patiently.

"What are somon? I know they are fish, but what are they and where do they come from? And what do they taste like?" he questioned.

81

"That is salmon, son, and they are the very best food in the world! Even better than berries."

"What are they?" Sparky again asked.

"Salmon are fish that come in from the ocean and swim up our rivers to lay their families in the form of eggs. Remember, we talked about that. There are four species of salmon that begin to arrive in our area when the leaves are starting to yellow, and by the time they are finished spawning, the snow will begin to fall, and we are ready to hibernate. The fifth species of salmon in our Pacific Ocean are sockeye salmon, but they do not spawn in the Khutzeymateen Valley."

"Species?" Sparky questioned.

"Species means types, and the smooth skins have given each of the five types of salmon in our area—the North Pacific Ocean as they call it—a name. sockeye salmon do not spawn in the Khutzeymateen River, but Chinook, coho, chum, and my absolute favorite pink salmon do spawn here. Last year there must have been one hundred thousand pink salmon come up Mouse Creek! I was in my glory! I just had to step into the creek, and presto, lunch was served. Their tender pink flesh is so yummy. It has a flavor like nothing else on Waipo. You will taste it when the leaves turn yellow up until snow time. Salmon to bears is like honey to bees. I must admit, I tend to pig out on salmon in the fall, but all bears do. The oily fish taste so good, especially since it will be starting to get cold and we need to fatten up for our snow time hibernation. I tend to eat anywhere from fifty to one hundred fish a day, and I put on at least one hundred pounds of weight in the fall eating those yummy fish," Lucy sighed.

"Fifty to one hundred fish! One hundred pounds of weight!" Sparky's eye bulged out of his head. "That's a lot of weight, Mom! Are you sure it is healthy to eat that much and put on that much weight?"

"Yes, it is a good thing, Sparks," Lucy laughed. "You will put on lots of weight, too. It is very important that we bulk up for our long snow time sleep because we do not eat from then until flower-blossom time arrives. You see, Sparks, without salmon, we would not survive through hibernation. We would not be able to get enough fat on our bodies to sustain us over winter. We would die in our dens. Salmon are the most important food to all bears that live near the ocean."

Sparky looked at his mom, then at Noni, and then at the sky. "Thank you, Taku, for making the plants, trees, salmon, and most of all for my very special mom. She is the best and she is so smart." He paused and continued to look at the sky. "I really love being alive, and without everything in nature, I would not be here. Thank you Taku, Waipo, and Universe." Then Sparky smiled at his mom and munched some more sedge grass. "Mom, I love you and these nibbly bits!"

Chapter 13:
The Bears and the Bees

Early morning sunshine broke through the low rain clouds as they slowly evaporated, allowing the mountain peaks a view of Sparky and Lucy's antics. Both bears chased each other at full speed. Their ears were slicked back on their heads as they ran full out with big smiles on their faces.

"Come here, you little purple porcupine!" Lucy yelled as she dashed after Sparky through the wet sedge grass and down to the mudflats.

The morning mist split in two as their bodies flew along the shoreline, and it then settled again behind the romping bears.

"You are as slow as a slug in the mud," Sparky giggled.

"Oh! That does it, you little green frog fart! You don't stand a chance now!" Lucy laughed as she tackled Sparky midstride, wrestled him to the ground, and began to tickle him and nibble his tummy.

"I'm teehee … not a … teehee … little green fr … teehee … frog fart!" he giggled. "I … can't … br-breathe! Then he wriggled free and ran off through the sedge. "You're as slow as a turtle in reverse!" he yelled as Lucy dashed after him.

A little farther down the shoreline, she tackled him again and pinned him to the ground, nibbling gently and quickly over his exposed baby bear belly.

"Slug in the mud! Turtle in reverse! Now you're in for it!" Lucy giggled.

Sparky struggled with all his might, but Lucy was much stronger. Finally she rolled on her back and let him think he had won the wrestling match. He stood on top of her tummy with all four feet and aggressively but playfully held her down. Sparky chewed on Lucy's ears, then pulled on her lips, and nibbled on her chest as they both giggled uncontrollably. Lucy finally rolled Sparky onto the ground, and then he rolled on top of her. They continued to tumble around in the sedge grass over and over each other. Suddenly Lucy stopped and stood up with her paw on top of Sparky's head so he could not move.

"Mom!" Sparky whined.

"Shhh!" she hissed. "Be still!"

Sparky heard a branch snap, and he froze. Lucy slowly removed her paw from Sparky's head and put her nose high in the air, scenting the approaching danger. Sparky stood up and moved in between his mom and the inlet. He peeked out in the direction Lucy was sniffing. Lucy stood on her hind legs, still sniffing deeply with her snout high in the air. Her head swayed from side to side as she squinted into the forest on the bank up above them where a bear trail followed the inlet. Sparky stood on his hind legs behind his mom and did exactly as she did.

More twigs snapped and a *huff, huff, huff* sound emitted from the forest. Lucy looked at Sparky with an uncertain look. Then she got down on all fours. Sparky did the same. He moved closer to her, and she whispered, "I think I know who it is, and if I am right, we are okay. They will just be passing through our area."

Sparky nervously nodded his head. He knew the huffing sound would only be coming from another bear.

Lucy and Sparky stood motionless in the sedge grass on the shoreline. They both saw something moving quickly toward Mouse Creek from the direction of the Khutzeymateen Estuary. The movement was on the bear trail.

"Look!' Lucy whispered to Sparky. "See the flash of light-colored fur through the trees? Watch. There should be another. There! And a third. There!"

"How did you know tha ...?" Sparky's words trailed off as he froze, and his eyes grew very large when he saw what was approaching. There was not one, but three bears coming. The three bears emerged into a clearing in the trees just above Sparky and Lucy. The large bear spotted them. All five bears froze and looked at one another. Ever so slowly, Lucy widened the stance of her front legs, lowered her head, stared directly at the large blond bear, and made a *huff, huff, huff* sound at the trio. Sparky mimicked his mom's stance but stood slightly behind her and made no huffing sounds.

The blond female also stood facing Lucy and Sparky with her head lowered, while her two blond cubs with a white frosting color on the tips of their ears hid behind their mom and peeked out shyly at Lucy and Sparky. The blond female huffed a couple of times, and then both moms relaxed their stance while Sparky stood up on his hind legs to try to get a better view of the two cubs that were his age. One was slightly smaller than Sparky and the other much smaller. The blond female turned back onto the trail and slowly began to walk back toward the estuary. She stopped and waited as both her cubs briefly stood on their hind legs and sniffed curiously in Lucy and Sparky's direction. The smaller cub tripped over a tree root and tumbled over sideways. The larger cub got down on all fours and *huffed* impatiently at the cub on the ground. The small cub got up, shook her fur off, took another look at Sparky and Lucy, and then quickly scampered over to her mom. All three disappeared into the forest.

"Is it safe, Mom?"

"Yes, Sparky," Lucy said as she took one more sniff in the direction they had gone.

"Who were those bears?" Sparky asked.

"That's Blondie and her cubs of the year. They both looked smaller than you, Sparky, so I think they are both females."

"Wow! They are both my age," Sparky said excitedly. I would have liked to play with them. The small one was so cute when she fell over."

"Well, Sparks, they are Blondie's first cubs, just like you are my first cub, so she is very nervous about them getting close to any other bears. Maybe somewhere down the bear path of life, you can meet her cubs, but right now Blondie is as protective of them as I am of you. We can't take any chances with our cubs, not even with other females with cubs."

"I know, Mom, but they looked so pretty. Their fur was so blond, and their ears were glowing at the top." He looked down at his own fur, "My fur is such a dark brown color compared to theirs. Why is that, Mom? How come we are not all the same color?"

"It depends on what color your parents are. The majority of the dominant males in the Khutzeymateen Valley, the boy bears that make most of the cubs, have very dark brown fur, as do most females in the area. Blondie has very light fur, so this time her cubs took after her color. You're right. They are adorable cubs." Lucy thought for a moment. "Sometimes if a set of two cubs have two different fathers, the cubs will look completely different from each other. I know of two sister cubs that had different fathers, and one sister is dark brown with short fur while the other sister is blond with shaggy fur. You would never know they were born from the same mother, at the same time."

"Two fathers?" Sparky questioned.

"Okay, Sparks, it's time for our bears and the bees talk," Lucy said and cleared her throat. "Every three flower blooms, mother bears leave their cubs and are able to make more baby bears with male bears. The male bears chase and fight each other, and the stronger or dominant male breeds with the female."

"Oh yuck!" Sparky exclaimed. "I'm not going to fight any male bears just to get close to an icky girl bear and get girl bear germs! What a stupid thing to do!"

"I think you will change your mind as you get older," Lucy smiled.

Just then Westy's head poked out over his stump that was beside the bears.

"Yo, Sparky! Let me tell you, you'll definitely change your mind when the girls—"

"Thank you, Westy, for your input," Lucy quickly cut him off midsentence.

"Jeez, Lucy! I was just tryin' to encourage the cub!" he said and then disappeared behind the stump.

"Now female bears mate with as many males as they can to ensure they get the healthiest, strongest male sperm to fertilize their eggs. So one week, a female might mate with one male, and one of his sperm will fertilize an egg, or possibly two eggs, and then the twins will look the same. If one egg gets fertilized that week and the next week she mates with another male and another egg gets fertilized by the other male, two cubs would be born that might look completely different. A fertilized egg reaches what is called a blastocyst, which will remain dormant in the mother bear's uterus until flower bloom and green time are over. When leaf-dropping season comes, if the female bear is healthy and fat, the blastocyst will implant into the female bear's uterus. For three moons, the bear cub forms inside the mother bear. During the fourth moon change, a cub is born while the mother is hibernating. The one-pound, blind, and bald cub crawls up the mom and finds a teat to suckle. When flower time arrives, mom and cub emerge from the den, and the cub is ten pounds and covered with fur. And very cute and cuddly just like you were, Sparks," Lucy said, lovingly nuzzling him until he tumbled over sideways.

"Stop it, Mom!" Sparky pleaded as he grabbed her nose with both his paws and gave her a big lick.

"Does all that make sense?" Lucy asked.

"Yes, Mom, it does," he paused and then shyly asked. "Well, maybe we could meet the two girl cubs next flower time. I would really like to play with them and see which girl bear I like more."

Westy suddenly popped up again. "See I told you he would—"

"Yes, Westy. Thank you again, but don't you have to clean some fur balls out of your stump?" Lucy stopped him.

"Ah jeez, eh! The weasel's just tryin' to be a male role model and offer some male thoughts on the subject. I mean you are dealing with the king of romance here!" Westy said regally.

"That's the issue, Westy. Now we are doing just fine without your help," Lucy insisted.

"Fine!" Westy said in a high-pitched hurt tone. "Have it your way, but I am a wealth of knowledge in the love department. I'm off to see Rosebud then!"

"I think he was just trying to help, Mom," Sparky said. "You might have hurt his feelings."

"Some thing are best discussed between you and I, Sparky," Lucy reassured Sparky. "Not to worry, he is a tough little weasel. He'll be all right."

Suddenly two loud squeaking voices came out of a huge Sitka spruce tree near Sparky and Lucy, causing them to look up at the tree.

"You're just saying that cause Lucy's talking to Sparky about the bears and the bees!"

"No! It's cause I like her more than you do!"

"Well! She likes squirrels with muscle! And that would be me!"

"Ah, that's pretty wobbly muscle, chub pot! She likes lean and mean, and that would be *me*!"

"You're so scrawny, she would sneeze, and you would blow away."

"Well, your so fat, you'd break her branch trying to visit her!"

"Oooo! *I'll show you*!"

Sparky and Lucy watched as a whirlwind of squirrel went up and down the tree, chasing and wrestling each other.

Sparky looked back at Lucy and said, "Mom, it looks like girls can cause some trouble. Maybe I will not worry about girl bears for a while. I think I will be very careful with them and other boy bears."

"Good idea, Sparky," Lucy smiled. "You will probably get to meet Blondie's cubs next green time. Until then, just enjoy being a baby bear."

"Okay, Mom. Let's go climb some logs and practice more wrestling moves."

"You're on, Sparky, but you gotta catch me first!" she yelled as she bolted away.

"Mom! That's not fair! Oooo! *I'll show you*!"

Chapter 14:
Sparky Meets Buffalo and Lefty

Sparky and Lucy ventured into the forest from their den at Mouse Creek and headed in the direction of the Khutzeymateen Estuary. They stayed high on the mountain side above the inlet and investigated interconnecting bear trails that lead to bear rub trees, other den sites, and popular intersections. Sparky was busily trying to remember everything and asked Lucy a million questions that would help him later in life. Suddenly they froze in midstride as a primeval thundering echoed throughout the valley. Lucy sat down and listened while Sparky stood motionless. As he listened to the vicious growling and roaring, every muscle in his body tensed and quivered with fear. His eyes were wide, and his heart raced in panic at the horrific noise bellowing from the forest.

"Mom! What is going on? What is that horrible sound?" he finally whispered in terror.

"Oh, the dominant male bears are at it again," she said and shook her head. "They are fighting over a female because it is mating season." She paused and listened. "It sounds like two very large males."

By now the hackles on the back of Sparky's neck stood straight up in fright.

"They sound like two very scary monsters!" Sparky said as he trembled.

Lucy pulled him close to her. "Oh, honey," she said and nuzzled Sparky gently with her long nose. "It is all right. We will just be careful to stay out of sight. Besides, they are too busy beating each other up and chasing each other to worry about us."

"What is mating? Why would they be fighting over a yucky girl bear? They sound so mad! What will we do if they come out and see us?" he said with panic in his voice.

"Not to worry, Sparks. We will hide in the forest right away just in case they come this way. I really don't think they would see us or chase us because they are too busy trying to fight each other and trying to mate the female. Mating is what bears do to make baby bears like you. The male bears have found a female who is ready to have a cub, and they are now fighting over who gets to make the baby."

"That sounds really stupid. I can't imagine any reason for having a big fight over a silly girl bear." Sparky shook his head and snuggled closer to Lucy.

Lucy smiled at Sparky's innocence. "Well, honey, some day you will understand. Now let's find a place to hide."

Lucy quickly looked around her for a safe place. She saw two enormous trees surrounded by dense bushes deep in the shadows.

"Come on, Sparks. Let's get off this bear trail and hide over here for a while until things settle down. If they start to chase each other, they will no doubt come down the bear trail. We will be safe and out of sight in those bushes."

Lucy and Sparky quickly scampered to the safety of the giant Sitka spruce trees and hid among the enormous leaves of the devil's club plant and dense foliage of the salmonberry bushes. Their thick bear fur protected their skin from the needle-sharp thorns that covered the canes of the devil's club. Sparky looked above his head at the plants' foot-wide leaves, and even their undersides were covered with the sharp thorns.

They lay down in a thick mat of bright green moss and peeked out from the shadows of the forest. Sparky looked at the trail about fifty feet away as the roaring continued to echo through the valley. "Are you sure we are far enough away from the trail?"

"We will be safe here, Sparky," Lucy reassured her cub as he continued to tremble. "The males will not see us in the shadows. I am not sure exactly where they are fighting, so it is safer if we just sit tight until they either calm down or leave the area. If they charge by here chasing each other, they will be too preoccupied with each other and the female bear to notice us."

"Do we have to stay by the trail?" Sparky whispered with great concern.

"Yes, love. I want to be able to see which way the males go if they do run by so we can go the other way. The sun will be in their eyes, and we are deep in the shadows here. They will never see us, Sparks, not to worry. I have done this many times."

"But, Mom, what if they smell us?" Sparky whispered in panic.

"Bear scent from the trail and the bear trees will confuse them. We will be fine," Lucy reassured her nervous cub.

Just then the roaring stopped, and Lucy and Sparky looked at each other.

"Now what, Mom?" Sparky whispered and snuggled closer to her. He could hear his own heart pounding in fright. Sparky resisted the urge to run and trusted his mother's judgment.

"Shhh!" Lucy whispered. "Be very quiet and very still. I hear them coming."

Sparky suddenly froze as a horrendous racket of trees crashing and breaking and deep grasping and snorting came bellowing through the forest not far off. The huffing and growling that emitted from the bowels of the forest was terrifying. Sparky sat motionless, too afraid to blink let alone move.

Then a sight appeared that Sparky had only seen in his worst nightmares, and it came straight down the bear trail toward them.

The monster came bursting through the dense forest. It was the biggest, meanest, ugliest bear Sparky had ever imagined. Sparky resisted the urge to scream and bolt to safety, knowing that if he tried to moved the massive thousand-pound (454 kilogram) male bear would rip him in two with one swat of his foot-long paw. The huge monster, resembling a heavily muscled mutant gorilla, thundered down the trail toward Lucy and Sparky's hiding place. The pair lay motionless. The creature's head was two feet wide, and it was missing its right ear and a large chunk of its upper lip. His eyes were wide with rage and fixed straight ahead. Sparky swore he saw an evil red glow in both of his eyes. The beast's mouth gaped open, drool dripped off his slightly protruding tongue, and froth foamed at the corners of his mouth and nostrils. As he ran by, a large fresh gash on his right shoulder revealed the pink flesh below. The bear's breathing sounded like the world's biggest dinosaur running as fast as it could go. The monster's muscles rippled as it bolted by and disappeared into the forest.

Sparky shuddered and began to relax for a moment, but he instantly tensed as a second gigantic male bear appeared from the depths of the giant spruce forest.

This male was taller than the first and even more heavily muscled. He too was frothing at the mouth and huffing deeply from exhaustion. His face looked normal compared to the first male bear. He did not have as many scars and did not appear as aggressive and mean as the first bear. The massive creature approached at full speed, seemingly fixated on the monster ahead of him. Suddenly his massive muscular body ground to a halt fifty feet in front of Lucy and Sparky's hiding spot.

The male bear huffed and, with its nose high in the air, sniffed deeply with great interest in the direction of Lucy and Sparky. He looked deep into the forest to where the mother and cub lay trembling. His eyes squinted, and his head swayed from side to side as his nose scented the air. The sunlight filtering through the trees from behind the hiding spot seemed to blind the huge male momentarily, and the creature shook his head and blinked. He refocused his energy on the trail in front of him and the large demon he was chasing. He looked once more toward the hiding spot and gave three low, aggressive huffs. Then he resumed his chase and disappeared from sight.

Not moving a muscle or making a sound, Lucy and Sparky lay still and quiet for a very long time until they heard the thundering fight resume a long way down the valley from their hiding spot.

Finally Lucy took a deep breath. Her cheeks puffed up, and she blew the air out slowly and steadily. Sparky could feel her body begin to relax. He tried to relax, but he was still much too terrified.

"I think they are gone, Sparks," Lucy whispered and tried to reassured her cub. "Are you all right?"

Sparky did not answer, so she lovingly nuzzled him with her nose.

After a minute Sparky was able to whisper, "That was so scary, Mom!"

Again they lay for a long time in silence. Lucy knew Sparky needed time to calm down. She patiently waited until her cub was ready to speak.

Finally Sparky's tiny voice whispered, "Who were those beasts?"

"Well," Lucy began, "the large bear in the front—"

"Excuse me, Mom!" Sparky exclaimed. "That thing was a monster, not a bear!"

Lucy chuckled quietly. "Yes, he is a bit of a fright, isn't he?"

"A bit! " Sparky shuddered. "Missing ear and ripped face! I know I will have nightmares about him!"

"Now, Sparky. You have to be a strong bear in this world to survive, so you must put him out of your mind," she said and hugged him close with her huge paw. "Okay then. The monster's name is Lefty."

"Why is he such a scary mess, Mom? It looked as though he had been hit by a bolt of lightening," Sparky said with a shudder.

"Well, honey, those bears are the two dominant males of the Khutzeymateen Valley. They get into a lot of fights with other bears. Lefty had his left ear bitten off in a fight with Buffalo about ten years ago. Then five years ago, Buffalo bit off the left side of Lefty's lip in a fight. And over the years, he has inflicted a lot of scars on Lefty's body. Male bears tend to get out of hand when they are fighting over females," Lucy said and shook her head.

"That is just so silly, Mom. Fighting is stupid, but to eat an ear is just gross! Who is this Buffalo guy, Mom? He was a very handsome bear compared to Lefty, but he sounds like a really mean and very strong bear. Judging from the mess Lefty is, Buffalo is much tougher. I would not want to make him mad at me," Sparky said with caution in his voice.

"Buffalo is the most dominant bear in the valley. Buffalo is a very strong bear, but he is only mean to other male bears during mating season. And, well …" She paused. "He would also eat cubs during that time to make the mother available to mate again," Lucy explained.

Sparky swallowed hard. "He would kill me?" He was now afraid again. "Is that why we hid?"

"Yes, Sparky, that is one of the reasons why we hid. Lefty would have definitely killed you, but I do not think Buffalo would have killed you."

Sparky looked at her with confusion. "Why, Mom?"

"Well, honey, that is Buffalo."

"What? Buffalo! Now I remember who Buffalo is!" Sparky said with shock. "He is my father!"

"Yes, honey. Buffalo is your father. That is probably why he stopped and sniffed the air. He must have smelled us, but he was too busy chasing Lefty to investigate further. He may have recognized you as his cub from your scent, but then if he was really mad because of Lefty, he may have still eaten you in a fit of rage."

"Well, I am glad he did not eat me! Stuck mussel! I can't believe I saw my dad! I am glad he is my father and not Lefty! At least Buffalo is strong and handsome. Lefty is just ugly and scary. Wow! He is my dad!" Sparky continued to say in disbelief.

"Yes, honey, your dad is very handsome. He comes from a long line of dominant male bears in the Khutzeymateen Valley. You have very good strong genes from your father. You have the potential to be a dominant male bear yourself."

"Wow!" Sparky exclaimed and stood up on his hind legs to make himself look bigger. "What do you think, Mom, am I big and scary like my dad?" Then he went down on all fours and began to strut around in front of Lucy. "Am I dominant male material?"

"Oh yes, honey. You definitely are," she giggled.

Sparky looked into the forest to where the roaring was coming from. "I will be a dominant male someday, Mom, but I am going to be a nice one," he insisted. "I am not going to fight and beat up other bears. I am just going to be really big and strong. Then all the other bears will respect me as a dominant male." He again looked down the trail and into the forest where Buffalo had disappeared. "Someday," he whispered. "I will be just like you dad, only bigger and stronger."

Chapter 15:
Nine-Headed Water Beetle

"Mornin', bear friends!" Westy greeted as he scampered up the trail headed into the forest. Sparky and Lucy were on their way down the trail from their den to the inlet shoreline. "Great morning to be on Waipo!"

"Hi, Westy!" Sparky said, excited to see his weasel friend.

"Hello, Westy," Lucy smiled and winked. "Off to visit Rosebud, are you?"

"Yep! Breakfast first. I'll pick up some fast food, like a running mouse or something, and then dazzle Rosebud with my incredible hunting skills by bringing her mouse in bed. She can't resist me coming to visit unannounced when I bring her food."

"That's my cone!" Mica's voice suddenly screeched.

"*Mine!*" Cliff yelled as he bolted under the branch where Mica had snipped off a big juicy pine cone. He scooped the cone into his mouth and scooted off into the forest. Mica roared down the tree trunk at full speed and dashed after him screaming, "*Give me my cone back!*"

"*No!*" came Cliff's muffled voice from behind the cone.

"*Jeez!*" Westy hollered after the squirrels. "Can't you two get along for at least one day so the rest of us can get some peace and quiet?" Then he looked at Sparky and Lucy. "They are enough to drive a weasel to eat fermented wild crab apples! I am off, mostly to get away from those two and find some solitude with my Rosebud! Later, bears." He disappeared under a devil's club bush.

The bears continued down the trail to the shoreline, across the sedge grass, and onto the mudflats.

"Mom, is it all right if I dig up a few clams for breakfast?" Sparky said as he squished his feet side to side into the gooey mudflats on the inlet shoreline. "The sea water has moved away, and the mud is showing again, so I want to practice my clamming moves."

Lucy quickly scanned the entire Mouse Creek area all around them. Then she listened for intruders and sniffed the air while Sparky also listened and sniffed deeply with his nose high. "Yes, Sparky. That sounds like a great idea. I will be right here in the sedge grass, eating. Mom will keep an eye on you." Then she grabbed a large mouthful of sedge and began chewing contentedly.

Playfully lifting his paws high and then gushing them in the mud, Sparky squished his way down to the shore. Suddenly a clam spurted water up through the mud out of its breathing hole and right into Sparky's eye. He shook his head and said, "Okay, clammy! You are about to become my breakfast." He started digging madly, causing mud and bear paws to fly in every direction. Sparky heard an odd humming noise coming off the water. He stopped, looked up, and squinted into the morning sun to see what was causing the racket. The wind blew the sound toward him, but the object was still only a dot on the horizon.

"Hmm, it must be one of those, what did mom call them ... er ... um ... oh yeah! Whale thingies. They sure make a funny loud noise!" he said and then began intently digging his portal to clamland.

"Urg ... uh ... phaaa," he groaned as he dug madly in search of the tasty clam.

Before Sparky knew it, he had dug a huge hole in the shore and still had no clam. Frustrated, he stopped digging and peered down into the hole.

"All right, Mr. Clam. This time you win. I think you have dug to the other side of the Waipo, so I am going to go find a lazier clam to dig up."

Sparky sat down to rest in the large crater he had dug with just the top of his head and ears poking above the top rim of hole. Instantly he heard the sound again, but this time it was very loud and right behind him. Sparky slowly turned his head, not knowing what to expect. What he saw horrified him. It looked like a huge water bug! It was twice as long as his mom, blue on the bottom, multicolored on the top, with nine heads and lots of arms everywhere. It came closer and closer to the shore, and as Sparky watched in terror, it stopped making its horrible buzzing racket.

Sparky's eyes grew bigger and bigger, and every muscle in his body froze with fear. He didn't know whether the monster was fast enough to grab him if he tried to run off up the mudflats to the sedge grass where Lucy was munching her breakfast, but he really just wanted to be by her side. Slowly he looked up from the monster to Lucy and back again. The bug's heads were moving up and down on long necks. Each head had two eyes, and funny sounds were coming out of the mouths.

This was enough for Sparky. He was terrified. Cautiously he looked at Lucy again, but it appeared she did not know the creature was lurking offshore. Finally Sparky could stand it no more. He slowly took one more peek at the bug, and then with legs almost around his ears from running so fast and mud flying in all directions, he bolted to his mother's side. Behind him he heard the creature making what sounded like laughing noises. Sparky was sure it was a pre-attack chant, and he was far too terrified to look back to see if the demon was chasing him.

"Mom! Mom! Run for your life!" he yelled as he bolted towards Lucy. "Run, Mom!" Sparky exclaimed.

"Oh my, Sparky! Whatever is the matter?" Lucy stopped eating sedge grass and looked at her panicked cub.

"Over there, Mom! The monster on the water!" Sparky said as he looked back where the creature was and in the process ran right into Lucy's large furry back end. "Ooof!" he exclaimed as the impact brought him to an abrupt stop.

"Oh, Sparky, calm down, honey. I am sorry. I forgot to tell you that the smooth skins would be here soon, and here they are. Remember we talked a bit about them. I also call them the pink ones, at least most of the ones that come here are pink, but these creatures also come in a variety of other colors. Apparently they call themselves humans."

"Smooth skins?" Sparky questioned. "Where do they come from? They are the weirdest-looking creatures I have seen yet. They are so … so … pink! And they don't look like they have any fur! Except for on the top of their heads and even then some of them don't have any! Don't they get cold?"

"That is why they wear clothes, Sparky. Clothes keep them warm because they don't have fur. When we come out of hibernation, they start coming in to visit us on their big fast-moving log. They seem to like to watch us. It is kind of creepy that they just sit there and stare at us, but they must be bored and lonely."

"That is really weird! Why would they just sit there and stare? How would they like it if we went to their den and stared at them? I have a bad feeling about them, Mom," Sparky said nervously. "What if they try to grab me?"

"Don't worry, honey. These pink ones are friendly. They will not hurt you," Lucy said as she sat down beside her panting, trembling cub. "It is okay. They start arriving when the sedge grass begins to grow and the skunk cabbage flowers are out. They visit us a few times a week until the leaves fall off the trees and we get ready to hibernate. See the tall one at the back? He has been visiting me for eight flower blooms, green times, and leaf droppings, ever since my family left Waipo. Remember me telling you that story?"

"Yes, I do, Mom."

"And once again the flowers have bloomed, and here he is again with more new friends. It is funny, though. The tall one always comes, but the other pink ones change every time. Until last year when the tall one started to bring in that pretty little female that I call the short one. I think he must really like that one because she is here all the time. They are all harmless, and they laugh when we do silly things, so try to give them some joy in their lonely lives and make them smile, Sparky. Besides, it is interesting to watch their behavior and interaction. We can learn much about the human species just by observing these ones. So just enjoy your new friends, honey." She paused for a moment and looked at the boat. "I must say though, I am glad I am a land creature. There is way too many of them living on that small log. I need a lot more space around me and lots of land to roam around on. There is far too many of them. Their home seems much too crowded for my liking."

"Gosh, Mom. They seem calm and placid now, but when they snuck up on me, they nearly scared the fur off me! Are you sure they are friendly? After you told me the story of the great Boris the rat, I don't trust them." Sparky paused for a moment and looked at his mom with worried eyes. "These pink ones are not going to try to grab me and haul me off to one of those horrible places and make my fur fall out, are they? Those lab-a-trees sound like things nightmares are made of!"

"Oh, honey. Have you been listening to Westy's nightmare stories again?" Lucy said kindly and nuzzled her son. "These pink ones are harmless. My mom used to tell me horror stories that were passed down through my ancestors that made me afraid of the pink ones, too. She said they were evil creatures that cut down and burned our homes. They would use some kind of stick that threw things at high speed. These objects would make holes in our skin, explode inside us, and kill us. But here in the Khutzeymateen we are safe. We do not have to think about evil pink ones hurting us.

"The tall one says many times that everything from Noni to the smallest mushrooms will be protected here forever. The tall one tells the others that we grizzly bears are a treasure on the planet. He says we will be protected and loved for all time. I also heard him say that our territory is large, but there is what he calls hunting nearby. I think that is the stick that hurls the exploding ball that kills us. You must always remember to stay close to this valley, especially when you are on your own some day. Do not wander far away from this magical place. But for now I promise these pink ones will not hurt you."

"I will be sure to stay close to the Khutzeymateen, Mom. These things sound really creepy and unpredictable. Why would they want to kill us? We never mean any harm to them. I certainly am more afraid of them than they are of me!" Sparky said and shuddered as he looked back at the boat. "They are so weird-looking. They don't have any fur, and they are ... well ... so ... so ... pink! They look like they are from another planet. And they only have two legs! That is really weird-looking!' Sparky exclaimed and wrinkled his nose up.

"Now, Sparky," Lucy said sternly. "Never judge a creature by its exterior appearance. These pink ones are actually very lovely, but you are right; they don't look very much like any other creatures on Waipo. However, you had best go over and get to know them better."

"Oh, Mom! Do I have to?" Sparky complained.

"Yes, love. They will be visiting regularly, so it is important for you to not be afraid of them. Now go on and have a visit. I am still very hungry, so more grass for your dear old mom."

Sparky looked at her longingly.

"Go on, young bear. Go visit the pink ones," she said sternly.

"Ah, Mom!" Sparky said in disgust as he turned and looked at the monster in the water that held eight adults pink ones and one smallish cub. "I will forever call that creature the bug."

"That is a good name, Sparky. It does look like a mutant water beetle," his mom said, chuckling as she turned to eat more grass. "Now go and make friends."

Sparky strutted toward the shoreline with his hackles standing straight up in the air. "Friends, shmends!" Sparky said with attitude. "I am going to charge them and see if I can scare those pink thingies off!" he whispered in a mischievous voice.

Sparky stopped and looked directly at "the bug" floating in the morning sunlit water. He made all his fur stand on end so he looked as big and scary as possible. He swayed his head back and forth and made loud huffing noises. Then with the fire of twenty grizzlies, he bolted to the water's edge at full speed. Much to his surprise, the bug and its occupants did not move.

"Huh! Not scary enough for you," he said to himself and strutted up and down the shoreline with his hair still on end. Sparky looked like a ten-pound cub that had been left in the fluff cycle of a dryer for just a bit too long.

Then he stopped and listened. Odd noises were emitting from the pink ones.

"They are laughing at me!" Sparky said with frustration. "They are supposed to be scared of me, not laugh at me! I will show them! I'll charge them again, but this time I will be much more fierce! This time I will scare them off!"

Still swaying his head and looking aggressively back over each shoulder with each step, Sparky retreated from the shoreline. Then he stopped and stared directly at the bug.

Sparky prepared for the charge. This time he got more distance between him and the water's edge. He glared long and hard at the bug and suddenly burst into a full-speed-ahead charge, huffing as loud and viciously as he could. He ran flat out at the Zodiac that was thirty feet offshore.

Hearing the commotion, Lucy looked up to see what antics her son was up to. Just as she did, Sparky caught a toe on a rock. As he tripped, he took a nasty tumble that caused him to roll over and over like a ball across the sand.

"Urg! Ump! Uph! Uar!," he yelled as he tumbled out of control head-over-tail-over–head-over-tail. Finally Sparky came to a very ungraceful stop, sprawled on the mudflats. He looked like a tangled starfish that had washed up on the beach with a confused tide. As he lay in the mud, stunned by his tumble, Sparky heard the pink ones laughing loudly.

Lucy rolled her eyes and almost burst into fits of laughter. She desperately held the giggles back as she yelled at her son. "Sparky! What on Waipo are you doing?" she said sternly.

Sparky looked up at his mother in a daze. Then he slowly stood up and shook the caked on mud off his fur. Embarrassed, he ran to his mother's side.

"Sorry, Mom," he said sheepishly.

"What were you doing?" Lucy questioned, still holding back her laughter. "I told you to make friends, not enemies!"

"I was just practicing my bear skills," Sparky pleaded. "I was showing my dominance by aggressively charging the pink ones."

"Sparky! Don't charge the tall one and his friends! They are our friends! Do you want them to think we are like those one-in-a-thousand bad bears that try to eat humans? If you are mean to these pink ones, they might stop coming to see us, and they might stop trying to protect us," she said sternly.

Sparky hung his head in shame. "Sorry, Mom," he whispered.

"Oh, honey," Lucy coddled. "I know you want to learn everything we bears need to know and practice, but these pink ones are friendly and harmless. They are good humans. Now please be kind and please go over and view them in a polite manner."

"Okay, Mom. I don't think I did any harm. They are all still in fits of laughter because I am so clumsy. I promise I will not charge them anymore. I will make friends instead."

"You are not clumsy. You are just growing into your bear paws and need to get better at balance and coordination. Now remember be polite and be good." Lucy smiled and began eating and humming to herself again.

Still very embarrassed about his crash, Sparky ambled down to the beach where the bug's occupants were still laughing. Suddenly one of them stood up and pointed a black object with a big eye at Sparky.

"Oh clam breath!" Sparky squealed as he panicked and jumped back. "It's gonna try and grab me, I am sure!"

Quickly the tall one made the pink one sit down, and Sparky quickly relaxed. He looked around and noticed a stump decorated with seaweed sitting at the water's edge.

"Maybe I will hide behind that stump," he whispered.

Sparky slowly walked toward the stump, carefully watching the pink ones to ensure they did not make any quick unexpected moves. His heart sped up as he nervously peeked at the bug from above the stump. Then he peeked at the pink ones out one side of the stump and then the other. He noticed they were smiling and making cooing sounds at something. He looked around at his mom, but she was still busily eating grass. Sparky peeked at the pink ones again and then hid behind the stump. They began emitting the same cooing sounds when he did this.

"Hey," he whispered. "They are smiling and cooing at me. Maybe Mom is right. Maybe these creatures are friendly after all. Maybe they aren't as scary as they look."

Sparky climbed up on the stump, laid his head on his paws, and looked at the humans.

"Gosh. Are they ever funny-looking. Various sizes and shapes and their faces all look so different. Funny small noses. I bet they can't smell the same things bears can smell. And they keep making that weird *ah* sound. I wonder why. I hope they are not in pain."

Sparky watched the humans for a long time. They seemed to do many things bears did. They sneezed, which startled him. They scratched and burped. One of the big females put her arm around the smooth skin cub and cuddled it, just like Lucy did to him. Obviously they loved their little ones as much as bears did.

Lucy's voice broke Sparky's train of thought. "Sparky, honey, come on. You have to eat and then it is nap time."

"Okay, Mom!" Sparky said, still looking at the bug. "See you next time, pink ones," he said and jumped off the stump and ran to Lucy's side.

As the two bears wandered into the forest, Sparky stole one more look behind at the bug.

"Mom?"

"Yes, honey?"

"You were right. Those pink ones are friendly. I am glad they come to visit us," he smiled mischievously. "Even if they are kind of funny-looking."

Chapter 16:
Slithery Snakes

At dawn, the bears left their snuggly den and ambled down Mouse Creek to the inlet shoreline for their sedge grass breakfast. The sky was bright blue, and the sun was about to peek over the mountain tops. Lucy put her long nose in the air and deeply breathed the crisp morning air. Sparky watched his mom, looked at the blue sky, put his little snout in the air, and breathed deeply.

"Mom, the air feels colder this morning," Sparky said as he gave a little shiver.

"Yes, Sparky, you're right, and did you notice the sedge grass is getting tougher and starting to turn a bit yellow?" Lucy asked.

"Oh no! What will we eat?" Sparky said in a worried voice.

"It's all right, honey. It just means we will be eating salmon soon."

"Oh bear!" Sparky bounced up and down with excitement.

Lucy chuckled. "I know you are looking forward to salmon, but we still have lots to eat until they arrive. Now, it's beautiful today, so I think we will stay here on the inlet for most of the day in the sunshine," Lucy said as she walked into the large spruce and hemlock trees above the inlet shoreline. "If we stay in the sunshine on the shoreline, we will need to dig ourselves day dens in the shade for napping."

Sparky strutted along behind his mom, trying to walk and look exactly the same as her. "What is a day den?" he asked.

"It is a safe cozy resting den in the shade that we will sleep in during the day. First, we have to find a spot in the trees with nice soft soil, like right here." Lucy scratched the ground with one paw then looked around. "This will be a good place for us because there are no bushes blocking our view. We can hear and see danger coming, and there is lots of shade from the big trees overhead."

"And there is a big old stump for me to play on," Sparky pranced over beside the stump then back to his mother's side. "How do we build the den, Mom?"

"First, you look at your tummy."

"Huh?" Sparky looked confused.

"You look at your tummy to see how big it is."

"Mom!" Sparky giggled.

"Really!" Lucy smiled and poked Sparky's tummy with her nose. "You have to judge how big your tummy is so you can dig a hole in the soil to fit it. That way, our tummies are in the hole and out of the way while we nap."

"What?" Sparky scrunched his nose up. "Oh, I get it!" Then he stood on his hind legs and put his paws at the top and bottom of his tummy and then side to side. "Okay, I am ready to dig!" he said as he got down on all fours again.

"You take this patch of ground, and I will dig here right beside you so we will be side by side while we sleep."

"Okay, Mom! Here I go!"

Sparky started to dig madly at the dirt. It flew in all directions, including all over his mother's back and into the hole she was digging. Lucy stopped to watch her cub through the dirt shower. Then Sparky stopped and looked up. Lucy burst out laughing when she saw her cub. He was covered with dirt from head to toe. All she could see were his eyes looking out at her. He carefully lowered his bear belly into the hole.

"Not quite deep enough!" he exclaimed and started madly digging again.

"Sparky, you are going to dig all the way to the other side of Waipo if you are not careful."

"I think it's just right now, Mom!" he stopped and carefully snuggled his tummy into the hole. "Yup! It feels just perfect! I could sleep here forever!'

Sparky lay proudly in his first day den and watched Lucy finish hers off. Then they headed down to the sedge grass, ate breakfast, and flipped rocks looking for crabs on the shoreline in the morning sun. At midmorning, they slowly headed back up to their day dens for a nap.

Lucy snuggled her tummy into her hole in the ground, curled her paws under her chin, and started to doze off.

Sparky lay his tummy in his day den and gazed out from the edge of the forest at the powder puff clouds drifting lazily across the blue sky. He looked at the high cliffs and the towering mountain peaks surrounding the inlet. One cliff caught his eye, and he squinted and shook his head.

"Mom!" Sparky exclaimed.

Lucy jumped with fright out of her nap. "For goodness sake, Sparky, what's the matter?"

"Mom, that cliff up there," Sparky pointed up with his nose. "It … well … it looks like three smooth skin faces. Well, I think they are faces."

"You are right, Sparky. They are the faces of three smooth skins that betrayed the laws of the unspoken trust and disrespected Universe, Waipo, and Taku. They were turned to stone to set an example for all to see."

"Wow!" Sparky exclaimed. "They must have done something very bad to be turned to stone!"

"Yes, they were very evil," Lucy said. "I will tell you that story another day. Now close your furry little eyelids and have a nap." She put her head back down and started to nod off again.

Sparky lay still for a few minutes. Then he stood up, lay down, stood up, did a circle, and lay back down. Then up, circled the other way, and then down. He turned his head upside down, rubbed the top on the ground, and then sighed with deeply.

"Mom!"

Lucy jolted awake again. "Yes, Sparky," she sighed patiently.

"I'm not tired yet, Mom, so can I please play on the stump for a while?" he pleaded.

"Yes, you can," she said sleepily. "Not Westy's stump though."

"I know, Mom. Westy would not like me snooping in his stump. I will play on this one beside us."

Every now and again, Lucy opened an eye to check on Sparky's antics as he climbed all over the stump and scratched it with his claws. Then he started to dig madly at the base of the stump.

Finally she said, "Sparky, what on Waipo are you trying to do? Why don't you come for a nap and relax for a while?"

"I will in a bit, Mom," Sparky puffed, "but I really want to see what's under this stump."

He sat down and puffed air out of his tiny furry little bear cheeks.

"Phew! This is hard work! What a tough old stump to move!" Then he stood up and started digging and pulling on the stump with all his might. "Urg! Umph! Ah! Come on ...urg ... stump ... you silly ... old thing!"

Lucy smiled to herself at her son's determination and tenacity.

"One thing about you, Sparks, you never give up." She smiled and lay her head on her paws and closed her eyes. No sooner did she close them than she heard a crash and then a scream.

"*Ahhh!*" Sparky yelled.

Lucy quickly opened her eyes, expecting to see her cub squashed under the stump with only his furry little legs sticking out. But instead she saw Sparky flying toward her at full speed. He took one leap into the air, sailed clear over the top of Lucy, and landed behind her, cowering and trembling as if he were hiding from something.

"Sparky! What in the name of Taku is the matter?" she said with great concern. "Are you all right?"

"Mom!" Sparky panted. "Over there! Under the stump I turned over!" he huffed. "There ... there ... is a big scary monster!"

"What?" Lucy questioned as she looked over toward the stump. "Sparky, I think you are imagining things. There is nothing in sight. Now calm down and have a nap, honey. I think you are just tired from all that digging," Lucy said gently.

"No, Mom! There really is a monster! It ... it is on ... on the ground! It was under the stump! It stood up and looked at me when I moved the stump! I think it might be an alien from another planet 'cause it doesn't have any legs or fur or ... It ... it is just really scary-looking, Mom!"

"Oh, Sparks," Lucy sighed as she got up and stretched. "You just won't let me get my beauty rest, will you? Okay, let's go have a look."

"No, Mom! It might eat us! I am not going over there!" Sparky said as he sat cowering and shivering in his day den.

"Come on, young bear. We are going to see what you found. I am not going over there alone. You have to come with me. It is important to face your fears, Sparks. Now come on," she said and looked at him patiently.

"Can I just—?" Sparky whined.

"Come on," Lucy insisted.

"But I could just—?" Sparky quivered.

"Right now, young bear," Lucy continued.

"Oh ... all right, but I don't think it is a very good idea. I really think we should just—" Sparky pleaded.

"Sparky!" Lucy exclaimed.

"—stay here," Sparky whispered.

"Now!" Lucy said sternly.

"Okay. I'm coming, but I am sure it is going to eat us," he said as he slowly tottered over to Lucy. "I'll follow you, Mom," he said sheepishly.

"No! You come up beside me." She motioned with her big bear nose. "Right here."

Sparky inched his way forward.

"That's it, Sparks. Now you must learn that grizzly bears are the kings and queens of the forest. There is really nothing that we should be afraid of. There are only things that we do not understand, so we must learn about them, and once we do, we will no longer be afraid. Now show me where your friend is."

"It is not my friend! It is a monster! I am sure as soon as we get close to it, the monster will get huge and swallow us both," he said and coward again.

"Sparky, what did I just say? Now calm down and let's have a look." Lucy took her long nose and gently nudged her son toward the stump. She could feel him trembling as he apprehensively inched forward.

"It is okay, Sparks. I am right here," Lucy reassured.

They slowly approached the stump, and Sparky climbed nervously up and peeked over the top and down the other side. Then he quickly ducked down and jumped beside Lucy.

"It is still there, Mom," he whispered. "It is lying there waiting to eat us!"

"Sparky! Stop being so silly," Lucy chuckled and peeked over the edge of the stump. "Oh, Sparky! For heaven's sake!" she said as she sat down and chuckled. "You silly goose! That huge scary monster is a harmless little garter snake. And by the looks of him, he is much more afraid of you than you are of him! The poor little fellow is so traumatized from being uprooted from his home that he is afraid to move." She stood up again and looked at him. "Poor little tyke."

Sparky hesitated and then climbed up on the top of the stump and looked down at the two-foot long snake coiled up and frozen with fear.

"Did I kill it, Mom?" Sparky said sadly. "I didn't mean to."

"No honey, he is all right," she reassured Sparky. "He is just scared. He will move soon, and if he doesn't, we will put his house back and leave him be."

Sparky looked closer at the snake over the edge of the stump. "He is kind of pretty, Mom. I like his yellow, red, and black body. And he is kind of shiny. What is a snake, Mom?" Sparky questioned.

"Well, Sparks, snakes are reptiles that live almost everywhere on Waipo except for the south and north poles," Lucy explained. "Reptiles are cold-blooded, which means their body temperature goes up and down as the temperature of the day gets hotter and colder. They become very cold at night, and they must rely on the sun to heat their bodies so they can move and survive."

"Wow! That is pretty cool, Mom! They don't have fur like us to help keep them warm. It is the sun that does that job." Sparky paused and thought for a moment. "Do all snakes look like this one? Are they all the same size?"

"No, Sparks," Lucy explained. "There are many different kinds of snakes on Waipo. This one is a red-sided garter snake. Taku adapted these snakes to be able to tolerate this rainy cool part of Waipo. Some snakes, such as the worm snake, are only half a paw long. Others, like anacondas, can be over thirty-six paws long or, as smooth skins say, feet long. They call their paws feet."

"Wow!" Sparky's eyes widened. "Now, Mom, you gotta admit that size snake is a monster!"

"Yes, Sparks. I wouldn't want to mess with a big snake like that. Not to worry though, they don't live in British Columbia. They prefer hot tropical countries."

"I am glad I live here then! Are all snakes the same color, Mom?" Sparky asked. "This one is pretty."

"Snakes come in a variety of colors, and their skin can be a solid color or have patterns."

Sparky leaned over the edge of the stump even farther. "I can't see any legs. How do snakes move? Or do they just lay around?" Sparky questioned.

Lucy chuckled. "All snakes have long bodies without legs. Most snakes move around by bending into an S-shape and pushing against the ground with several body parts. They use strong muscles to propel themselves and slither across the ground."

"Cool! Slithery snakes!" Sparky whispered as he dug his claws into the stump and leaned over the edge even farther. Then suddenly he jerked up beside Lucy.

"Whoa!" he exclaimed. "That snake just stuck his tongue out at me! It was red and shaped funny. It looked like he had two tongues on the end!"

Lucy laughed. "He was tasting you, Sparky."

"What!" Sparky questioned and wrinkled up his nose. "He never licked me!"

"No, but he tasted your vapors. Snakes have forked tongues, tongues that are split in two at the end. The split gives them a bigger surface area for scents to land on. The snake tastes the air and then tries to identify the intruder entering their personal space. I am not sure why they are red, but maybe it is to help frighten off the intruder."

"Are snake skins slimy like oysters and slugs?" Sparky asked and scrunched up his little bear nose. "If they are, snakes are yucky."

"No, honey. Snakes are not yucky and slimy. They have scaly skin that is dry to the touch. And do you know what?" she paused.

"What, Mom?" Sparky exclaimed.

"Snakes shed their entire skin at least once a year."

"Wow! That is so weird! You mean their skin comes right off! How can they do that without all their guts falling out all over the place?"

Lucy laughed. "You silly willy. Their new skin forms under the old one, and then the old skin splits, and the snake wiggles out with a shiny new set of clothes on."

Sparky giggled. "That is funny, Mom. How come we don't shed our skin?"

"We do, Sparks, every day. Ours just flakes off in small pieces, so we don't notice it as much. Most creatures shed their skin as new cells grow and old ones die off."

Sparky lay his head on his paws and looked down at the garter snake. "He still is not moving, Mom. Are you sure I did not kill him?"

"He is fine, honey. Trust me. He is just nervous," Lucy said reassuringly.

"Maybe he is hungry. Maybe if we gave him something to eat, he would feel better." Sparky thought for a second. "What do snakes eat anyway? His mouth looks pretty small!"

"Snakes eat bugs, small or large animals, depending on the snakes size, and eggs. Some snakes bite their prey and this kills the creature. They are called venomous snakes. Constricting snakes wrap themselves around their prey and squeeze, so the prey cannot breathe."

"Yuck! That's not nice either way!" Sparky exclaimed.

"Yes, Sparks, but everything on Waipo, including snakes, needs to eat. They don't have paws to catch their food like we do, so Taku devised other ways of making sure they could eat."

"How do they eat without paws? How can they get the food into their mouths?"

"Snakes are actually very efficient eaters, Sparks. They can dislocate their jaws so their mouths wrap around the food. Then powerful snake muscles contract, and the food is swallowed automatically. But I think our little friend here can find his own food, honey," Lucy reassured him.

Sparky leaned over the log even farther and looked at the snake very closely.

"I wonder if he's lost. He looks pretty small. I wonder where his mom is," Sparky said with great concerned.

"All snakes hatch from eggs, but some mother snakes carry the eggs inside their body until they hatch. And don't worry your cute little furry head off about this little one. All baby snakes can take perfectly good care of themselves as soon as they hatch."

Sparky looked even closer into the snake's eyes as it sat motionless on the ground. Then suddenly, the garter snake stuck its tongue out to taste the air, and before Sparky could realized what was happening, the little creature uncoiled his body and bolted off, slithering in an S-shape across the ground into the forest. The snake's fast movements caught Sparky completely off guard, and he startled. The hackles on the back of his neck stood on end, and his little bear body jumped. At that moment his claws dislodged from the rotten stump, and he tumbled into a heap on the ground landing right where the snake had been.

"Umph! Ow!" Sparky cried.

Lucy looked over the log. "Are you all right, honey?" she asked with concern.

Sparky looked around and shook his head, then rubbed it with his paw. "Yes, Mom, I think so."

Once Lucy knew her cub was all right, she burst out laughing.

"Mom! It is not funny! That snake nearly scared me out of my skin!" He pouted. "I think he did it on purpose."

Lucy managed to contain her laughter.

"Sorry, cubby, but from this angle, it was very funny." She paused and wiped the giggle tears from her eyes. "I really don't think the snake meant to scare you, honey. Put yourself in his little snake skin. How would you feel if a big eyeball attached to a furry head suddenly lowered from the sky and spoke to you?"

Sparky got up and shook the moss out of his fur. "That is true, Mom. You are right. I would bolt out of sight faster than he did. Poor little guy, I scared him again!" Sparky said and felt very bad.

"It is okay, Sparky. It is all part of learning about life and how to treat others that live with us on Waipo. Always remember to think about what consequences your actions will create. Always put yourself in the other creature's mind and body to see how you would feel if that was done to you. If you remember those two things your whole life, you will never harm another creature mentally, spiritually, or physically. Now, my love, give me a paw, and we will turn this stump back over where you found it just in case our little friend comes back."

"Yeah!" Sparky smiled as he ran to help Lucy. "I want my new friend to have a safe home again. I hope he will forgive me for scaring him."

"Oh, I think he will, sweetie," Lucy smiled. The two bears lined up beside each other with their paws on the edge of the stump ready to pull it into its original position. "I'll say 'barnacle, mussel, clam,' and on 'clam,' we will pull together. Ready? Barnacle, mussel, *clam!*"

The stump rolled back upright and landed right where it started.

"That was easier than doing it myself!" Sparky exclaimed. "I sure hope I see that snake again, Mom. I really hope he is okay, and well, maybe he will remember me and not be mad at me for moving his den, and well, maybe we can be friends."

"Honey, some day you may see him again, but not today. I think he was pretty frightened, but I don't think he will be mad at you," Lucy reassured him.

Sparky looked hard into the forest. "I don't see him." Then he gently said, "I am sorry for disturbing you, Mr. Snake. Please forgive me. I sure hope we can be friends some day."

Lucy knew how bad Sparky was feeling, so to take his mind off the snake, she decided to tell him about the adventure she had been scheming for the two of them.

"Sparky, since it is getting near leaf-change time, how would you like to go on an adventure to explore the Khutzeymateen Estuary?" she said with great excitement in her voice.

"Ah … the estuary sounds like it is a long distance away. Don't you think I am a little young for that kind of thing?" Sparky looked nervously at Lucy and shook his head back and forth. "I don't think so, Mom. I would rather wait until I am a big bear to do that, like my second green time."

"Sparky, we are not waiting until next green time. We are almost through this green time. It is best we go visit the estuary now because come salmon time, we are not leaving Mouse Creek until we hibernate. There will be too much good food. We will need to eat as much as we can, get big and fat, and conserve our energy for hibernation during snow time. I think now is the best time to go explore the estuary, and I also think you are big enough to make the journey. It is good for you to know the whole Khutzeymateen area so when you leave me, you can feel comfortable in your territory and become a dominant male bear quickly. Part of being a leader is having the power and confidence in your home area," Lucy said encouragingly.

"Well, I guess you are right, Mom. I still don't think I will ever leave you, but I guess it is good to know the estuary," he said apprehensively and paused in thought. "What if we run into a male bear?" he asked nervously.

"I will be on the lookout the whole time, and if we do run into trouble, we will have to deal with the situation. I will try to keep us out of danger. The best way to avoid problems is to avoid the cause as best you can," she reassured him. "We will leave tomorrow when the sun lights up the sky."

Chapter 17:
Hairy the Meddler

Lucy and Sparky woke early to the *rat-a-tat-tat* of a pileated woodpecker knocking loudly on trees trying to find breakfast. They crawled out of the entrance to their cozy den, sat on the soft moss, and looked up at the large busy bird. He swiftly flew from tree to tree, pausing to drill holes in each one and looking for insects under the bark. His red-crested head reverberated so quickly with each *rat-a-tat-tat* that it became a blur.

"He is so noisy. How come he doesn't get a headache from hitting his beak on the bark and making all that racket?" Sparky asked as he yawned and stretched. "I am getting a headache just watching him."

Lucy laughed and then explained, "That is how woodpeckers search for food. Their head moves so efficiently and precisely that the pecking does not hurt them."

"I am glad I don't have to hit my head against a tree to eat. Can we go down to the inlet to get some quiet?"

With Sparky in tow, Lucy began to walk down the bear trail that hugged the edge of Mouse Creek. A fine mist filled the air, and patches of fog danced in the treetops along the trail. The humid air settled on the plants with a shiny dampness and quickly moistened the bears' fur enough that it looked heavy and wet.

"We will eat a little grass and then head up the inlet toward the Khutzeymateen Estuary. We have to leave soon because it will take until the sun is high above us to get there," Lucy said as she negotiated a stretch of moss with deeply etched bear footprints.

Sparky followed close behind, still having to leap from footprint to footprint but finding it easier than when he was first out of the den.

Lucy poked her head out of the forest, sniffed deeply, and checked the shoreline for danger. As the bears munched on the sedge grass and watched fog rise off the inlet surface, Sparky asked apprehensively, "Mom, are you sure this is a good idea?"

"Yes, Sparky. You will love the estuary. Now let's head out."

They left Mouse Creek and followed the inlet shoreline, cutting up into the forest onto bear trails or swimming where the shoreline was too rugged and steep for Sparky to negotiate. Lucy patiently waited as Sparky continuously stopped to look at the high mountains that rose straight up out of the salty ocean water and inquisitively sniff at all the new smells along the way.

After a time she said, "Come along now, Sparky. We have to keep moving in order to make the estuary by midafternoon. Then we can relax in the sun, and you can investigate all the new sights and smells you want."

While sniffing a lupine flower, Sparky suddenly paused and looked at Lucy and with great concern asked, "Mom! Where are we going to sleep tonight?"

"Not to worry, Sparks. Your old mom has dens all over the Khutzeymateen. I have a perfect spot just up in the trees near a lovely marsh area beside a small pond. We will be nice and comfy for the time that we are at the estuary."

Suddenly they heard a branch snap just up ahead, and both bears froze in their tracks. Lucy put her nose high in the air and sniffed deeply, trying to get a scent of the intruder.

"I think it's a male bear. Be very quiet," Lucy whispered as another branch snapped, this time closer.

Sparky froze with fear and stood as close to Lucy as possible without climbing onto her back, which he really wanted to do. He cowered behind his mother, briefly peeking around her furry hind leg in the direction she sniffed. Sparky nervously fidgeted and checked behind and beside them for movement in the salmonberry bushes that lined the trail.

Lucy stood up on her hind legs to get a better view of the trail and forest ahead. Sparky did the same, not knowing what he was looking for, but if Mom did it, surely, he should be doing it too. Lucy's bulging tummy was bald from months of Sparky's abrupt quick movements rubbing the fur off while he suckled. From the side, her chubby tummy looked like she had swallowed a round oversized beehive.

Her seven-foot upright stance allowed her to see above the bushes. Lucy twisted side to side at the waist, with her nose still stretched up scenting the air and her ears perked upright and alert, listening for clues of the location of the intruder. She squinted and could see movement in the bushes just off the trail not far ahead. Suddenly a loud whoof, whoof, whoof! came from the forest, and a wiry tough-looking male subadult bear stepped out of the bushes and on to the trail. The bear glared at Lucy and Sparky. He stood squarely on, with his head hung low. He swayed it back and forth and popped his teeth together, growling aggressively.

"Oh, it's you, Hairy," Lucy said as she remained calm. She got back down on all fours and stood her ground, looking straight at the male bear. "Stop trying to look so tough. Where is your mother?"

Sparky stood down and timidly peeked out at the male bear from behind his mother.

"Yo, Lucy!" the bear said cockily and kept his stance. "I ditched the old lady. Now I'm free to terrorize the valley and"—he looked at Sparky and licked his lips—"look for cub burgers like the one behind you. Tasty-looking little tender morsel. Come on out, lil' fella, and let Uncle Hairy eat you … er … I mean meet you!" he hissed through clenched teeth.

"Now look, Hairy," Lucy said patiently but kept her shoulders square and maintained direct eye contact. "You know if you try anything with my cub, you will have to come through me first, and you won't look so handsome after I am done with you. So don't try your tough talk with me because I will run you off faster than you can run, and that means you will be in huge trouble. Oh, and by the way, I know it is your third summer, so your mother weaned you and chased you off. You did not 'ditch' her. So just wander on your way. And if you are smart, you will try to stay out of trouble and harm's way and stop meddling in other bears' business."

Hairy suddenly shrunk down from his tough bear act and turned slightly sideways to Lucy and Sparky, but he still glared at them. "Well … er … you better watch out … uh … cub burger … 'cause some day this will be my territory … so … so … you better watch behind you 'cause … er … yer on my food list."

Sparky poked his head out a little farther from behind Lucy and stared curiously at Hairy. At the same time, he closely watched Lucy's body language and listened to how she handled the troublemaker.

"Oh, for spruce sake, Hairy! Just be on your way!" Lucy warned as the hackles on the back of her neck rose up, and she stood even squarer and larger-looking.

Hairy stood his ground and stared back.

"Now!" Lucy ordered.

Slowly and reluctantly, Hairy gave way on the trail. As he steeped off into the forest, he poked his head out one last time and looked at Sparky. "I'll be watchin' you!" he threatened.

Lucy sighed, rolled her eyes, and said, "You better be, Hairy, because I'll be there protecting my cub and I will also be teaching him all about defending himself against bears like you, so you better be watchin'. And you are a newly weaned cub, so you should be watching for big male bears that want to turn you into a cub burger. Now get on your way! Now!"

Hairy woofed at them one last time and then disappeared into the dense bushes.

Lucy listened for a few minutes to make sure he was gone for good. Then she turned to Sparky and asked, "Are you all right, Sparks?"

"Yes, but I am afraid. He sure wasn't a very nice bear. Would he really try to kill and eat me, Mom?" he asked nervously while stepping from foot to foot and squishing his tiny paws into the ground.

Lucy could see by Sparky's natural nervous reaction that he was very upset and just wasn't admitting it. She gently nuzzled him. "Unfortunately yes, honey. Male bears are very aggressive toward cubs and younger bears. Hairy is a little over the top with his attitude. This is only his third summer, and he is just newly weaned. He is still a fairly small bear with not much muscle, but he is acting and talking big and tough like he is king of all bears. I really do think he is scared silly and trying to cover it up with a tough attitude, but if he provokes some of the other bears in the valley, he will be flattened in no time and put in his place or even killed."

Sparky listened intently and then whispered, "Can I always stay with you, Mom, so I will not be eaten? I would really like to live here in the valley for a long time, but I can see there will be all sorts of bears that would like me not to."

"Well, Sparky, we have two flower blooms and two salmon runs together. During that time I will teach you all I can about survival: how to protect yourself, how to use body language to show you are not afraid, how to eat properly so you grow big and strong, and most of all, how to avoid trouble. Not to worry, Sparky. By the time you leave me, you will know everything you need to about bear life and survival. Now, are you ready to continue on up to the estuary?"

Sparky looked nervously around him and said, "I guess so, but I am staying really close to you in case Hairy jumps out behind us."

"Good idea, honey. Now let's go."

Sparky took one more look around and scampered after Lucy.

Chapter 18:
Mac and Croaker

The estuary's vibrant green sedge grass hugged Sparky and Lucy as they lay in the warmth of the afternoon sun. Every now and again, Lucy tugged off a huge mouthful of sedge and lazily chewed, and then Sparky did the same. While he gnawed at the sedge, Sparky strained his neck to look all around at the steep snowcapped mountains rising sharply out or the valley on three sides. Tumbling waterfalls spilled down their granite cliffs, and the remains of avalanche debris from the winter snow lay in numerous deeply etched gulches. Then he looked ahead at the inlet stretching away before him. In the distance he heard the low roar of the Khutzeymateen River. Beside them, a minor channel of the river meandered by with harlequin ducks floating silently in the current. On the opposite side, a short distance away, a marshy pond glistened in the afternoon sun. Sparky watched as a great blue heron fished in a pond. Its stilt legs, blue body, and long neck were poised so still on the shore that it could have been made of stone. Then the bird burst into action. Its head shot below the surface and emerged with a fish in its beak.

"Sparky, how did you enjoy your trip to the estuary?"

"Other than running into that bully bear, Hairy, it was great. He wasn't a very nice bear at all. I never want to be like him, Mom. I am always going to try to be a nice bear."

"Some of the subadult bears in the valley don't have very much confidence in themselves, so they try to be tough and bully other bears around. They will try to kill cubs, so you always have to be careful and stay close to your big old mom. Waipo is a wonderful place to live, but you must watch for many dangers. Now, it was a long trip. Should we have a little nap?"

"I think I'm too excited to nap. Can I just check out and sniff the area around the pond while you nap?"

"Well okay, cubby, but make sure you don't stray far. The grass is taller than you are. Don't go any farther than the pond because I can see you and it is close enough that I can get to you quickly if need be."

Lucy lay her head on her paws and closed her eyes.

"I will stay close, Mom," Sparky said. He sniffed a rock with a green and orange bug on it. The bug moved along as Sparky sniffed deeply. He crinkled his nose in disgust at the foul smell the stink bug emitted.

"Yuck!" Sparky sneezed and shook his head, trying to get the smell out of his nose. "What a stinky little bug!"

Something zipping across from one grass tuft to another caught his eye, taking his mind off of the terrible smell up his nose.

"What was that?" he whispered to himself as he slowly crept up to where the creature disappeared, and stared into the grass.

"Hey! What are you lookin' at?" the grass patch said, startling Sparky. He jumped back. "Can't a mouse have any privacy around here?" the tiny voice grouched, but Sparky still couldn't see what the creature was. Finally a tiny face with a pointy nose, beady eyes, and large ears poked out of the grass and yelled rudely at Sparky, "Beat it, buddy! This is my grass tuft!"

"Um, ah, sorry, Mr. Mouse. I was just trying to make some new friends," Sparky sulked.

"Ah, all right, all right. Sorry, kid. I'm just a little tired. The lil' moussus just had twelve kids, and I am run off my feet trying to feed her so she can feed the kids. Sorry I was rude to you. The name's Mac."

"Hello, Mac. I'm Sparky, and that's my mom, Lucy, over there sleeping."

"Where are you from Sparky? I haven't seen you around the estuary before."

"My mom's territory is Mouse Creek, half a day that way," Sparky motioned with his nose down the inlet toward the ocean.

"I must say you live in an area with a classy name," Mac said and sat up on his back end while combing his front paws regally through the fur around his face.

"Yes, I do," Sparky agreed eagerly with his new friend. "I'm sure it is named after you, Mac Mouse."

"Well, if not me, probably after all my long line of thousands of ancestors," he said with his nose high in the air. "What brings you to the estuary, Sparky?"

"My mom wanted to show me the estuary. It is my first summer, and this is my first big adventurous outing."

"Good for you. I'm sure we will meet up again in the future. You will have a lifetime of adventures ahead. Great to meet ya, Sparky, but I gotta run. The lil' moussus will be wondering where I have gotten to. I'll see you around," he yelled as he zoomed off to another grass tuft.

"Bye, Mac. Nice to meet you too. Good luck with the kids!"

"Thanks! I'll need it!" another tuft said.

Then it was quiet except for the distant waterfalls and a red-winged black bird trilling as he clung to a group of reeds in the pond.

Sparky snuffled his way down to the edge of the marshy pond. He was sniffing a rock when suddenly it exploded into the air and landed two feet away.

"Stuck mussel!" he gasped as he jerked back in fright and fell over onto his butt.

"Are you trying to give an old toad a heart attack?" the rock grumpily croaked. "I was just nodding off when I felt your big cold nose on my back. Good gravel! There goes another ten weeks off my life! Young bear, what are you doing sneaking up on toads?"

"Well ... I ... er ... I wasn't ... er ... trying ... um ... I thought you were a rock," Sparky finally blurted out.

"Oh my shivering sea stars! How could you possibly mistake a distinguished toad for a ... a ... a ... rock!" the toad exclaimed in disgust, his pride obviously hurt.

"Well ... um ... I am sorry, Mr. Toad, but it is my first summer and I am still learning about Waipo, and that's my mom over there sleeping, and we are on an adventure from Mouse Creek, and this is all so new, and I didn't do it on purpose, and well, I am really sorry." Sparky pouted, upset that he had offended the elderly toad.

The old toad softened toward Sparky when he realized the cub had not snuck up on him on purpose.

"Oh, it's okay, young fella. I really should be more alert to danger. After all, some animals would have eaten me. Maybe you are a good luck bear sent by the Great Rigget to make me more aware. You see, as I ... mature ... I tend to let my guard down and I ... forget to look around. I tend to doze off instead. Perhaps you are a messenger sent to make me pay more attention to my surroundings. The name is Croaker McPondhopper the 172nd."

"Nice to meet you, sir. My name is Sparky."

"My pleasure, young bear, but please, call me Croaker."

"Can I ask you a question, Croaker?"

"Of course you can."

"Who is the Great Rigget?"

"Rigget is the great spirit of all toads, Sparky," Croaker said with much respect.

"Hey! That's like the great bear spirit, Taku."

"That's right, Sparky. All creatures have their special spirits that they look up to."

"Do you live in this pond all year, Croaker?"

"Sure do. During the summer I hop around eating bugs, look at the view, watch for predators, and of course nap. In the winter I hibernate under the mud or under forest debris."

"I hibernate too, Croaker. My mom and I just came out of hibernation not too long ago. But we have a warm cozy den to sleep in." Sparky thought for a moment and looked questioningly at Croaker. "Don't you get cold in the mud? You could probably come into our den and hibernate with us. I am sure my mom wouldn't mind, and there is lots of room if you have a family. I could go and ask my mom right now if you like. I really don't want you to be cold and freeze to death."

"Sparky, that is very kind of you, but I am fine in the winter. Some toads even freeze solid and then thaw in the spring, so we have all adapted to surviving the winter. Thank you for your offer. I also have quite a large extended family, so it would be awfully crowded in your den. There are hundreds of us."

"Wow! You have a big family! Do you really freeze solid in the winter?"

"Yes, Sparky, some toads do. Then you would think I was a rock," he laughed.

Just then Sparky heard a branch break not far away. His head snapped up, and he stared into the forest. Not far from them, he saw a large dark figure step into the shadows.

He whispered to Croaker, "Nice to meet you, Croaker, but I gotta run back to my mom."

"I heard that, too," Croaker whispered. "Good to meet you too, Sparky. Be safe, cubbo!"

Sparky dashed back to Lucy, who was still snoozing.

"Mom," he whispered. "Wake up, Mom. There is a bear coming this way!"

Quickly Lucy sat up and peeked over the tall estuary sedge grass.

"Good job for hearing him, Sparky," Lucy whispered. "Let's see if we can recognize who it is."

Another branch broke closer to them, but the bear could not be seen. They sat frozen for a long time.

"I feel like somebear is watching us," Sparky whispered.

"I can't see anybear," Lucy squinted. "We haven't heard anything or seen any movement for a while, so I think we are safe. The bear must have left without us seeing it."

"That is creepy," Sparky whispered. "Maybe it was that freak Hairy."

"I don't know, honey, but we will keep our eyes and ears alert. Now let's go down to the shore and dig some clams before we go up to our den for the night. Stick close to me, Sparky."

"I will, Mom."

Lucy cautiously stood on her hind legs and looked for movement in the estuary and forest all around them. Sparky stood on his hind legs and mimicked her movements, but he was too short to see over the tall grass.

"All clear. Okay, here we go. No dawdling."

The bears made their way down to the exposed mudflats of the estuary and dug for their dinner. Sparky watched his mom intently to make sure he did not get too far away from her. Every time she sniffed the air, Sparky sniffed the air. Every time Lucy stood on her hind legs and looked around, Sparky did the same.

"Sparky, the sun is going to sleep soon and so should we," Lucy yawned.

"Where's the den, Mom?"

"Follow me. You will like it," she said and began to walk up toward the forest.

Sparky quickly cracked open his last clam with his sharp claws and slurped it down. Then he trotted after his mom.

The den was a short distance inside the forest above the estuary. It was tucked under a large rectangular boulder in a rock slide near a marshy area next to a small lake. The boulder was balanced on two other boulders, making a perfect cavelike den that was lined and covered with thick moss inside and out.

Sparky hopped into the den excitedly and kneaded his feet into the moss.

"This is perfect!" he squealed and looked out at the estuary and mountains.

"I said you would like it. Now can I come in too? Or does your poor old mom have to sleep outside?"

"Come on in!" Sparky giggled.

Lucy snuggled in beside him, and Sparky leaned his back into Lucy's side as she wrapped her paws around her cub. He lay his head on her paw, and as he fell into a deep sleep, he began to snore softly.

Chapter 19:
Swamp Monster

Sparky woke early the next morning, excited to explore more of the estuary. He lay quietly for a long time, looking out the den entrance at the wide lush green valley and mountains surrounding it and listening to Lucy's deep peaceful breathing.

"I can't stand it any longer," he whispered. "I have to go and look around the estuary. I will be careful and well. Mom won't mind."

With care, he wiggled very slowly out from beside Lucy so he didn't wake her. Before leaving the den, Sparky poked his head out the entrance, listened intently, put his snout in the air, and sniffed deeply. He stepped out of the den and circled his tiny body to look all around. Then he stood up on his hind legs, with his front feet dangling for balance, and clumsily repeated the circle check. Satisfied that no other creatures were in the area, Sparky slowly and cautiously negotiated the short trail to the lake. He sat nervously in the warm morning sun and looked back the few steps to the den, just to make sure he could bolt back if he needed to. Sunshine glistened off the olive green lake, and a mountain bluebird clung sideways to a cluster of sedge grass and trilled a beautiful morning song. The lake shore was surrounded by tall sedge grass, except for the narrow opening where Sparky dreamily sat. A branch moving across the far side of the lake caught his eye.

"That is weird. There is no wind." He squinted for a better look. "There must be something carrying it, but I don't know what it is. Maybe it's one of those beaver thingies Mom talked about."

Suddenly the sedge grass right beside him began to make noise.

"Uh-oh" he whispered nervously to himself. He wanted to run back to the den, but instead he stood petrified with fear. He watched as a huge brown hairy swamp monster's back rose out of the grass right beside him. The monster did not realize Sparky was next to him. It slowly began to turn its head and body toward Sparky. Sparky's eyes were as big as moons as he remained frozen in his tracks. As the creature turned around, its gigantic mouth opened wide, exposing a huge set of teeth. This was to much for Sparky.

"*Ahhh!*" he screamed and bolted behind a large rock beside him.

"*Ahhh!*" the swamp monster screamed, dashing back into the water and disappearing completely under the water in hiding.

Sparky slowly peeked out from behind the rock as the monster's big long ears, beady eyes, and giant nose surfaced for a peek. Then they both quickly disappeared again to hide.

"I wonder if I can make it back to the den before the swamp monster eats me," Sparky nervously whispered to himself as he peeked out over the rock. "Oh no, there's its head again!" he said and quickly ducked down behind the rock. He closed his eyes and sat very still, wishing he had stayed in the den snuggled with his mom and wondering if he could get safely back. Raindrops hitting the top of his head brought him back to reality. Then he remembered it was a blue sky day. How could it be raining?

"Uh-oh!" he whispered as he slowly opened his eyes and cautiously turned around to see a big wet nose right above his head.

"Hi!" the big wet nose calmly said. "Whadija scream for? I waza just wakin' up. I was da middle of a nice yawn, anya nearly scared me outta my moose skin. Now I'z ah soaked, and well, I'z don' usually get wet 'til I wake up and have breakfist."

Sparky slumped as far away from the big wet nose as he could without being rude. "Sorry I scared you ah, Mr. ... ah ... what are you? A swamp monster?" he asked nervously.

"Ah jeez eh, unless somethin' happened overnight. Ah here, lemme check," the creature said as its huge head looked all around itself up and down and under its tummy and around to its bum. "Ah yup, I'za still a moose. Morse iz da name. Morse da moose. Wazyer name, lil' bear?"

"My name is Sparky. Sorry I frightened you, Morse. I'm just visiting the estuary with my mom. She is up in the den sleeping, and I thought I would come down and look at the lake. I didn't think any other animals were here."

"Cool name, Sparky. I'za not from these parts either. Iwuz spozta take the left valley yesterday, but I went right instead, cuz I'z thought forshor Iwuz right. Iwuz doin a big adventure with da cousin, Mable. Her and me had a big dizcushin bout left or right valley, and well, oops,"—the embarrassed moose chuckled— "here I iz. Got here late last night, wolf tired, and flopt off in thiz here grass. I'za gonna have some grass and head back up to take the left valley. Da cousin took da right valley, she wuz right, and'll never hear da end ovit."

"Well, I better go back up to the den and see if my mom is awake. She doesn't know where I am, and if she wakes up, I don't want her to worry. It was nice to meet you, Morse, and good luck finding Mable," Sparky said as he stood up and looked at Morse's knees. His gaze followed Morse's stilt legs up to his massive chest, on up to his long neck, and all the way to his big floppy nose and beady eyes.

"Yah, I should be off too and seems I'z wet, I'z goina swim ta th'other side ovta lake and eat along the way. Good t'meetcha too, Sparky. Watch out for da swamp monsters." He chuckled.

Sparky watched Morse's gangly legs disappear as he waded into the lake. When half of the moose's huge body was submerged, he effortlessly swam off. His big rabbit like ears twitched from side to side, listening for danger while his long bulky snout with the floppy nose smelled the sweet morning air for intruders' scents. Every now and again, Morse's head disappeared below the surface and came back up with a large mouthful of reeds from the bottom of the shallow lake. When he got to the other side, Morse stepped out of the lake, gave a great big shake, turned and nodded to Sparky, and then disappeared into the tall sedge grass.

"Wow, that was cool and scary at the same time. I think I will stay closer to my mom until I am big enough to see over the sedge grass," Sparky said as he scampered back to the den.

Sparky climbed in beside Lucy, who was snoring so loudly that Sparky lay down and snuggled his ears under her paw.

Lucy moaned a "It's not time to get up yet, Sparky," and then started to snore again.

Sparky gave a little smile and said, "I know, Mom. I'm still wolf tired." Then he fell back into a sound sleep.

Chapter 20:
Saved by the Pink Ones

Sparky and Lucy spent the next two days exploring the estuary. They followed new bear trails, practiced swimming in the current of the river, and ate lots of sedge grass and clams. The morning of the third day, Lucy decided it was time to make their way back to Mouse Creek. They left midmorning and slowly ambled out of the estuary. When the bears reached the inlet shoreline, they began to follow bear trails.

"I think we will stop on the next grassy knoll for a break and a snack," Lucy said.

Suddenly the loud snap of a twig alerted Lucy to an approaching intruder. She stood on her hind legs and sniffed the air deeply. Sparky cowered nervously beside his mom, peeking out from behind her leg to see if he could see anything.

"I smell trouble coming, Sparks. Let's get out of here! Now!"

Sparky knew better than to ask questions. His mother's tone of voice told him a male grizzly bear was nearby.

The sound of branches crashing to the ground suddenly filled the air as the large male approached the area not far off. This put even more fear into Lucy and Sparky, and they ran through the forest at full speed.

"Come on, Sparky. Let's go down to the shoreline. We can swim and maybe he will lose our trail."

Sparky

"I'm scared, Mom," the tiny cub puffed out through breaths as he bolted after his mother.

"Come on, honey," Lucy encouraged. As she ran, she momentarily looked back and saw a flash of a very large male bear coming toward them. "We will be fine, but we have to go now."

A loud crack of a branch behind Sparky made him run even faster to keep up with his mother.

The pair ran to the water's edge. Lucy jumped in, but Sparky was afraid to swim and ran along the shoreline. She glanced behind and saw the male bear gaining on them.

"Sparky! Get in the water! Quickly!" Lucy yelled. "If you do, he will lose our trail!"

"I can't swim good enough!" Sparky nervously yelled back.

"Then jump in and hold on to me, son! Come on, quickly!" Lucy insisted.

"I am so tired," Sparky panted. "I think I have to stop, Mom!"

"No, Sparky! You can't! The male bear will kill you if he catches you! Now jump in the water and hold on to me!" she yelled to the exhausted little cub.

Sparky heard a large rock fall into the water not far behind him. He gasped and quickly stole a look behind and saw the huge dark brown bear quickly coming down the shoreline. It was enough to encourage him to jump. Without a second thought, he stretched out full and splashed into the water right beside Lucy. The cub struggled for a moment and then managed to grab his mother's fur with his teeth. He pulled himself onto her neck and grabbed two tuffs of fur with his tiny paws. He held on for dear life as Lucy swam as hard and fast as she could to escape the male. They could hear the loud growling and huffing of the pursuing male. Sparky got his breath back and looked ahead. He let go with his teeth and yelled.

"Mom! Up ahead! It's the pink ones, and they are coming toward us! The tall one and the short one! Look!"

"I bet they know we are in trouble!" she said breathlessly. "They are pulling up to the grass patch just ahead. We will stop there for a break. The male grizzly will not bother us if the pink ones are around. I think it is Scarface, and he is afraid of humans."

The pair swam quickly to the grass patch as the pink ones drifted into shore. Exhausted, Lucy and Sparky dragged themselves out of the water, sat down, and took a deep breath. They looked back and saw the male bear darting out of sight into the forest not far behind them. The sound of trees being snapped in half by the frustrated male filled the air, and then it became quiet except for his huffing.

"I am exhausted," Sparky gasped.

"I knew they would come over to us," a voice said.

Sparky's head snapped around in surprise. He looked at the pink ones. They were talking, and he could understand them!

Then Sparky looked at Lucy.

"Mom!" I can understand what the pink ones are saying! Can they understand us?" Sparky questioned.

"Don't be alarmed, love. All creatures on Waipo can communicate. We all can speak each other's languages because we are all interconnected by Universe. Except for smooth skins. The poor things have become so disconnected from the circle of life, they no longer have the sixth sense of interspecies communication. You see, Sparky, we need no audible words to communicate if we choose to. All species are able to do this, except human. The smooth skins have lost their ability, and now they must speak aloud. So, son. you can understand them, but they cannot hear us."

"I feel sorry for the pink ones," Sparky sighed. "They have really lost touch with the most important thing in universe. Living a healthy connected life on Waipo. Without that, what else is there, Mom?"

"It is true, Sparky. Being interconnected with all species on a healthy Waipo is the only way everything will survive and Waipo will stay healthy," Lucy concluded.

Movement on the shoreline caught the bears' eyes, and they looked back again. The male bear, who was huffing loudly and popping his teeth, repeatedly skulked from the forest onto the shoreline and back again.

"I am sure glad the pink ones came along. That bear is really angry," he said nervously. Then he looked at the Zodiac.

"Mom!" Sparky whispered. "They are talking again!"

"The poor babies," the female pink one said. "They look so tired from running. I wish the males would leave moms and cubs alone."

"Well, Wendy, you have to remember that is the way of the forest," said the male pink one.

"I know. Nature has its way of balancing life on Earth, but it seems so unfair!" She pointed at Sparky. "Look at that adorable little cub. He is exhausted. He doesn't deserve to be chased all over the inlet!" She smiled at Sparky, who looked sweetly back at her. "Look at him! He is so adorable and innocent," she cooed.

"Hey, Mom!" Sparky giggled. "Did you hear what the pink ones said? They feel sorry for us. The female said I was adorable!" he giggled. "Her name is Wendy. Mom, can I go over for a closer look at her? I like her."

"Yes, Sparky, but move very slowly and don't scare them. Most smooth skins seem to have a very small safety zone. We don't want them to do anything drastic like leave. We need a rest."

"Okay, I promise, Mom. I will be cautious."

Sparky began to nibble at the grass and slowly inch his way closer to the female pink one.

By now the Zodiac had drifted near shore in the wind. Sparky ambled over to the boat.

"That is close enough, Sparks," Lucy cautioned. "They are showing signs of stress. Don't push the pink ones."

Sparky sat down on the shore not ten feet away from the female pink one and looked her calmly in the eye.

"She looks peaceful and friendly enough," Sparky said and then took a nip of grass and continued to size up the female pink one. "I wonder why you don't have fur like me and my mom? You are very pretty, but you would look much better with fur. You would be beautiful like my mom." Sparky turned his head from side to side and checked out the female pink one from head to toe. "Well, I hope you are not sick. You also look a bit too skinny. You certainly must get cold with no fur or fat to keep you warm! How do you hibernate? My mom is a much healthier female than you are. She has a beautiful fur coat and lots of fat to keep her warm." Sparky thought for a moment. "Hmmm. I wonder." Then he looked over toward Lucy and asked, "Mom, should I offer the female pink one some grass or maybe dig her a few clams? She is pretty small and fragile to be wandering around out here in the rugged cold mountains and forest. What if she gets lost? She needs to fatten up some. The male pink one must not be a very good hunter. He does not take good enough care of her."

"No, Sparks. Don't interfere with nature. It is survival of the fittest in this world," Lucy reassured. "Not to worry, she will be fine. She looks healthy enough."

"No, she doesn't, Mom! You look healthier. She looks skinny and starving!" Sparky said adamantly.

"Sparky! Be respectful!" Lucy warned. "If she could hear you, she would be hurt. Now be nice and think of other creatures' feelings. Remember, before you say or do something, always think of how you would feel if someone said or did it to you. That way, you will never carelessly hurt anyone. Besides, there may be a reason for her being thin."

Sparky looked questioningly at Lucy and scrunched up his nose.

"Why would that be, Mom?" Sparky questioned. "Why would anyone want to be skinny when there is so much good food around and you can eat lots for hibernation time? I would rather be fat!"

"Well, you must realize that apparently thin smooth skins are much more appealing to their mate. If a female pink one is thin, more male pink ones will be attracted to her."

"That is the silliest thing I have ever heard!" Sparky said and shook his furry little head. "I think we should take this female pink one salmon fishing in the fall with us and stuff her full of salmon! She could use a hundred pounds. How will she make it through hibernation?" Sparky said with great concern. "I like her because she likes us. I would like to help her to survive through the winter!"

"Sparky that is very sweet of you, but smooth skins do not hibernate. She does not need one hundred pounds of weight," Lucy reassured him.

"What!" Sparky said with shock. "Why would anyone chose to stay out in the cold and snow all winter when they could be fat and happy in a nice cozy den curled up to their mom?"

"Well, honey," Lucy chuckled. "Smooth skins don't just curl up with their moms in dens. I really don't know what they do all winter long, but that is their choice and who am I to say it is wrong?"

"But that is even more reason to fatten her up! If she stays out in the cold all winter, she will freeze to death!" Sparky insisted. "Look at her! She is so skinny, she will die for sure!"

"No, no, Sparks," Lucy explained patiently. "You must understand. Smooth skins live in heated dens, or houses as they call them, where it is really warm. They are nothing like our dens. Smooth skins don't stop eating like we do. They continue to graze all winter, so they do not need extra weight to survive. A few smooth skins migrate south to warmer climates like the birds and whales, but most just stay in their dens all winter." Lucy suddenly paused and looked up at the forest.

"I think I hear the male bear skulking in the forest again, Sparky. Maybe we should slowly move down toward Mouse

Creek, and with any luck, the pink ones will follow us, and we will be safe."

"Okay, Mom, but just a minute." Sparky looked at the female pink one right in the eye. "Please, please, please follow us to Mouse Creek," he said with strong persuasive determination.

"What are you doing, Sparky?" Lucy giggled.

"I am trying something, Mom. Maybe I can make them follow us," Sparky said hopefully.

"It is worth a try," Lucy encouraged. "Now come on let's go, Sparks," she said and nervously looked around. Then she started to walk slowly down the inlet.

Sparky stood up and again looked deep in the eyes of the female pink one.

"Please, please, please, follow us to Mouse Creek," he said again. "If you do, I will be your friend forever."

Sparky slowly began to follow Lucy. Then he turned, took one more look at the female, and began to walk again. As he did, he heard the female pink one say, "I think we should follow them for a while. I just have a feeling that they will be safer with us around. Let's follow them to Mouse Creek so they will be safe."

"Mom!" Sparky yelled excitedly to Lucy. "It worked! The female pink one heard me! They are following us to Mouse Creek! We will be super safe now!"

"Good work, Sparky!" Lucy encouraged. "Now let's go so we can get home where it is really safe."

"I like those pink ones, Mom," Sparky said happily as he followed his mother down the shoreline. "Especially the female pink one. She is really nice. She will be my friend forever."

Chapter 21:
Whale Tales

Heavy gray clouds jostled by a cold north wind rushed passed the mountaintops as Sparky sat quietly on the inlet shore, contemplating the wind on his fur and the wonder of Waipo. He looked at the massive high mountain peaks towering above him and then gazed at the water that stretched out of view on both sides of his tiny body. Then he glanced behind to make sure he was close enough to Lucy, who was dozing in the sedge grass.

The large aggressive male that had chased them nine suns ago was still lurking up and down the inlet. They had not seen him for two suns, but they had heard branches and trees breaking nearby. However, when the bears had come out of their den earlier that morning, his dark silhouette slipped into the shadows of the forest not far from them.

Sparky stood on his hind legs and did a quick check all around him for danger and then sat back down, peacefully sighed, and stared back at the inlet. Suddenly the surface of the water where Sparky was looking broke into a spray of mist that flew high into the sky. Then a loud *pwwaaff* broke the silence.

"Whoa," Sparky exclaimed as another spray close to the first one broke lose, then another, then another. He watched intently until a huge triangular object came above the surface and then disappeared below the inlet water.

"Mom!" he yelled. "Mom! Hurry! There are sea monsters!"

Lucy woke with a start and bolted sleepily to her cub's side.

"What is the matter, honey?" she asked with concern.

"Look!" Sparky exclaimed as another triangular shape surfaced. "What is that monster, Mom? It looks scary! Will it hurt us?"

"No, Sparky!" Lucy said excitedly. "It is our friends the humpback whales! They have finally come home. This is exciting, Sparks. Do you know why?"

Lucy's excitement was contagious and Sparky quickly said, "No, Mom. Why?"

"They come when the leaves start to turn yellow, and they stay until the snow dances in the air. When they come home, it means the salmon are not far behind. The salmon will be here soon!" she exclaimed excitedly. "Soon we will feast."

"Oh boy, salmon! Soon I will taste them for the first time!" Sparky said. He watched the whales for a minute as they continued to surface. "They are beautiful." Sparky sighed. "So shiny, smooth, and black. Can we call them to shore for a visit, Mom? I would love to meet them."

"They look like they are traveling up the inlet to check for salmon, Sparks. We will stay here until they come back down the inlet later in the day. Then we will say hello, and they can tell us whether or not the salmon are starting to arrive. While we are waiting, I can tell you all about our whale friends," Lucy suggested.

"That will be great, Mom! I have lots of questions," Sparky said excitedly. "The whales look really huge! How big are they?"

"Well, our friends the humpback whales are usually forty-five paws, or feet, long, but they can reach up to sixty-two paws."

"Wow!" Sparky's eyes bugged out of his head. "That is a big fish!"

"No, no, Spark's. Whales are mammals like you and I. Their babies drink mother's milk like you do. They are also warm-blooded like us."

"Cool!" Sparky whispered.

"Do you know how much they weigh?" Lucy asked.

"Uh." Sparky frowned as he thought. "Five hundred pounds?"

"No, Sparks," Lucy giggled. "I weigh five hundred pounds. Humpbacks average thirty tons (27 tonnes), but they can reach fifty-three tons (48 tonnes). That is one hundred and twenty to two hundred and twelve of me. At birth Humpback babies weigh one to two tons (.9 to 1.8 tonnes), and they are thirteen to sixteen paws (4 to 4.9 meters) long."

"Spurtin' clam! They are hugemongous! And so are their babies!" Sparky stopped for a moment in thought. "Mom, they are much bigger than us. They could eat us!" he said with great concern. "Maybe we should not invite them over to say hello. Maybe we should just go hide in the forest right now!"

"No, no, you silly willy wittle one," Lucy said with a smile and nuzzled him with her long nose. "Don't be afraid. The whales are gentle giants. They would never hurt us. Humpback whales don't have teeth to eat you, but I do!" Lucy said and gently began to nibble at Sparky's neck. He began to giggle uncontrollably as she nibbled down to his ribs. Sparky giggled and giggled until he fell over sideways with laughter. Then Lucy started to nibble his tummy and took a deep breath and blew as hard as she could on his belly button. Sparky broke out into more fits of laughter.

"Mom!" he managed to squeak out. "Mom! Sss ... sss ... stop! I ... can't ... brea ... breathe!"

"Oh, the poor baby bear is getting eaten by his mommy," Lucy laughed.

Giggling, Sparky stood back up, shook the mud off his fur, and looked at Lucy. "Mom, when I get to be bigger than you, you will be in big trouble!" he finally managed to say. "I am going to hold you down and sit on you and tickle you until your fur falls out!"

"You will have to catch me first," Lucy said smugly. "Oh, come here, cubby," she said and scooped him over with her huge paw.

Sparky giggled and snuggled in close to Lucy. "You are such a fun mom. I love you sooooo much." He sighed. "Even if you tickle me until I can't breathe. Now, I have more questions about whales. Do you promise not to tickle me anymore?" Sparky questioned.

"Yes, Sparks. I promise," Lucy smiled.

"Are your toenails crossed, Mom?" Sparky said and gave Lucy a shifty sideways glance he checked her paws.

Lucy held up her paws. "See, no crossed toenails. I promise not to tickle you. Bear's honor."

"Okay, Mom. Now, we were talking about food. What do whales eat?" Sparky questioned.

"Well, Sparky, let's take it from the top. There are many types of whales. All whales, dolphins, and porpoises are called cetaceans. There are two types of cetaceans—toothed and baleen. Toothed whales include sperm whales, beluga, narwhals, orca, beaked whales, dolphins, and porpoises. Baleen whales include humpback, gray, blue, fin northern right whale, and bowhead. There are more of each type, but this gives you an idea that there are many kinds of whales in the world."

"Wow!" Sparky said. "What do the humpbacks eat, and how do they eat if they don't have any teeth?"

"Well, like I said, humpback whales have baleen—huge sieves inside their mouths—instead of teeth. The humpback has 270 to 400 plates of baleen on each side of their upper jaws. They are mostly black in color, and each plate grows up to seventy centimeters long.

"Skippin' scallop!" Sparky said. "Everything on whales is big! What is the baleen made of?"

"The baleen is made of keratin, like our fur and nails. It grows down from the roof of the whale's mouth. When a baleen whale opens its mouth, the baleen make it look like the whale has a huge moustache, like the male pink ones seem to like to grow on their upper lips."

Sparky giggled. "That's funny, Mom!"

"Yes, but the baleen works very well. The whale gulps a mouthful of seawater and food into its mouth. Humpbacks eat schooling fish, like herring, sea lance, capelin, mackerel, cod, salmon, and krill. When the whale has its mouthful, the flexible baleen traps the food, but the water is able to escape through the sides of the whale's mouth."

"Cool! Do the whales stay here in the Khutzeymateen Inlet to eat, Mom?"

"No, honey. I think they are probably just checking for salmon today. They usually live in Work Channel, the next inlet from us, for August, September, and October. Work Channel inlet is very rich in nutritious food that whales need to survive. That is why the humpbacks are there every year before they do their long migration to Hawaii. You see, Sparky, the whales eat all fall, and then they do not eat again until they reach Hawaii—their winter home where they mate and have their babies."

"They don't eat all the way to Hawaii! Don't they get hungry?" Sparky asked with big eyes.

"Well, Sparks, it is kind of like us when we hibernate. We make sure we have enough fat stored so we make it through the winter. Whales are very smart survivors, like all furred, finned, feathered, and shelled are. I have seen humpbacks catch their dinner by bubble feeding, and it is amazing."

"What is bubble feeding, Mom?" Sparky asked, scrunching his nose up.

"Well, Sparky, a group of two or more whales come together. They all decide who will be the main feeder for the dive. Then all the whales take a big deep breath and dive down into the depths of the ocean. When they come to the school of fish that they want, say a school of herring, all the whales swim around the fish and blow a ring of bubbles. The bubble net holds the fish in a group. The fish become confused and disoriented and can't escape through the net of bubbles. The whales slowly guide the school to the surface of the ocean. Once they are at the surface, the main feeding whale comes up through the middle of the bubble ring with his mouth open and scoops up most of the fish. In the meantime, the other whales try to catch as many escaping fish as they can around the edges. The whales sieve the water out of their mouths and eat the fish. After a couple of minutes' rest, they pick a new main feeder, and the whole process starts over again."

"Cool!" Sparky said with awe. "Whales are so smart. How do they find the school of fish they will eat?"

"Whales live in the dark depths of the ocean. Because of this, they use their senses much differently than we do."

"What do you mean, Mom?" Sparky questioned.

"Well, Sparks, we have a very highly developed and adapted sense of smell. That is why we have our long noses," Lucy said. She wiggled her nose and then nuzzled Sparky with her snout. "Lots of smell sensors allow us to smell things a mile away if the wind is good. We are therefore able to smell danger coming, and we are able to snuffle out good-tasting food, like baby bear cubs." She nibbled Sparky's ear.

"Mom! You said bear honor, so no tickling!" Sparky reminded Lucy. "And I thought Taku gave you a long nose to tickle me with!"

"Well, that too, Sparks"—Lucy laughed—"but mostly to smell danger and find food." She paused and looked at Sparky. "Do you think whales use their noses much?"

"Hmmm," Sparky looked at Lucy and thought deeply. Finally he said, "I don't think so, Mom. If they are mammals like us, they can't breathe in the water, so they could not smell scents very well."

"Very good, Sparks!" Lucy exclaimed. "Now what sense do you think the whales would use most?"

Sparky thought hard again.

"It must be very dark in the ocean, so they would not be able to see very far," he reasoned.

"Very smart, Sparks. That is correct," Lucy encouraged. "But whales do have highly developed eyesight that they probably use when they are near or at the water's surface to find their family or food. And small toothed whales and dolphins can see as well underwater as they can above the water. This helps them hunt successfully. That is, except for river dolphins. River dolphins live in muddy water, and therefore, their eyes have evolved to be tiny slits. They are virtually blind."

"Wow!" Sparky exclaimed. "That is amazing. Waipo is an incredible planet! Everything is so perfect and well balanced. Taku thought of everything." Sparky sighed and then continued. "Well, let's see. Taste would not really be necessary for survival, except if the whale got a rotten fish," Sparky giggled.

"Right!" Lucy laughed. "We don't know for sure, but whales may leave messages in the water that can be tasted by other whales. I have never got the courage to ask such a personal question. I know the pink ones are busy trying to figure out if whales do that."

"Hmmm," Sparky mused. "I think touch is very important for all creatures in order to be healthy." Then Sparky looked at Lucy with a big smile. "Nothing beats a big hug and lots of licks from your mom!"

"That is very true, my special baby bear," Lucy smiled and nuzzled his ear. "And whales are as loving as us bears with their babies and each other. Except of course when male bears are fighting over something silly or when a mother bear is protecting her baby bear." She looked at Sparky. "We all need lots of love all through our lives in order to stay healthy. But do you think it is the most important sense for a whale?"

Sparky thought hard.

"Hmmm ... let's see. I have said sight, smell, taste, touch, and the last obvious one is ... er besides all our sixth sense ... oh ... er ...""

"Sparky," Lucy whispered in his ear.

"Hearing!" Sparky yelled. "Of course. Hearing would be the most important for whales!" Then he stopped and looked at Lucy. "But, Mom, how can whales hear underwater? Don't their ears get full of water? I can't stand getting water in my ears!"

Lucy laughed.

"Sparky, whales are aquatic mammals, so they have evolved differently than us. They have different ears than us, so the water does not bother them."

"But how do whales hear?" Sparky questioned.

"That depends on what the whale is up to and if the whale is baleen or toothed. There is as many different whale sounds in the world as there are whales. Our friends the humpback whales make omnidirectional, loud, long, low-pitched sounds that travel through the water and are received by other whales. Sometimes if conditions in the ocean are right, the sounds they make can travel for hundreds or even thousands of miles. This is the humpbacks' way of keeping in touch with friends and family."

"Whoa! That is a long way to talk to your buddy!" Sparky exclaimed. "I wish we could do that!"

"Yes, Sparks, that is a long way. Now, toothed whales and sperm whales send out special directional clicking sounds that they use for hunting. You see, Sparky, the whales can tell what kind of prey they have in their sights, its size, location, and speed of travel just by listening to the reflected echoes that are bounced off the prey."

"Slippery slug!" That is so cool, Mom! Whales can draw a picture in their minds just from sound! They are amazing! Hey! Our friend Skite the bat did the same thing!" Sparky exclaimed as he looked out to the ocean to try to see the whales.

"That's right, Sparky."

Sparky looked at Lucy with a puzzled look on his face. "But how do the whales make sounds underwater, Mom? They can't breathe under there!"

"True, Sparks, but when the whale is at the surface of the ocean, it can take a big enough breath to let it stay under the water for fifteen minutes or more. So a whale with lungs filled with air can make all sorts of noises and be under the water. Some make long low sounds, others make fast clicking sounds, while others sing like birds. All whale sounds are produced in various ways. Whales use their nasal passages in their heads to make sounds by varying the opening of the nasal plug. They can also force air out their blowhole in the top of their skull. Like us, they can 'talk' through their larynx. They also have an area on their head called the bulbous melon."

Sparky scrunched his nose up and said. "That sounds gross. What is it?"

Lucy laughed. "The bulbous melon is a structure of fat and muscle located in a whale's forehead. The structure may help the sound to focus into a beam for echolocation."

"Cool!" Sparky looked down and began to nibble at grass. Then he looked up at his mom and said, "But I still don't see how whales can hear underwater with their ears full of water."

"No, no, Sparks," Lucy giggled. "Whales hear by receiving sound waves through the water. The sound vibrations enter the whale's head mainly through their lower jaw and continue to their inner ear or bulla. The bulla is free-floating and surrounded by a bubbly foam substance. It is not attached to the skull in any way. Hearing ability varies with each species of whale. Some whales hear much the range that we do, and others are capable of hearing ultrasonic sounds much higher that we can hear. The variety of sounds may serve different purposes, such as navigation, food finding, or communication. They also may sometimes just sing for the joy of being alive."

"That's like we do some days, Mom! I just love being alive!" Sparky smiled and playfully rolled on his back with his tiny feet in the air. "But I still don't quite understand how a whale can hear an object and know what it looks like. That eco ... ecer ... eclo ..."

"Echolocation, son," Lucy helped. "Okay, I will try to explain it again. The whale makes a loud ticking sound. The sound travels through the water and hits the object the whale wants to test. The sound bounces off the object and returns to the whale. This is the echo part. Depending on the strength of the echo and how fast it returns, the whale can construct a picture of the object in its brain. The object's size, shape, density, and distance all affect the picture created in the whale's brain."

"I get it!" Sparky smiled then paused thoughtfully. "So the whale can actually almost see the object in its mind just from the different sounds the whale sends out."

"Exactly, sweetie."

"Whales are amazing, Mom," Sparky said and then thought for a moment. "But their size is what really gets me. I thought we were big, but we are tiny compared to a whale! Are the humpbacks the biggest whales in the world?"

"Oh heavens, no, love. The blue whale is the largest mammal on Waipo. This baleen whale can reach 110 paws (34 meters) long and average weight is 120 tons (109 tonnes), but they can reach 200 tons (181 tonnes). Their hearts are as big as I am—500 pounds (226 kilograms). Their tale can measure 20 paws (6 meters) across from edge to edge. Blue whales' throat pleats can expand to hold 40 to 50 tons (36 to 45 tonnes) of water and krill, and they can eat up to 8 tons (7300 kilograms) of food per day. Baby blues start out large. The bouncing baby blues are 23 paws (7 meters) long and weigh 2.5 tons (2.26 tonnes). Baby blues drink 50 gallons (190 liters) of milk a day, which allows them to gain 8 pounds (3.5 kilograms) and hour. That is 200 pounds (91 kilograms) a day."

"Wow, Mom! That is a lot of weight in one day!" Sparky said with amazement.

"Yes, it is, Sparks. They grow very fast. Other whales have big body parts also," Lucy continued. "The right whale's eye is about seven inches (eighteen centimeters) wide. A sperm whale's brain weighs seventeen pounds (eight kilograms). That is five times heavier than a pink one's brain."

"Look, Mom!" Sparky said excitedly and motioned with his nose. "The whales are coming back!"

Lucy walked down to the water's edge and stood quietly looking over the inlet toward the whales. She stood there for a long time without saying a word.

Finally, Sparky curiously wandered up beside her.

"Mom! What are you doing?" he whispered.

"Shhh, son. I am asking the whales to come and meet you," Lucy whispered back.

"But you are not saying anything," Sparky continued.

"Sparky, mind communication is a skill you will develop before you are weaned. Now be patient. Shhh. I hear them!" she whispered.

The whales surfaced and sat motionless for a few moments quite far offshore. Then they all disappeared from sight into the depths of the ocean.

"I guess they didn't want to meet me," Sparky said in a very disappointed little voice.

No sooner had Sparky spoken than the water right in front of the two bears erupted in a spray as eight whales surfaced at once with a loud *pwwaaff!* The spray from the air rained down on the bears, and the fishy smell of whale breath filled their long snouts. Then the whales disappeared under the surface of the water again.

"Wow!" Sparky exclaimed with excitement. "The whales are huge! And they have come over to meet me!"

"Shhh, son. Be calm, silent, and very polite," Lucy whispered.

The whales all surfaced again, but this time, they all floated on the surface of the water and looked at the bears.

"Welcome home once again to the Khutzeymateen Valley, sister and brother whales," Lucy said with great respect.

A kind voice of much greater power then spoke, and Sparky cowered closer to his mother.

"It is with much joy and honor that we again meet, sister bear," the female whale voice said. "We see you have a handsome son to teach the ways of Waipo, Universe, and Taku. I can see that one day he will be a mighty leader of all bears."

At this, a broad smile spread across Sparky's little bear face. He stood tall and puffed out his tiny bear chest.

"She is a very smart whale," Sparky whispered to Lucy.

"Son, shhh," Lucy whispered. "My apologies, sister whale."

The whales laughed.

"The wee bear cub does not know how good our hearing is," a male whale voice said. "He is a character and will be a great bear leader. Do not worry, sister bear. Let the young bear speak his mind."

"What is your name, wee bear?" yet another whale voice asked.

"Sparky!" Sparky yelled proudly as he stood up straight and tall.

"Ohhh!" the whales moaned.

"Sparky," Lucy said quietly. "Keep your voice calm and low. Remember the whales have sensitive hearing."

"Oops. Sorry, Mom," Sparky whispered. "I am very sorry for yelling, sister and brother whales," Sparky apologized.

"That is fine, wee Sparky bear," the wise female whale again spoke. "You did not know to speak quietly." Then the large female whale rolled on her side and took a good look at Sparky.

"Oh yes, sister Lucy bear, he is a fine young bear." Then she rolled back and said, "I too have someone for you to meet. Seanna, please come here." She beckoned and a small whale swam up beside her. "This is my new granddaughter, Seanna. Daughter of my daughter Zalu," The whale said proudly "Seanna, this is sister bear Lucy and her son, Sparky.

"Hello, Sister Lucy. Hello, Sparky," the baby whale said shyly.

"Hello, Seanna!" Sparky said enthusiastically. "It is great to meet you! Are you learning all sorts of baby whale things like I am learning all sorts of bear skills?"

"Yes, Sparky," Seanna giggled. "I am. And my grandmother has also told me lots of amazing things about your species, too."

"Yeah, my mom told me how awesome whales are, too." Sparky had a hard time containing his excitement at meeting a new friend that was a youngster like him. "I am really happy to meet you and your family!"

"Your granddaughter is gorgeous, Sister Bilka," Lucy smiled at the whales.

"Thank you, Sister Lucy. But you must now excuse us. We must be on our way back to Work Channel. It is almost dinnertime, and you know our appetite," Bilka said with a laugh.

"Excuse me, Sister Bilka," Lucy said very respectfully. "Could you be so kind to tell us if many salmon have arrived in the Khutzeymateen Inlet? Sparky is looking forward to his first fish, and we are hoping that will be soon."

"Of course, Sister Lucy. There are twice as many salmon as last year at this time. In seven to fourteen sunups, we should see the salmon in full spawn."

"You will love salmon, Sparky," Seanna said excitedly.

"I know I will, Seanna. I can hardly wait. Maybe if I see you when we are older when I learn how to fish, like maybe next leaf-dropping season, we can fish together. I will be onshore, but I could watch you and your family bubble feeding, and you could see my moves in the mouth of Mouse Creek."

"That would be fun, Sparky. That is if it is all right with Bilka," Seanna said as she looked at her grandmother.

"That would be just fine with me. So Sparky will have to practice his fishing for next leaf-dropping time. Now we really must be on our way."

"Thank you for the salmon update and for stopping by," Lucy said with great respect. "Please come again anytime."

"You are always welcome at Work Channel for a visit if you are roaming," Bilka replied.

"Bye, Sparky," Seanna said quietly.

"Bye, Seanna. I hope to see you again soon. I can't wait until we meet up, to see how much we both grow!" Sparky said excitedly.

"Me too, Sparky!" Seanna giggled. "Bye, my new friend!"

As the whales began to swim off, they all rolled on their sides and waved their front flippers at Lucy and Sparky. Then, perfectly synchronized, they all took a breath, and eight triangular tails surfaced and then disappeared under the green-black inlet water.

"Wow! Mom! That was the coolest!" Sparky exclaimed. "Did you see how long their arms were!"

"Yes, honey," Lucy smiled. "The humpback whales have the longest arms, or flippers, in the animal kingdom. Their flippers can grow up to sixteen and a half feet (five meters) long."

"Holy! That is long! And the patterns on their tales, were they all different-looking?" Sparky questioned.

"You are an observant baby bear, indeed. The whale tails are like snowflakes, no two are alike. That is how the pink ones keep track of the many different individual humpback whales."

"Cool!" Sparky exclaimed and watched as the whales playfully danced on the surface of the inlet a half a mile away. "Mom!" Sparky suddenly said with a concerned look on his face.

"What is it, son?" Lucy asked.

"Well, it looked like the whales had something growing on their skin. They aren't sick, are they?"

"Oh no, honey," Lucy said reassuringly. "Most animals host parasites and bacteria. You and I have all sorts of minute critters living on us right now."

"Oh gross!" Sparky squirmed and rolled in the grass and then stood and shook. "Did I get them all off! I don't want things living on me!"

Lucy laughed. "It's okay, Sparks. We need the microscopic critters living on us in order to survive ourselves. They are part of the cleaning and maintenance crew that helps to keep us alive."

"Really?" Sparky questioned.

"Yes, honey. We would not survive. Think of it in this way. Think of yourself as Waipo or Universe. You are your own little planet where there are all sorts of things happening, and all sorts of critters living that you are not aware of, but everything happens for a reason and for the survival of your planet."

"Cool! I am a planet all of my own. Do the pink ones and all smooth skins have creatures living on them, too?" Sparky questioned.

"Of course they do. Everything on Waipo has something that lives on it, and that brings us back to the whales. Whales are so big that barnacles and cyamids—whale lice—form colonies on their bodies. That is what you saw on their skin. They do not hurt the whales, but the whale is the host where these creatures live."

"Wow! We eat barnacles." Then Sparky sat and thought for a moment. "Mom!"

"Yes, Sparky?"

"I really liked meeting the whales. Are there a lot of humpback whales on Waipo?"

"Well, Sparky, like many creatures on Waipo, the humpback whales are endangered. The smooth skins killed so many that their numbers went from an estimated 115,000 to approximately 10,000. We are lucky that 7,000 of those humpbacks left on Waipo live in the Northern Hemisphere."

"Urg!" Sparky said angrily. "Won't the smooth skins ever learn? I am just a baby bear, but I can see the importance of balance in the whole scheme of things. Why can't the smooth skins, Mom?"

"Well, Sparky, the smooth skins are much different than all other species on Waipo. They are kind of like the consumptive parasites on any creature. Without control they will eventually kill their host, and in the smooth skins' case, their host is Waipo."

"What is a consumptive parasite, Mom?" Sparky crinkled his nose and asked.

"That is something that take much more than it needs to and doesn't give enough back to its host. Eventually the parasite kills its host," Lucy explained.

"Yeah well, Waipo belongs to all of us, not just them! Maybe we can make the baby smooth skins see how important our planet is. Maybe we can make the smooth skins realize how much we have to lose by losing Waipo and all the species on her. They have to realize that they can't just go around killing everything; otherwise, there won't be anything left on Waipo but smooth skins, and how boring would that be?" Sparky said and his hackles stood on end. "I hope Seanna will be all right. She was beautiful, and I hope to meet her again soon."

"You will see her again, Sparky. The whales come every year to eat fish and visit the Khutzeymateen. As long as there are fish and oceans, the whales will come to visit. Now, young wee bear that will someday rule the Khutzeymateen Valley, you need some mother bear milk and a good nap, so let's go to our day den, love," Lucy said and wandered towards the forest.

"Yup!" Sparky sighed. "Those whales are really smart. Someday I will be a dominant male bear in the forest. King of the Khutzeymateen!"

Lucy chuckled. "Come on, King Sparky! Time to eat so you can grow into a king. Now get your little furry body up here right now!"

"Coming, Mom," Sparky said sheepishly.

Chapter 22:
I'll Starve

The golden light of dusk slowly began to pour itself over the granite mountains of the Khutzeymateen Valley and spill carelessly into the icy waters of the inlet. Autumn had arrived, and she busily stole the summer's green hues, splashing instead her favorite colors—yellow, orange, and red—over the vegetation in the valley. Her chilly breath made the leaves of the deciduous trees shiver so hard that many began to lose their grips and fall off the branches to the ground.

Sparky stood on the shore of Mouse Creek and watched as Lucy nimbly hopped from boulder to boulder across the creek. She stopped on each rock and peered into the rushing water, just as she had been doing for the last week. She was anxious for the salmon to arrive because the berry season was coming to an end and the fall sedge grass had become tough and dry. Lucy knew the salmon must arrive soon so she and Sparky could begin eating and put on enough fat to be able to survive the winter. Without the salmon, the bears would die of starvation in their den.

"Can you see any yet?" Sparky yelled excitedly to his mom and stood up tall on his hind legs to try and get a better view. His furry little legs quivered with enthusiasm while his sharp hind toenails dug into the mud for balance. Sparky patted his tiny pink bear tummy with his front paws. His round teddy bear ears listened, and his nose sniffed higher and higher to see if there was a fishy smell in the air.

"Can you see any yet, Mom?" he nagged again. "I am starving. I can't wait to taste the salmon!"

"Patience, son!" Lucy laughed. "You can't rush nature. So far I haven't seen any salmon."

"But I really want a salmon! I need to put on some weight for my first winter hibernation, or I will die! What if the salmon don't come, Mom? I will starve to death! I am too young to die! Look at my tummy. It is so tiny! I am gaunt and starving! I need a fish, Mom, or I will die!" Sparky whined incessantly.

"Sparky! Stop it now! You are being way too melodramatic, and you are distracting me! Now be quiet!" Lucy said sternly. She was losing her patience with Sparky's whining. "Now let me be so I can check for salmon!"

"Sorry, Mom," Sparky said sheepishly. "Starvation makes me crazy. I just really want a salmon! I can't wait to taste one! I'll see if I can smell them!"

Lucy rolled her eyes, ignored her cub, and continued to search the water of Mouse Creek for any movement of spawning salmon.

Sparky ran down to the water and stood up to his knees in the icy creek. He peered into the rushing water and then stood up on his hind legs once more. With his nose high in the air, he sniffed the air deeply. Without thinking, he closed his eyes. Sparky's little hind legs wobbled under him in the swift current of the creek. He opened his eyes quickly, but it was too late. The movement of the creek threw his balance off completely, and he tumbled backward over a rock.

"Whoa!" he screamed as his furry little body flew through the air and then completely submerged in a deep ice-cold pool of water.

Lucy quickly looked around just in time to see Sparky in flight, upside down with all four paws in the air, before the tiny cub completely disappeared under the water's surface. Then, as if Sparky had been shot from a cannon, his wee body exploded from the creek. He shot six feet up the bank and onto the shore. His fur clung to his body from the weight of the water, causing him to look like a dejected drown rat.

Lucy laughed so hard that she almost fell off her rock.

"Sparky! What are you doing!" she finally managed to say before the laughter hit again.

"It's not funny, Mom! I could have drowned! I was just helping to look for salmon, and I lost my balance," Sparky pouted and vigorously began to shake the water from his fur. "It is so cold when you get wet and the big glowing ball has gone behind the mountains!"

Lucy hopped the rocks back over to her son and cuddled him close with one paw. "Come here, darlin'," she said kindly and began to lick Sparky dry. "I know you were only trying to help, and I appreciate it. Now give another big shake."

"That water is so cold." Sparky shivered, and then he vigorously shook his head to get the water out of his ears. "I got half the creek in my ears and up my nose," he whined and began to sneeze. "I can't ... *achoo* ... st-st-st ... *achoo* ... stand water in my eeee ... *achoo* ... ears and up my nose!" He gave a big shake and then sat as Lucy licked his face dry. "I could have drowned or been swept down the creek with the current. Then you would be missing me," he pouted.

"Oh, sweetie, you know I love you, and I would have rescued you." Lucy nuzzled her shivering son with her nose and began to lick the water off his tiny bear tummy.

"Mom! That tickles!" Sparky giggled.

"Mommy wuvs her baby bear," she coed and licked even harder.

"Mom! Stop! Don't you have to go check for more salmon?" he pleaded through his giggling.

"Are you going to stay snuggy and warm here onshore in this nice patch of soft moss?" Lucy said and continued to lick her wriggling cub.

"Yes, Mom! I promise!" Sparky said as he lay down on a cushy vibrant green bed of moss. "I will stay right here."

"All right, Sparks. Mom is off to rock hop for salmon," she said and hopped on to a rock close to shore. "If you get to cold, call me and I will come snuggle you. Okay?"

"Yes, Mom, I will call you."

"Good baby bear. Mom will have one more look, and then I will come and snuggle with you and keep you warm. I will be back soon."

Sparky lay in the moss for a moment. It was so soft and warm.

"Maybe I should try and dry my fur off on the moss," he whispered.

Sparky flopped over on his side and began rubbing his wet fur coat on the moss. "Ah, this feels so good. Oh, my back is itchy and wet," he said and rolled on his back and began to frantically wriggle and jiggle with all his feet cavorting in the air. Rolling on the other side, his tiny furry body jerked in a circle as he inchwormed his coat dry. He stood up and pushed one shoulder along the ground and then the other. Then he pushed the top of his head along the moss, but he did it just a little too hard. "Whoa!" he exclaimed as he unexpectedly and ungracefully somersaulted forward his legs flailing in all direction. Sparky lay in a dazed heap. "Huh, I guess I got a little carried away with the fur drying. Maybe I better just watch my mom for a while." Quietly he snuggled in the moss and began to doze off as Lucy intently looked for salmon.

Chapter 23:
Not Just Another Pretty Fish

As the sun moved closer to the mountain peaks for the evening, a golden glow illuminated Mouse Creek with rich warm light. Lucy hopped from boulder to boulder, peering into the water for fish. After a few minutes she yelled. "What's this?" Then with lightening speed, she plunged her head and front feet into the water.

Sparky looked up and thought Lucy was falling off the rock into the creek. He jumped to his feet with panic and yelled, "Mom!" Then his eyes grew huge as Lucy emerged from the golden creek. In her mouth was a six-pound (2.7 kilogram) male pink salmon. The fish flipped up and down in Lucy's strong grip until it finally gave up and became limp.

"Wow! Cool! A salmon!" Sparky yelled excitedly as he watched Lucy bring the huge fish to shore. "That is the most hugemungous fish I have ever seen! You are an awesome fish catcher, Mom!" Sparky exclaimed as he excitedly bounced up and down on the shore like a rubber ball. "I can't believe I finally get to taste a salmon!"

Lucy walked up the beach to Sparky and plopped the fish down in front of him. "Well, what do you think of that?" she asked her quivering cub.

"Stuck mussel! This fish is almost as long as I am!" he whispered as he sniffed and inspected the salmon.

"They are a good size, honey. Most pink salmon weigh about five pounds (2.27 kilograms), and their length is twenty inches (51 centimeters). The biggest salmon are the Chinook salmon, or as some call them spring or king salmon. On average they are about twenty two pounds (ten kilograms) and three feet (one meter) long. But the biggest Chinook ever recorded by the pink ones was 127 pounds (58 kilograms). It was caught right here in northern British Columbia.

"Wow! That record Chinook was a huge fish, Mom! We could eat that one Chinook salmon and not have to fish for the rest of the day! How come they are so much bigger than the pink salmon?"

"Well, honey, life span varies depending on the species of salmon. Pink salmon only live two years. Chinook salmon live six to seven years. So the Chinooks have a chance to grow much bigger."

"But where do the salmon go, Mom? How come they are not in the river all the time?"

"Salmon begin their life in a freshwater river or lake, then swim out to the ocean for their adult life, and finally return to the river or lake where they were born to spawn."

"How many kinds of salmon are there, Mom?"

"In this area there are five, but Boris told us a sixth kind has been brought in from another ocean. The smooth skins raise them for food. This might not be a good idea because it could change nature's balance and affect the native fish, which would affect all of the creatures that rely on the salmon. Everything in the Khutzeymateen needs salmon to survive."

Confused, Sparky looked at his mom. "If there are five different species of salmon in British Columbia, how come the salmon don't dig up each other's nests? And if that many eggs are laid, do all the salmon come back to the same river? There should be millions of fish."

"Mother Nature staggers the spawning distances. The bigger and stronger the fish, the higher upriver they will spawn," Lucy explained. "You must remember there are many animals and birds and even other fish that eat the eggs and salmon. Very few baby salmon live to be adults. Population control is important on Waipo. Only enough salmon to carry on survive."

"Mother Nature is so smart with everything on Waipo," Sparky said respectfully.

"Yes, she is, Sparky," Lucy paused and thought. "Once the eggs are laid and fertilized, the male and female salmon have completed their journey, and they die."

"Really!" Sparky exclaimed. "That seems sad. Why can't the salmon live to see their babies?"

"As with every species on Waipo, life, reproduction, and death are all part of the life cycle of the salmon. You see, Sparks, everything on Waipo has a life span, and everything in nature is balanced. Once the salmon have reproduced, they do not need to live anymore, and they die. Their purpose has been fulfilled—procreation of the species. Spawning is the last step in a salmon's life, and they then become food for other creatures."

"I understand now. It is not sad, it is just part of the life cycle," Sparky sighed. "Just like some day you and I will die and become part of nature in another way. I guess the planet would become very overpopulated if everything that was ever born survived and lived forever."

"That is right, son. Everything will eventually move from one energy form to another. When the salmon die, we eat them and they become part of us, which helps us to survive. Plants get eaten or die and become part of the soil again. Energy needs energy to survive," Lucy explained.

Sparky thought for a moment then said, "I still don't understand how an egg in the freshwater gets to be a big salmon in the ocean."

"Once the egg hatches, the salmon leaves the freshwater and lives in the ocean between two and seven leaf droppings. Then they return to their home freshwater source where they were hatched," Lucy explained.

"Cool! Salmon are not just another pretty fish. They are really smart!" Sparky looked down at the salmon. "The male salmon are kind of scary-looking, Mom. They have such big teeth."

Lucy looked down at the fish. "Yes, they are scary. When they leave the ocean to spawn, the males get longer jaws and big teeth for fighting. They get a hump on their backs, and both the male and females become more colorful."

Sparky carefully inspected the salmon. "He has a beautiful iridescent yellow-green color, but what are these spots here, Mom?" he asked and pointed with his nose.

"Those marks on his skin are decay, and it is a natural part of the spawning process. Once the salmon leave the saltwater to return to the spawning rivers, bacteria and fungus begin to attack their skin. Their body prepares to die, and the skin starts to decay."

"They start to rot while they are still alive!" Sparky said with horror in his voice.

"Yes, Sparky. It is all part of Mother Nature. She has her way of cleaning up Waipo. It has worked for millions of years," Lucy explained. "There are so many thousands of fish carcasses, the flesh-eating bacteria is necessary to speed up the decay of the dying fish so they quickly become part of the planet in another way."

"I guess so, but it sounds so gross. Poor fish. It sounds like something in my nightmares." Sparky stood on his hind legs, stretched his front legs in the air, and scrunched his face up like a monster. "I am the monster mutant salmon with flesh-eating disease all over his body that ate all the bears of the world!"

"Oh, Sparky, for goodness sake! You are such a spruce nut bar," Lucy laughed. "You just wait until you taste how delicious the fish are when they are well-aged and rotten. You will love the flavor."

"Yuck!" Sparky said with disgust. "I am not eating any rotten fish!"

Lucy laughed. "We all say that at first, but you just wait. You will see how delicious they taste."

"Let's talk about something else. I feel sick!" He paused and then said, "What do salmon eat?"

"When they are first born, they live off the yoke sack of the egg. While in freshwater, the tiny salmon will feed on insects and water organisms. Salmon that reach the ocean will then eat shrimp, squid, and small fish. When the salmon return to the freshwater to spawn, they stop eating and survive on their fat reserves only. And this is amazing, because some salmon travel thousands of miles to return to their spawning beds where they were born."

"Holy! That's a long way to travel just to meet a lady fish, have babies, and then die! I think I would just stay out in the ocean!" He paused in thought. "How do the fish know where they are going underwater? And how do they find their way back to the river where they were born?"

"Well, honey, there are a few different ways. The fish have a pineal gland located in their brain. This gland senses changes in daylight, so the fish can tell when the days are getting shorter. It is believed fish can navigate by using the currents of the ocean, the position of the sun, and by accessing a magnetic imprint in their brain. Like the pink ones using a compass, the salmon can find their way home by using the magnetic field of the planet. Birds and caribou do this as well. One last thing is that salmon have an incredible sense of smell. When they reach the coast, they follow their nose. They will pick up the odor of their home stream and follow the scent until they reach the spawning bed where they were born."

"Wow! Their noses are as good a sniffers as ours! How many fish will come back to spawn, Mom?"

"Well, that depends of a lot of variables, honey. An average year in Mouse Creek is about 50 to 80 thousand salmon. In a really good year, we might see 100 to 150 thousand salmon."

"Wow! The water must be black with fish backs!"

"Yes, Sparky. I can almost walk across the creek on their backs. I just have to step into the water, and within a second, a fish is in my mouth. This is very important because we need to eat lots of salmon to survive the winter hibernation. No salmon means it would be very difficult for coastal bears to survive. It would also make survival very hard for eagles, seals, whales, sea lions, and other species that depend on the salmon for food. Even the trees along the shoreline benefit from the fish being dragged up. The fish break down and make great fertilizer. Salmon are very high in nitrogen and other nutrients from the ocean. These nutrients and minerals are important in the growth and development of all plants. The trees along the shoreline of a salmon-spawning river or creek seem to be larger and healthier than trees farther back in the forest."

"Mother Nature is so smart! She has everything so balanced." The little cub looked thoughtfully at his mother. "Mom, salmon are very important for a lot of reasons. I hope they never stop coming to the Khutzeymateen Valley and Work Channel where Seanna lives in the fall. I want our friends the whales to have lots of salmon to eat. Seanna needs lots of salmon to grow just like I do." He paused again, and a concerned look spread over his innocent tiny face. "Mom, I really want all our friends in the forest to have enough food to survive. Is there any way we can keep the salmon healthy and coming to spawn every fall?"

"Well, honey, that depends a lot on the pink ones. If they take care of the salmon and the ocean, then all the creatures that depend on the salmon will survive. Without a healthy ocean, nothing on Waipo, our water planet, can survive."

"That is scary, Mom. Those pink ones are nothing but trouble!" he said with a frown.

"Now, Sparky, be nice. Remember how they helped us that day when we were being chased by the aggressive male bear. They stayed with us until we got to Mouse Creek. Do you remember? You would not want to see anything happen to that nice female smooth skin that you liked."

"Yes, I remember. They were very kind to us. And, no, I would not want her to get hurt," Sparky sulked.

"There are good pink ones and bad ones. Some of the older pink ones made some bad decisions and mistakes, but hopefully the baby pink ones will see into the future and realize that the survival of Waipo and all species lies in their hands. For that matter, the survival of the pink ones lies in their hands. Mother Nature is very well balanced, but precariously balanced as well. The honest truth is that if nature becomes too unbalanced, Waipo will die, and along with her, all life as we now know it will also die."

She paused thoughtfully for a moment and looked at Sparky, who looked very concerned. Then she continued. "Sparky, this is neither bad nor good; it just is. So do not worry your little furry head off. When I say Waipo will die, I mean Waipo will die in the form of what we know her now, but Waipo will always win in the end. She will come back in some new form, but it may take millions of years. You see, honey, we are all just minute specks in time on Waipo. Everything on the planet is pretty insignificant in the whole scheme of Universe and time. Sparky, in pure reality of Universe, time does not exist. Universes exist on universes in the continuum of all. For example, take your cute little furry body. It is actually a mini universe."

Sparky looked down at himself. "Me?" he questioned.

"Yes, you," Lucy smiled. "There are all sorts of different things going on that you don't even know about. There are happy cells, each one doing there own little job to keep you alive. Blood is moving throughout your body, transporting nourishment and oxygen. Your skin and fur sheds on a regular basis and new grows back. Pollution in your body is being constantly removed. Wars are being fought by your immune system. Sparky, so many other things are going on as well that you are not aware of, but it is your little universe functioning and surviving. Everything on Waipo is always changing and moving. Nothing on Waipo stays the same for long. Nothing is superior or inferior, and everything will eventually die for one reason or another. Like this fish. He died to give us life. And if life on Waipo as we know it dies, another form of species will then be given a chance to carry on."

Sparky sighed deeply. "You are so wise, Mom, and I have so much to learn."

"Yes, honey, but the main lessons we must learn are all the positives. Like happiness, sharing, caring, giving, kindness, and of course the most important one, love." She smiled and nuzzled her long nose into Sparky's furry pudgy little neck. Then she sat down and looked at him. "So because I am happy with my son and care about him so much, I will be kind and share this fish with you. And because I love you so much, I will give you the first bite of the first salmon of the year. Your first salmon ever!"

"You are so smart, Mom. Thank you for the salmon. I love you." He smiled and sighed and looked at the fish. "Thank you, fish, for feeding me. Thank you, fish, for being my first yummy salmon ever! Okay. Here it goes! My first salmon ever!"

Sparky sunk his teeth deep into the dark peach-colored flesh of the salmon then stopped suddenly. His eyes closed, and then he began to gnaw contentedly at the fish. He lay down on the ground and held the salmon with his two front paws.

"Well, son? What do you think?" Lucy smiled.

Sparky opened his eyes and got a dreamy look on his face. Then without removing his mouth from the fish, he mumbled, "Gish ish sha tah vest mehl I haf efer eafen!" Then he closed his eyes and continued to chew the salmon.

Lucy laughed. "I knew you would love it, honey. Well, I guess I better go catch myself another salmon. Looks like this one is taken," she said and then turned and hopped onto a rock in the creek.

Chapter 24:
Grampy Gimpy

Lucy sauntered down the inlet shoreline, and Sparky followed close behind, stopping frequently to nip at the salmon berries that dripped like large orange and red raindrops from plant branches. Sparky could reach most of the berries on the bushes that grew spottily on the forest edge of the shore, but some of the bigger juicier berries were too high up on the bushes. He had to stand on his hind legs and reach high on his tiptoes and even jump up to pull the branches down to reach the fruit.

As the bears approached another side stream near Mouse Creek, Lucy suddenly stopped in her tracks and gave a low, muffled *huff.*

Sparky knew this meant to go quickly to her side. He scrambled up as close as he could and whispered, "What is the matter, Mom?"

"Look over there." Lucy motioned with her nose. "It's Grampy Gimpy. I think he is deaf as a stone, but we will keep our voices down just in case."

Sparky looked to where Lucy was pointing and saw the biggest, fattest old bear he had ever seen.

He began to giggle.

"Mom he is so big and ... well ..." Sparky hesitated and tried not to be rude. "Well, Mom, he is so ... *fat!* His belly is almost dragging on the ground!"

Sparky continued to giggle as Lucy spoke. She giggled, too.

"Yes, Grampy Gimpy does tend to plump up in the fall, but that is probably why he has lived so long."

"Who is he, Mom?" Sparky asked as he watched Gimpy pick up the remnants of rotting salmon parts and swallow them.

"His name is Grampy Gimpy, and he used to be the King of the Khutzeymateen Valley, but now he is too old and crippled to be a competitor during mating season. He is about thirty years old, and he is a retired dominant male. He only comes down to this area when it is salmon season. Otherwise, he stays far back in the forest, avoiding trouble." She hesitated for a moment. "And it just so happens that he is your grandfather, Sparky."

"*Really?*" Sparky said with surprise and shock. "That big huge monster is my grandpa?" He stopped, and with huge eyes, he looked at Lucy. "I mean ... er ... I am sorry, Mom. I did not mean to insult you or Grampy Gimpy ... but he is just ... and well so ... that is my grandpa! Your dad?"

Lucy laughed. "Yes, Sparks, he is my dad. I was his last daughter, and then he sired two more sons before he was dethroned by Buffalo, your father, and Lefty. You remember seeing them."

"Yes, I remember those monsters, and they were very scary! Grampy Gimpy looks like an old pussycat compared to them. A very large old pussycat that is." He paused and then said, "Mom, I know I have to run really fast when I see Buffalo and Lefty. And I know we couldn't go say hi to my dad for that reason, but can we go say hi to Grampy Gimpy?"

"Well, Sparky, I think it is better if we don't bother him. Grampy Gimpy can be a bit cranky if his routine is interrupted. Older male bears are very set in their ways. They have a schedule, and if anything upsets it, they tend to let it ruin their whole day and sometimes their whole week. He is very old, and I think it is just better to leave him be. He looks very content and relaxed, so we will be respectful and let him eat his salmon in peace."

"Okay, Mom. That sounds like a good idea, but can we at least watch him?" Sparky pleaded. "I may never see my grandpa again. He is so old. He could leave Waipo at any time."

"Yes, sweetheart. We will be quiet and watch him for a few minutes." Lucy smiled at Sparky.

They peeked through the bushes again, and Gimpy was in the creek trying to catch a salmon, but his old body was just not fast enough to grab the one he was after. The fish scrambled out of his reach and swam up the stream.

"I wish I could go catch a fish for my grandpa," Sparky whispered to Lucy.

Lucy licked Sparky on the forehead. "That is very sweet of you, Sparky. Not to worry though. By the looks of dear old Dad, he is doing just fine getting ready for his winter nap."

They looked back just in time to see Grampy Gimpy pick up a very large rotten salmon carcass and slurp it down in one gulp. He looked up with a contented grin on his face and stood silently for a moment. Then from somewhere deep within his tummy, the biggest loudest most disgusting burp came rumbling out of his mouth. He gave a big shake as if he was relieved. Then he turned and limped into the forest. Fat waves rippled down his body like the nonstop huge monster-size waves in the ocean.

The burp was too much for Sparky to handle. He burst out laughing and rolled on the ground. After a few moments, he managed to gain enough control to force out words between his belly laughs.

"I can't believe I got to see my grandpa!" Then he giggled again, out of control. "And what a funny character he is! He is so big, and he burps really loud, and he is so funny and … he is my grandpa!"

"Yes, Gimpy has always been a character," Lucy said between her own giggles.

"I sure hope I live to be as old as Grampy Gimpy!" Sparky finally managed to say after he slowed his laughing down.

"You will, Sparky," Lucy said, "just so long as you eat enough salmon in the fall to keep you healthy and strong through your long winter nap."

Sparky sat on his haunches and looked at his tiny bulging bear belly and poked it with his paw.

"Well, Mom, I have a long way to go until I catch up to Grampy Gimpy! We better go and eat lots of salmon for the next month! And I guess I will even try one of those rotten ones. Grampy Gimpy seems to enjoy them, and they sure have not done him any harm!"

Chapter 25:
Salmon Walking

A week passed, and Sparky sat on a rock enjoying the warm morning air. He stared intently at Mouse Creek.

"One hundred and sixty nine, one hundred and seventy. Oh forget it! Mom!" He exclaimed. "There must be a gazillion salmon in the creek today!"

Lucy laughed. "Yes, honey. We are at the height of the salmon run," she said as she chewed a few bits of grass. "Come and eat some grass, my baby bear. You still need your roughage, vitamins, and minerals."

"No, thank you, Mom. I am pretty full of fish. Is this a good salmon run? Are there usually this many?" he asked still looking into the water.

"Not this many usually. This is a good year. We will be very fat by the time we hibernate." She looked at Sparky mischievously. "Sparky, do you think you can run across the salmon backs to get to the other side of the creek?"

"Mom!" Sparky giggled. "The fish would sink with me standing on them!"

"If you run really, really, really fast, I bet they wouldn't," Lucy coaxed.

"Mom! Are you trying to drown me? Or just get me soaking wet?"

"Oh, baby bear. Mommy is just kidding, but the water is so thick with salmon that I have often wondered if we could not run across their backs. But I think we are both too fat now for them to hold us up."

Sparky giggled and poked his pudgy bear tummy and sighed. "Those salmon sure are good. How many salmon are there, Mom?"

"In the creek or in your tummy?" Lucy kidded.

"Mom! In the creek! I know how many have gone into my tummy. Lots!

"Yes, I know, you piggy wiggly. Mom has been catching them nonstop for her baby bear." Then Lucy made snortlike piggy noises.

"Mom! You told me to eat lots of salmon."

"Yes, but not the whole creekful!" Lucy continued to kid.

Sparky rolled his eyes. "You said it was good for me. And besides, I am a healthy, growing baby bear cub, and you said I need lots of protein. All twenty salmon a day," he said proudly.

"Twenty! It is more like one hundred!"

"Mom! That is how many you eat! I would blow up if I ate that many in one day." He giggled. "Now how many fish are in Mouse Creek right now?"

"Well, honey, judging from my calculation this morning, I would guess at least 150,000 salmon have come up to spawn so far. I have not seen this many fish for a long time."

"Wow! That is so cool!" Sparky licked his lips. "Can we stand on a rock in the middle of the creek and look at the salmon? Can we practice catching fish again? I am sure I can catch one myself."

Lucy smiled at her son's enthusiasm. "Sure, Sparks. Let's go down to the point and you can practice all you want."

Chapter 26:
Tricksters and Steak Bones

Every morning, as the leaves grew more and more yellow, Sparky woke bright and early, ready to eat as many salmon as Lucy could catch.

"Come on, Mom. Let's go!" he whined. "I am really hungry for salmon, so you have to catch me lots of fish today."

"Okay, okay, Sparky. Let your old mom wake up a bit. Stop being such a nag this morning," she said and smiled at his urgency to fish.

"All the fish are going to be gone to the other animals! Let's go!" he said and headed out the den door.

"No worry of that, Sparky. There are thousands of fish in the creek," Lucy said as she squeezed out of the den entrance and walked quickly to keep up with her cub. They briskly made their way down the trail to the mouth of Mouse Creek.

The tide was very low, and the mudflats were alive with gulls, ravens, crows, eagles, and smaller shore birds that darted around in an exhausting stop-start fashion.

The noise emitting from the gulls was deafening.

"Egg over here! And here! Here! And here!" they yelled to one another. "Another one here! And here! Here are two!"

"Jeez!" Westy yelled at the gulls as he scampered around the shore, scrounging leftover fish parts. "Da ya think we could have a little quiet? The weasel's gettin' a headache from yer squawking!"

He looked up and saw the bears coming toward him. "Morning, Sparky and Lucy! The fish this morning is mighty fine tasting!" he said then tucked into a big fish tail that some animal had left behind.

"Morning, Westy," Lucy smiled as they walked by him.

"Morning, Westy!" Sparky squealed. "Mom's catching me lots of fish today!"

"Good! Leave some for the old weasel, 'kay, bearo? Good luck, Lucy!" Westy said.

Sparky shook his head and looked at the gulls. "Why do they have to yell so loudly all the time?" he complained. "It makes my ears hurt."

Just then two young Glaucous gulls that had been scurrying around in the water chasing loose salmon eggs that washed out of nest and down the creek started to peck each other and squabble.

"Mom! Rocky took my egg!" one said.

"No, I didn't! Barney's just being a poor little baby bird."

Nearby, a big fat old-looking bald eagle pulled his head up from devouring a rotten salmon carcass. "For heaven's sake! It is not like that was the only egg in the creek. There are thousands!" he yelled grouchily.

"Well, I wanted that one!" one of the gulls whined.

Disgusted, the eagle looked over at the squabbling gulls' mother. "Lady! Will you shut those two up! It is already noisy enough around here without them fighting!" he scowled.

"Oh, the poor grumpy, grumpy, baldy brain is a little testy today," two crows squawked as they landed on each side of the old raptor that was at least four times their size.

"Get lost, you two," the eagle grouched, but the crows pursued their harassment of the giant bird.

"Grumpy, grumpy, grummm-peee," they sang in chorus and hopped cockily around the eagle.

The eagle gave the two tricksters a long angry look, and then he sighed, shook his head, and flew off.

"Yes!" they said in unison. "We can eat his salmon!"

"Mom!" Sparky whispered. "Did you see those two little crows scare off the big bald eagle?"

"Yes," Lucy laughed. "Those two are smart brave tricksters. Here. Sit for a minute on this nice soft mossy patch beside your mom, and I will tell you a story about those two. We will fish in a minute after the story."

"But, Mom, I want a fish. I am hungry," Sparky whined.

"Okay, son. You wait here and I will be right back."

Lucy sauntered over toward the creek while Sparky snuggled on the soft vibrant green moss. Then he rolled on his back and squished his head and body into the soft cushion. As his legs wriggled in the air, he sighed, "Ah, this feels so good! Mom said goose feathers are really soft. I bet if I rolled on a goose, it would feel like this!"

As Lucy approached the crows, they paused from aggressively pecking at the salmon carcass and looked at Lucy.

"Morning, Lucy!" one of the crows squawked.

"You look gorgeous as ever. Your fur is turning a lovely chocolate brown color from all the salmon oil. Very attractive," the other crow said with much respect.

"Morning, fellows. Thanks for the compliments. Are you boys over visiting from the Kwinamass River?" she asked.

"Yup, just flew over to terrorize the area," one said.

"Thought you all needed some new crows to liven things up," said the other.

"Well, I am sure you two will do just that. Now you two boys stay out of trouble." Lucy smiled.

"Never!" they both said at the same time. "Life is far too short for that kind of nonsense!" They chuckled and went back to pecking the salmon.

Lucy laughed and walked into the creek.

She looked around for a moment. Then with lightning speed, her head dove below the water and emerged with a twelve-pound salmon flipping aggressively up and down in her jaws. She began to walk back to Sparky, who was still madly rolling around and giggling with his legs flailing.

"Hey! Nice fish, Lulu!" one of the crows exclaimed.

"Wooo!" whistled the other. "Lucy, you truly are one of the great fisher bears of the world!"

Lucy nodded at the two, walked up beside Sparky, and plopped the fish on the ground. Seeing the fish, Sparky stopped his rolling antics, flopped over on his side, and then quickly hopped to his feet.

"Yummy, yummy, *yummy!*" Sparky exclaimed and stepped off the moss to eat the fish. "Now I am ready to hear your story, Mom."

Lucy shook the water off her fur, took a bite of the salmon, and then sat down beside Sparky, who was peacefully devouring the fish.

"Now our two friends down there are brothers named Ebb and Flow," Lucy began and motioned toward the crows with her long nose. "I have known them since their mother brought them to meet me ten years ago. In that time, they have had many adventures, and I have heard about every one about one hundred times. I have most of the memorized in detail because they talk about them over and over and over again. I must say, they are good adventures and most of them are very funny." She paused and took a nibble of Sparky's salmon, chewed, and swallowed it before continuing. "The first thing you must realize is crows are very intelligent creatures. They will go to great lengths to make a point or to get something they want, which you just witnessed with poor old Reginald the bald eagle."

"They were brave to challenge him. He looked really grumpy!"

"Well, Sparky, ever since his lifetime mate passed away, Reg has been a lonely eagle. Reg is an older bird who doesn't want to put up with the antics of the youngsters. He has lost his patience in his old age." She paused in thought then continued. "Now back to the story. When Ebb and Flow turned two, they decided to experience city life and see how the city slicker crows lived. After leaving the Khutzeymateen and flying over numerous mountain ranges, they arrived in Prince Rupert and landed on a sailboat at the Rushbrook Docks. Being young crows, they didn't realize the dangers of roosting on a pink one's boat."

Sparky's eyes grew big, and he stopped eating his fish. "What happened, Mom?" he said with great concern.

"Well, they landed and began discussing how they would spend their time in the city—important crow things like which dumpsters they should raid, if a bag of garbage was found how to break into it quickly, how to dive bomb cats and dogs, and where to meet if they got separated. Anyway, as they talked, the owner of the sailboat came running out of nowhere and yelled at the two brothers. Then he had something in his hands that made a very loud bang, and suddenly most of Ebb's tail feathers disappeared."

"Whoa! That is scary! What happened next?" Sparky said with big eyes. "That pink one wasn't very nice for doing that!"

"Ebb and Flow were shocked at the rude welcome. They quickly flew to a nearby tree. They were, of course, very scared. Ebb could not believe the mess his tail feathers were in. They were both just really glad the flying object that hit Ebb's tail did not kill them. As they sat trying to calm down, a voice came from behind them. It said, 'Hey, you boys must be new in town.' Ebb and Flow turned to see a wise older crow sitting on a branch behind them. He ruffled his feathers and then continued. 'If you weren't new, you would know to not sit on Harry the Grouch's boat. Not to worry. Most of us locals have lost our tails at one time in our lives. They will grow back.'

"'Why is he such a grump!' Ebb crowed. 'His bloomers must be on way to tight!' Flow scowled. 'Well,' the old crow said, 'he is frustrated with his life. He works way too hard and too many hours. He does not have a pink female in his life. And, of course, he is afraid we are going to poop on his boat. He doesn't realize that only those rude gulls do that sort of thing, not us sophisticated crows.'

"The old crow paused for a moment and regally rustled his wing feathers. 'Say, how long are you boys around for? My flock and I are planning a little trick on old grumpster Harry. We want to get back at him for all the tail feathers he has removed from our bottoms over the years. Want to join the fun?'

"Ebb looked at his back end. 'I would love to get back at that miserable man!' he said. 'I am in!' 'Me, too!' said Flow. 'We are here for two weeks.'

"'Great!' the old crow smiled. 'Meet here in five suns coming over the mountains. There will be at least twenty of us, so two more will be even more fun.'"

Lucy looked at Sparky and smiled. "Ebb and Flow went back in five sunups, and they were informed of the devious plan. The scheme was perfect for their trickster antics."

"What did they do, Mom?" Sparky excitedly asked.

"Well, the local crows had been watching grouchy Harry for a long time. They knew that some days he worked nights and slept during the day. This was one of those days. They all waited quietly in the pouring rain and watched as a dripping wet Harry grouched up the dock, grumbled something as he boarded his sailboat, and disappeared below. They waited and waited until they heard loud snoring coming from Harry's boat. Then one of them flew to the porthole to double-check that Harry was sleeping. He confirmed Harry was asleep and gave the wing signal to start the plan in motion. The old crow gave the *caw-caw* signal, and six crows flew off to the dumpster and got six large old rotten steak bones. The rest of the crows positioned themselves so they could see Harry coming out of his boat.

"The six crows with the steak bones worked in teams of three. They all flew high in the air above where Harry slept on the sailboat. The first two crows took aim and dropped the steak bones, dead center on the target above Harry's bed. When they flew down to pick up their bones, the second crows dropped their bones. As the second two came down and the first two flew up, the third crows dropped theirs on the target. They repeated this rotation over and over again."

"Oh, that is so funny!" Sparky squealed with laughter as he flopped down on the moss beside Lucy. "That would fix that grump for knocking the crow's tail feathers out! How long did the crows drop bones on the sleeping monster? I bet he was even grumpier after they played their trick on him!"

"Well, honey, they continued to drop bones until the watch crows spotted Harry throw the doors of the boat open in a storming rage. The watch crows sounded the alarm, and all the birds quickly scattered to safety. From the trees, they laughed as Harry, wearing only his underwear in the rain, went into a rampage on deck. He exploded with anger. Pacing back and forth, he fired the tail remover in all direction, as if shooting invisible crows. Harry's pie-shaped face was scarlet red with rage. His fat belly jiggled up and down with his jerky aggressive movements as his skinny, knobby knees and chicken legs danced awkwardly around the deck looking for crows. Finally, Harry gave up and went back inside the boat.

"But the crows were not finished yet. They waited until the spy crow gave the wings-up sign that Harry was asleep. Then they started the whole process over again one last time and got an even better result. This time when Harry flew out of the boat in a rage, he slipped on the wet deck of the boat and fell off the edge into the icy cold ocean. The crows all began cawing with laughter as Harry dog-paddled awkwardly to a ladder on the side of the dock and hauled his fat body, with his underwear clinging to his rolls, out of the water."

Sparky rolled on the ground laughing. "That is such a funny story, Mom! Those crows are so smart! Can you tell me another story about Ebb and Flow?"

"I thought you wanted to practice fishing, young man."

"Just one more story … and … well … er … then can I meet Ebb and Flow before we go fishing?"

"Okay, Sparky. One more story and of course you can meet them."

She closed her eyes and thought for a moment. "Okay, I have one! Are you ready?" she asked mischievously.

"You bet, Mom!" Sparky said and listened intently.

Lucy cleared her throat and began. "Pink ones insist on having what they call pets."

"What are pests, Mom?"

"That is pets, Sparky. They are animals called cats and dogs. The cats are distant relatives to wild cats—lions, cougars, tigers, and bobcats. The dogs are related to wolves." She paused for a moment in thought and chucked. "Among the bear community, we have a joke that because the cat family is a true carnivore, if domestic cats were larger, they would eat their pink ones."

"Yuck!" Sparky wrinkled his nose. "I would never want to eat a pink one. They just don't look very tasty at all! And from what I hear, they eat really bad stuff, so they must not be healthy to eat."

"The smooth skins also hold other creatures hostage. Mice, rats, hamsters, birds, fish, and even snakes and spiders, just to name a few."

"That is just weird, Mom! They don't keep bears hostage, do they? I can't imagine living with a smooth skin my whole life. It would be horrible and boring not being able to roam freely in our beautiful home. I am going to stay well away from the smooth skins just in case they try to grab me for a pet!"

"Don't worry, honey. They would have to get past me first. And besides, you are too big to be a pet. Now, a zoo or circus would take you," Lucy kidded.

"Mom, that is not funny! I think that would be worse than being a pet! Please stop. You are going to give me nightmares. I am definitely staying away from the smooth skins!" He pouted and snuggled in closer to Lucy.

"Honey, don't worry. We are very safe here in the Khutzeymateen, and Mom will always protect you from harm.

And when you are a big bear on your own, I will make sure you are wise enough to avoid trouble." Lucy gave him a reassuring smile. "So where were we? Oh yes, cats and dogs. As I said they were originally related to the wild cats and dogs. Then over the centuries, for what ever reason, humans decided to breed them to be different shapes, sizes, breeds, and colors and hold them hostage in their homes. Some dogs and cats are very fortunate with good homes. Others are much less lucky and are mistreated and abused. Apparently some humans cut their pets' fur into ridiculous 'fru fru' hairstyles that are extremely embarrassing to the animal. Things like pompoms on their heads and tails."

"That does it! I am definitely staying away from those pink ones! They are weird! I like my fur just as it is!" Sparky exclaimed.

"Yes, honey. I have been told the wolves do not like to talk about what has been done to their breed." Lucy sighed. "And what else is interesting is that besides our species, the wolf—the domesticated dogs' ancestor—is one of the most feared animals to the pink ones. But now the pink ones call the dog man's best friend. Pink ones will kill wolves, and yet they love their dogs more than anything else. Sometimes I think the pink ones are very confused."

"They are just weird!" Sparky shuddered. "They don't seem very smart, Mom."

"Now, Sparky. Don't be disrespectful. The smooth skins around Waipo are still learning to fit in on our beautiful planet. Now back to the story." She paused. "Now where were we? Oh yes, while Ebb and Flow were in Prince Rupert, every morning while doing their scrounging route, they flew over a yard that had a big huge bowl of fresh dog food sitting out in the open. This would make a fine free meal for two young hungry crows out exploring the world. The only problem was that the food was right beside the house where the giant slept."

"Who was the sleeping giant, Mom?" Sparky asked nervously with eyes the size of large clams.

"It was a huge dog the size of a small moose!"

"Whoa! That's a lot bigger than Ebb and Flow!" Sparky exclaimed.

"Yes, it is, honey, and every time the brothers would try to borrow some food, the greedy dog would try to eat them. So the birds came up with a plan to trick the dog. The crows sat high in a tree and watched the monster that was attached to a long chain. Every time something went by the monster's yard, it would bolt out of its house and run until it choked itself and fell over sideways at the end of the chain. Then it would frantically bark at whatever was passing by."

"See! You go crazy when you live with smooth skins!" Sparky squirmed. "You can't run free and explore, so you go crazy tied up."

"Yes, honey. This dog's brain was definitely made out of squirrel food. Poor neurotic thing was probably insane from being tied up all the time with no exercise. His chase game was most likely the only exercise, excitement, and entertainment the poor bored soul got. Ebb and Flow decided they would spice up the dog's life and at the same time get a free meal. Ebb flew into the yard just far enough out of reach of the end of the dogs chain. He started squawking making a big fuss while hopping up and down on the spot. When the dog spotted him, it bolted out of its wooden cave and flattened itself at the end of its leash. Then it stood up and started barking wildly at Ebb. Meanwhile, Flow flew down to the food bowl and stole as much food as possible. He flew back and forth, hiding enough food in the trees that the crow brothers would eat well all day long. They did this every day for the two weeks they were in Prince Rupert, and the dog never caught on. It was too busy trying to eat Ebb. Flow always made sure he took just enough for the day so the monster could eat too."

"Wow! Ebb and Flow are smart and brave!" Sparky giggled. "I would be to afraid the monster would get lose and eat me!"

"Ebb said the first time he landed, he wondered if he was too close. So when the dog ran at him, he flew up in the air then came back down when he knew he was safe, just in case." Lucy smiled. "Should we go and meet my two fine feathered friends?"

"Yeah! I know I will like them." Sparky stood and looked at the fish bones. "Should I take the remaining fish to Ebb and Flow as a gift?"

"No, honey. We can catch them a nice big fresh one. Just leave that salmon there so the smaller animals, insects, and birds can pick at it. We will share that carcass with them and get a fresh fish for Ebb and Flow."

"Okay, Mom!" Sparky exclaimed. "I like sharing!"

Chapter 27:
Sparky's Big Catch

Lucy and Sparky tottered down to the shore.

Sparky sniffed the air deeply. "I love the smell of leaf-dropping time when the salmon are here. Fish smell everywhere. It is great!"

"Just wait until the salmon start to decay. It smells even better then," Lucy assured him.

"I don't know about that, Mom. The thought of rotten fish makes me want to be sick," Sparky groaned.

The crow brothers were still pecking madly at the half-eaten salmon carcass on the mud beside where Mouse Creek entered the inlet. A young nervous bear traveling through the area some time that morning had abandoned the salmon and ran down the inlet when it heard Lucy and Sparky coming along the trail from their den.

"Hey, Lulu!" Ebb said when he spotted the bears coming toward them. "Who's the cute little fur ball trotting along beside you?"

"Whoa! He's good-looking, Lulu!" Flow exclaimed. "Definitely dominant male material, that one!"

"Boys, this is my cub. I hope you don't mind us intruding on your breakfast, but he really wanted to meet you. I told him a couple of your adventure stories, and he couldn't resist coming over."

"Bonus!" said Ebb. "Name's Ebb. What's your name, little dude?"

"Sparky!" Sparky said proudly.

"I'm Flow and that's a cool handle you got happenin' there, partner!" Flow said. "I can tell it fits you. You will go far with a handle like that!"

"My mom and I are going fishing. My mom is teaching me how to fish and where all the good fishing spots are in Mouse Creek. She is a very smart mom." Sparky smiled and looked up at his mom.

"You got that one right, little dude." Ebb winked and nodded at Sparky. "She is the greatest fisher bear in the area. Everyone knows Lucy is the Queen of the Khutzeymateen."

"Yup, Sparkmister!" Flow continued. "We always love to follow Lulu around when we are in the area. If we do, dinner is pretty much assured."

"I am going to be a great fisher bear just like my mom when I grow up," Sparky puffed his furry little chest out. "I am going to catch you two a big fish right now!"

"Bonus for us, lil' buddy. Twice as much fish to pick at! Go get 'em, Sparkmister!" Ebb prompted.

"Dive deep!" Flow encouraged.

Sparky and Lucy walked down to the edge of the creek.

Sparky looked nervously at the fast-flowing deep cold water bubbling and boiling over the boulders. Watching the moving water made him feel a bit dizzy. He found a spot that had a small pool where he could see salmon milling around, waiting to make their move upstream.

"Okay, Mom. This is the spot." He swallowed hard.

"Now remember, Sparky, not too big. Once it is in your mouth, tighten your jaws, and when you are underwater, breathe out through your nose," Lucy encouraged.

"Right, Mom! I've got it!" he said enthusiastically. Very slowly and carefully he waded out into the creek.

"Good luck, my little love bug! Mom will be right here eating grass if you need me. Have fun!"

"Go, Sparkmister!" the crow brothers yelled from their salmon.

"Okay," Sparky reviewed. "Not to big, bite hard, and breathe out."

He peered at the water intently as a chorus of comments came from his friends onshore.

"Good luck, good luck, good luck," said all the gulls.

"Jeez, Lucy! If the cub's gonna get wet, he might as well get a big one! Go big, Sparks!" Westy encouraged.

"Westy, he has to start small," Lucy said patiently to the weasel.

From a large spruce on the edge of the forest, Cliff's voice squeaked, "Mica! Sparky is trying to catch a fish all by himself! He could ... you know do that ... *d* ... thing! Get ready to save him!" Cliff worriedly chirped as he hung off the end of his branch to watch Sparky.

"Cliff! Stop being such a drama squirrel! The cub's fine. Now eat another cone and relax. You look gaunt and starving. Ha ha," Mica sarcastically said from his branch in the same tree.

"Oooo! I'd show you if I was not so concerned for Sparky!" Cliff threatened.

Sparky was so focused on catching a fish that he didn't hear all his friends cheering him on. He tried to see the size of the fish through the rushing water.

"There, that looks like a small one," he whispered, plunged his head into the water, and then quickly came up coughing. Lucy looked up from her grass eating and calmly said, "Remember to breathe out, honey."

"*Achoo! Achoo! Aaaachoo!*" Sparky sneezed the water out of his nose.

"Hey, kazoo-tight, little buddy!!!" came a chorus from the crows. "Go get those fish, tiger!"

"Zoomtight, zoomtight, zoomtight!" said the gulls.

"*Ah jeez!*" Westy said as he nervously clutched his paws into the sand. "Sparky! Careful, cubby!

"See! I told you, Mica! I can't look!" Cliff turned away.

"Oh, Cliff, stuff a cone in it!" Mica chirped. "Go, Sparky!"

Sparky looked at the water with great determination. "I will catch the next fish!" he whispered to himself.

Then he spotted a salmon and lined up for the catch. He plunged his tiny face into the icy water, but this time, he remembered to breathe out. Water filled his ears, but the only thing he felt was his teeth around the fish. He tightened his grip so it did not get away. The fish was huge, and Sparky struggled to hold on and bring his head above the water for a breath. He inched his way out of the creek with the salmon in his mouth. He battled the resisting fish the whole way. The huge salmon tried to escape, flipping its body up and down so hard that Sparky was almost pulled over into the water by the massive fish. Sparky dug his bear claws into the mud and pulled up with all his might to keep his head above the water.

"He's got a big one!" the crow brothers yelled together.

Everyone onshore, except Cliff, watched and cheered Sparky on.

"Come on, baby bear! Come on, baby bear!" they all chanted.

With great effort, Sparky backed out of the water and onto shore. Both the head and tail of the salmon dragged on the shore as it hung limp in the cub's mouth. Slowly he struggled toward the crows, proudly carrying the huge salmon.

When he reached them, Sparky dropped the salmon and stood looking at the fish in disbelief. "I did it!" he whispered. "I did it!" he yelled.

"You sure did, young fellow!" Ebb cheered.

"Congrats, lil' dude! You are now officially a great fisher bear!" Flow said.

Lucy came over and gave Sparky a big lick across his cheek.

"Way to go, son!" she said very proudly. "I love you!"

"Yea, Sparky! Yea, Sparky! Yea, Sparky!" the gulls cheered in chorus and then continued their other chorus of "Egg, egg, egg here, and here."

"Jeez! That's a monster! I knew the cubbo would go for a big one! Way to fish, Sparks!" Westy said proudly.

"Can I look yet? Is he safe?" Cliff said nervously.

"Oh for gnat's sake, Cliff! We've all moved on to other things already!"

"I missed it! I missed Sparky's first fish! Oh no!" Cliff said disappointedly, then he looked at Mica and whined. "Why didn't you tell me he caught a fish?"

Mica rolled his eyes and just continued to eat his spruce cone.

Sparky looked down at his fish and then at Ebb and Flow.

"The first fish I caught is for you, my new friends," Sparky said proudly with a smiled.

"Oh no, little fellow, you have to eat your first fish, not us. You and Lucy can share it, then we will have the leftovers," Ebb smiled.

"We insist," piped up Flow.

"Mom?"

"Honey, you just caught a whooper. There is more than enough for us all, Westy included," Lucy said as she ripped the fish into five pieces and tossed them all a chunk.

"What about Mica and Cliff and the gulls, Mom?" Sparky asked with concern.

"Squirrels don't eat fish, and the gulls are to busy bobbing for eggs to want fish. It's all right, honey. Everyone has more than enough food," Lucy reassured her cub.

"Okay then, let's eat!" Sparky yelled. "Sharing is truly the best thing on the entire planet!"

Chapter 28:
The Faces in the Mountain

Long, low shadows, short sunups, and fewer salmon in the creek made Sparky and Lucy aware that hibernation time was coming soon. They lay in the soft cuddly moss on the edge of the forest near Mouse Creek. Sunshine warmed Sparky's tiny pudgy body as he snuggled in closer to Lucy's tummy and rolled onto his back with his legs in the air. Out of the corner of his eye, he saw the cliff that looked like smooth skin faces.

"Mom, can you please tell me about the faces in the mountain?" He flopped over on his side, laid his wee head on her big furry soft paw, and gazed up at the faces etched in stone.

"Well, my special love," Lucy began, "the legend has been passed down through many generations of our ancestors. There was a time when Waipo was much younger and only our brother and sister species joined us to inhabit Waipo."

"You mean only bears were on Waipo?" Sparky asked.

"Oh no, my Sparks. All that had fur, feather, fin, scale, and shell shared Waipo along with those that ate light. Everything lived in peace and harmony. There was an unspoken word on Waipo that all of her species shared and cared for the planet. There was peace, trust, and respect for Waipo and each other. Life and the planet were a gift from universe. Waipo was lent to all species by Universe so that all of us here could experience the gift of life. All species knew that Universe ruled all life. Every species on Waipo knew that in order for all to live, some must give their lives, but all understood that in order for life to continue on Waipo, greed would never become a spoken word. Harmony reverberated over Waipo, and all on Waipo lived together and took only what was needed to survive and no more than that. All species survived for thousands of years in balance. Every species formed the tight circle of life that kept Waipo healthy and strong. Every species respected the universal rules of survival."

Sparky thought for a moment. "Mom, what is greed?"

Lucy looked very seriously at Sparky. "Greed is if we took more fish than we really need and left none for other animals. Greed is if we ate every bit of sedge grass possible, even if we were not hungry, just so others creatures would not have the sedge for food and homes. Greed is if we ate every scrap of food and killed off all the creatures just so we could have Waipo to ourselves, for our use only. Greed causes the imbalance of all that Waipo and Universe have balanced for millions of years. Every destruction of greed causes loneliness and emptiness."

Sparky sat up and looked at Lucy. "Mom, greed is a horrible thing. Why would anyone want it?"

"Sparky, sometimes creatures become weak and lose control of themselves. Then greed sets in. It is such a negative thing that nothing good ever comes of it."

Sparky looked at Lucy with a great question. "Mom, the smooth skins don't have fur, feather, fins, scales, or shells!" he exclaimed. "Do they eat light? Weren't they part of Waipo?"

"It is very true, Sparky. They don't look like the rest of us on Waipo. But let me continue and I will explain everything. You are a very observant, smart cub," she smiled. "Now snuggle in and enjoy the sun while I tell you the legend of the faces."

Sparky licked his mom's cheek and lay back down on her paw.

"I love you, Mom," he sighed.

Lucy nuzzled his tummy with her long nose as he giggled, "I love you too, Sparks. Now where were we? Ah yes, the rules of survival on Waipo and in Universe." She cleared her throat. "Respect for Waipo was the most important rule of all inhabitants because without a healthy Waipo, none would survive. Balance was another rule. Universe had all species balanced over every landmass on Waipo so that harmony would prevail. There were just enough of all forms of life, and they were strategically dispersed over the planet so that the population balance would be controlled and all species would live and share a healthy planet and Waipo would enjoy perpetual life and give perpetual life to all species."

"Waipo is really important to us all isn't she, Mom?" Sparky whispered as he intently listened to Lucy's every word.

"Yes, Sparky. Waipo is all species's only home. It does not matter if we are here in the Khutzeymateen or our koala brothers and sisters are in Australia. Waipo is our universal home. Everything that we do to our water, our land, or our air does not only affect us, but it affects all life on Waipo. You see, Sparky, Waipo knows no boundaries. She only knows balance, and she is only trying to stay alive so that we all may live in peace, health, and balance. Every species that is removed will affect the survival of Waipo and us all. This is where the smooth skins and the faces in the mountain come in.

"Every landmass on Waipo had its own breed of smooth skins that fit in like every other species. Most lived in synergy with the laws of Universe, but the smooth skins, particularly the males, always seemed to be discontent with just being on Waipo. They seemed to always want more and would fight and kill to get it. The female smooth skins would temper the males' aggression, but they could only achieve this to a point. As in most species, the female is the bearer and main nurturer of the species. She is the one who struggles to maintain balance so that all may survive. But sometimes, there is only so much that can be done, and then things get out of control."

Sparky looked at his mother questioningly.

"You will understand as I tell the story, Sparks," she reassured him and then continued. "We are not sure where the first smooth skins on our landmass came from, but they lived in peace with all species and lived by the laws of the circle of life set by Universe to be lived by on Waipo. That is until three of the smooth skins did the unspeakable."

Sparky's eyes grew very large, and he looked at Lucy. "What happened, Mom?"

"On Waipo, our great ancestors were revered as sacred beings. No other creature would take the life of a grizzly for we were, and still are, the indicator of all life on Waipo," Lucy explained.

"Really!" Sparky exclaimed.

"Yes, Sparky. If our species remains healthy on Waipo, every other species will live and be healthy."

"Wow! We are important!" Sparky smiled and pushed his furry little chest out.

"Yes, we are important, but let's stay humble. Remember only the positive, humble, good, will survive, young bear," Lucy cautioned. "Now deflate your furry chest and listen to the wisdom." She gently nudged Sparky's tummy with her long nose.

Sparky fell over giggling. "Okay, Mom. I will always remember that. Now please tell me more of the story."

"As I said, the unspoken laws of Universe and Waipo state that the negatives like greed, dishonesty, violence, and aggression shall never enter the thoughts of any species on Waipo. This was the only way for all to survive in peace and harmony. Those three smooth skins"—Lucy pointed at the faces in the mountain with her nose—"broke this vow."

"What did they do?" Sparky questioned.

"Well, Sparky, the Khutzeymateen Valley has always been a sacred home for our kin and all other species that live here. It is one of the extremely powerful valleys on Waipo, and all species love this valley. It was a valley that the smooth skins called sacred. Their word *Khutzeymateen* has two meanings: place where seal meets bear and place where long inlet joins steep mountains. They feared and respected the valley and all creatures that lived here, especially our ancestors. The smooth skins knew we were more powerful and stronger than them in our sacred land. They knew the valley, Waipo, Universe, and Taku would protect us and all other species that dwelled here. No harm would come to any species, including the smooth skins, just as long as all lived by the rules of respect and balance."

"Then what happened, Mom?" Sparky's eyes were huge with anticipation.

"Many hundreds or years ago," Lucy continued, "three smooth skins decided to break the laws of Universe to prove their own strength and try to gain power over all the land. The three were great warriors who were trusted and respected by all smooth skins over a vast expanse of land. It is thought that an evil force entered the weakened mind of one of the smooth skins, and he then convinced the other two to follow his plan. The three smooth skins let all the different negative energies enter their bodies—greed, selfishness, hate, dishonesty, anger, deceit, and violence." She paused and looked at Sparky. "Remember to always stay in the positive side in life. Love, happiness, honesty, kindness, generosity, sharing, and good will to all species will let you live a much happier, content, and complete life. Be a good bear to everyone and everything, and you will be well-loved and respected. You will never have to be dishonest to cover up hurtful things you have done."

"I will always remember that, Mom. I know it is true because when I saved that butterfly from the river the other day, it felt really good. Especially when he dried off and flew onto my nose to say thanks and then flew away. I felt like I had done something very important." Sparky sighed. "It feels wonderful to be good and kind."

Lucy smiled at Sparky and licked his cheek. "That is the best way to live, Sparks. If you are good, Universe and Waipo smile on you always. And the rest of the story will prove this. The three went to their clan leaders and told them they would go out on a hunting expedition to bring home deer and moose to the clan for winter. They were supplied with a canoe, much food and warm clothing, and many spears to hunt the creatures. After a big celebration and feast to bring them lots of luck, they headed off with the blessing of their clan. They paddled off down the river, but instead of going to their traditional hunting grounds on the Skeena River, they took a fork of the river and paddled toward the sacred Khutzeymateen River Valley."

"Uh-oh!" Sparky exclaimed. "I may be a baby bear, but I can tell this means trouble!"

"You are right, Sparks. Uh-oh is right! The three smooth skins entered the valley and paddled up the inlet to the estuary where many of our ancestors roamed freely in peace. They went onshore and fashioned a hole in the soft ground of the estuary. Two dug while one watched for our brothers. When the hole was very deep, the smooth skins put sharp spears in the bottom that pointed to the sky, and then they covered the hole with a mat of sedge grass. They planned to kill a grizzly bear and take the body back to their clan to prove their strength and power over Universe, Waipo, and the great grizzly spirit Taku.

"They decided this deed would prove them superior beings. They thought the clan would fear them because of their incredible victory over the powerful forces of Universe. With this new power, they could control their clan, as well as others, and all the land. However, they did not realize the consequences of their actions. Not only the punishment they would receive, but also the shift in respect for continuity between all species and smooth skins on the planet. They did not understand that they would shift the entire balance to spiral out of control."

"That's disgusting!" Sparky said in shock and disbelief. "How could anyone be that selfish, stupid, and cruel?"

"Once the hole was covered, the men left for the night in their canoe and planned to come back in the morning for the body. They decided to sleep in the middle of the inlet where they thought they would be safe from the great grizzly. In the middle of the night, the smooth skins were awakened by the flash of lightning and the roar of thunder that filled the sky all around them. The clouds swirled and stirred in chaotic circles over the three smooth skins' heads. Panic filled their bodies as the chaos engulfed them. Then suddenly Universe opened, and a blinding light broke the night sky in two, and the great lightning bird dove from the heavens and hovered over the canoe. A voice echoed through the valley as the three smooth skins huddled together in fear. It was the voice of the great grizzly spirit Taku, and the voice boomed as it spoke in the smooth skins' tongue."

Sparky's eyes widened with fear, and he moved in closer to Lucy and listened intently. Lucy spoke in a deep loud voice as if she were Taku.

"'You have broken all the rules of Universe and Waipo,' Taku thundered. 'Tonight, you three smooth skins have killed a scared grizzly bear—the first to be killed by a smooth skin. This act is unspeakable, and you will now be punished for your deceit, greed, and selfishness. You will now face the penalty for breaking the unspoken laws of Universe. You have killed a great one, and you have killed to satisfy your own egos and negative emotions. It is well-known throughout Universe that the great grizzly is one of the sacred creatures of the Waipo. You shall also be punished for the second law you have broken. Universe says that to kill for any other reason than to survive is murder. For these broken laws you must pay with your lives, and you will be set in stone for all others to see that the laws of Universe and Waipo are much stronger and more powerful than all species. For Universe and Waipo will always have the last say in all that occurs. Universe in the end shall, for all time, rule and survive.'"

Lucy paused and snuggled Sparky who was wide-eyed, trembling, and speechless.

"Suddenly the lightening bird dove toward the canoe, and as it neared, lightning bolts shot from its talons and the boat burst into flames. At that moment, the souls of the three evil

199

smooth skins were hurled at the mountain, and their faces were etched into the stone. Then their spirits evaporated into thin air. The lightning bird flew to the bright light in the heavens, and Universe again closed and all was calm."

Both bears looked up at the faces etched in stone.

"Wow!" Sparky said with fear. "There is so much more going on than we know." He sat up and looked at Lucy. "Mom, what is Universe? Who are the smooth skins? What is the lightning bird? Do I have to worry about being punished by Universe because I have eaten too many fish? I mean I have been killing another species, like all the clams, mussels, and barnacles?"

Lucy nuzzled her cub. "Now calm down, honey. There are many questions that do not need to be answered. Things just are. The main thing that we all must remember is that if we take care of Universe and Waipo, they will take care of us. It is when we do not respect that punishment and hardships occur."

Lucy looked at Sparky. "It is the little things that count. Like when we walk in the footsteps of our ancestors through the moss. Not only does it make us proud and comfortable, but we are also respecting Waipo by not trampling all her beautiful greenery flat. And do not worry about the salmon. We take only what we need to survive. There are many salmon for all just so long as greed does not occur. The three smooth skins that broke the creed did not need to kill the grizzly, and that is why they were punished. Everything is very delicately balanced in Universe and on Waipo so that all may survive. Unfortunately the smooth skins are causing countless upheavals on Waipo. There is nothing we can do to stop this, but Universe and Waipo are becoming extremely angry as their patience is tested. The geese and birds have told me much chaos and turmoil is occurring on Waipo as her and Universe's tempers flare at the smooth ones."

"What is happening, Mom? I am scared." Sparky whispered.

"Now, Sparks," Lucy cooed and snuggled her cub. "There is no reason to be frightened. We are safe. Waipo is doing what she has always done, but with more ferocity."

"Like what, Mom?" Sparky questioned.

"Well, the geese say her temper is heating up and the planet is getting hotter. As a result, hurricanes, rainstorms, and other weather events are becoming more severe. Fires, floods, volcanoes, and earthquakes are occurring more frequently. The smooth skins think they are causing these problems, and they are, but not in the way they think. You see, Universe and Waipo are being very patient with the smooth skins as they test the boundaries of the laws of Universe, but the smooth skins are pushing too far. Universe and Waipo are giving the smooth skins much warning before they really lose their tempers. They are hoping that the baby smooth skins will begin to take better care of Waipo as they grow and start to turn the degradation of Waipo around so all species left can survive.

"Why are the smooth skins so silly, Mom?" Sparky questioned. "I mean the tall one and the short one seem to love and respect us and Universe and Waipo. I thought all smooth skins would be the same."

"Unfortunately not, Sparky. You see, in smooth skins, the delicate balance of feminine and masculine has been severely altered. In their species, the female has been removed almost completely from important global decisions. This shift has altered the delicate balance necessary for all to survive. Most smooth skins on Waipo have let all the negative emotions control them, especially greed. This makes them forget the importance of keeping Waipo healthy, so we can all survive and be happy. Smooth skins have many lessons to learn. The first and most obvious lesson that they will just not see is that they must share the planet with other species, not just fill Waipo with their own species. And they must learn that they have to give, not just take. They must also learn the meaning of the phrase, 'It is not just about me, it is about we.'"

Lucy stood up and stretched then mischievously looked at Sparky and said, "Now, young bear! It is time for lunch! And since there are no more salmon spawning and we have eaten most of the salmon carcasses off the shore, I will race you to the beach for a clam feast!" She took off running.

"Mom!" Sparky giggled and bolted after her. "That's not fair!"

Chapter 29:
The Long Sleep

Sparky yawned and stretched as Lucy nudged him along the path. All the plants of the rain forest were tattered, and most of their leaves had fallen to the ground. Piles of squirrel stashed pine cones spilled out of holes where bulging tree roots had made hallows in the soft red cedar-colored earth. Dried mushrooms, berries, and roots hung in the tree branches like Mother Nature's Christmas decorations—winter snacks for the birds and rodents who had hidden them. A heavy blanket of snow already covered the mountain peaks surrounding the valley. Ice had formed on the puddles of rainwater that had fallen the day before.

As they walked along, Sparky and Lucy suddenly heard yelling coming from above them in a big old spruce tree and more coming from a separate stump near the base of the tree.

"Mom, stop for a minute," Sparky yawned again and then giggled. "Listen. They even fight when they're hibernating!"

"Stop snoring!" Cliff ordered.

"No! You stop snoring!" Mica screeched back.

"Could you inhale a spruce cone then, to plug up that big rumbling cavern!"

"No, 'cause you ate them all, lard breath!"

"I'll show you!"

"Jeez! Wouldja two stuff a seal in it! Da weasel's tryin' ta get his winter beauty sleep! Jeez! The best part of hibernating is not having ta listen ta you two!" Westy hollered from the stump below.

"Let's say good winter to our friends before they fall asleep again," Lucy suggested. "Ready? On *clam*, we'll say 'Good winter, Mica, Cliff, and Westy.' Okay?"

"Yes, Mom, I'm ready."

On *clam*, both bears chimed their winter wish to their friends.

"Good winter, bear friends!" three squeaky voices yelled back.

"I am so tired," Sparky moaned as his butterball body jiggled its way down the trail. Waves of fat washed up and down his back with every step.

"All the excitement of fall and the salmon season has caught up with you, honey. Now it is time to say good winter to all our friends and head into the den for our long winter nap." Lucy nuzzled her cub down the trail. "It's not much farther now, my sweet cub. You can make it."

"Can you carry me, Mom?" Sparky whined. "I am so tired."

"You are much too big to carry, so just keep on walking, sweetie. We are almost there. Look, there is Noni!"

"Good winter, Noni," Sparky sighed and yawned again. Wearily, he tried to move his sleepy head to see all his forest friends. "See you in the spring. Good winter, animal and bird friends and all my plant friends. Have a great winter"—*yawn*— "han I will see you in the—" *yawn* "—ss ... ppp ... rringg."

"Okay, honey, here is our big old Spruce tree and our den. Now let's get you inside before you fall over right here."

"Oh, hold on, Mom!" Suddenly Sparky's tired little eyes grew large with concern. "I forgot to thank all the salmon for giving their lives so I could survive. And thank you, Universe and Waipo, for giving me life." Sparky looked sleepily up at the sky. "Good winter, Universe. Please take care of all my friends, and I will see you and them all in the spring."

As Sparky and Lucy entered their cozy den and snuggled in together for their long winter sleep, Sparky sleepily looked at Lucy and said, "Good winter, Mom. Thank you for teaching me all about Universe, Waipo, and Taku. Thank you for being my mom and giving me life and keeping me safe. I love you."

"Sweet dreams up until the spring. I love you too, my little King of the Khutzeymateen," Lucy said then she snuggled Sparky in close to her.

"Good winter, Mom," Sparky whispered.

And they fell into their long winter sleep.

Afterword

For now, Sparky and Lucy are safely snuggled in their cozy den until spring.

The legacy of the great grizzly bear and all the creatures in the Khutzeymateen Valley will continue for thousands of years to come if the Khutzeymateen Grizzly Bear Sanctuary remains protected for all time.

Appendix—Lucy Says

More on Big Beautiful Waipo

"Mom. What is a planet?"

"Waipo is one of nine planets in our solar system that is part of Universe. A planet is a round sphere composed of minerals. It is on a set orbit around the nearest star, in our case the sun. Waipo travels at approximately 28.5 kilometers a second around the sun."

"That is enough to make your head spin!" Sparky exclaimed and shook his tiny bear head.

"All nine planets are held in their orbit around the sun by gravity. Waipo is the third planet from the sun. The sun is a star in the Milky Way Galaxy, which is composed of a lose spiral of 100,000 million stars."

"Whoa! That is a lot of stars!" Sparky said with big eyes.

"Yes, it is, and they are spread out over a diameter of approximately 100,000 light-years. Our sun is located approximately 30,000 light-years from the centre of the Milky Way Galaxy. The whole galaxy rotates, and it takes the sun 225 million years to make one revolution around the center of the Milky Way. "

"Light-years?" Sparky wrinkled his nose up. "What is that, Mom?"

"A light-year is the distance light can travel in one year, at about three hundred thousand kilometers per second."

"Wow! That is a long way, Mom! And the Milky Way Galaxy is huge!"

"Yes it is, Sparky, and do you know what else?"

"What?" Sparky questioned eagerly.

"At least a hundred million other galaxies have been estimated to exist in Universe and probably many, many more. So there may be the probability of life on other planets. And that means that somewhere out in the sky, another Sparky could be lying on his mom's chest just waiting to be ... tickled!" Lucy said and began to rub her paws up and down Sparky's ribs.

He giggled and squirmed as she continued.

"Mom! Stop!" he wriggled and pleaded. "Tell me more about Universe! What is it and where did it come from?"

"No one really knows what Universe is and where it came from, but I can tell you a myth about Universe that was handed down from my ancestors."

"Oh boy!" Sparky was excited. "I love your stories!"

Lucy smiled. "But I would rather tickle you!" She gave him one more rub on the ribs and then thought for a moment. "Let's see. Okay. It is said that at one time Universe was a dark empty abyss that harbored and protected the great spirits of the animal and plant kingdom who dwelled in silent darkness in a tiny corner of the large black void. All was quiet and calm, but after millions of years, Universe became tired and unhappy with the darkness. Universe grew weary and began to sleep for long periods of time. Concern grew among the spirits that their keeper would soon die if something was not done. While Universe slept, all of the spirits were summoned to meet and come up with a solution to cheer Universe back into happiness. They decided that each of them would be given part of the blackness to create a masterpiece of cosmic art to honor and cheer up Universe, but one section of the darkness would be set aside for Universe to create a masterpiece. Each spirit skillfully began to decorate the void with stars, moons, planets, galaxies, comets, and a variety of other cosmic wonders. Carefully, the spirits mixed an array of minerals and gases and sculpted and painted beauty and light and peace and chaos onto the black empty canvas of Universe.

"When Universe awoke and looked at the beauty all around, joy soared so high in Universe that the stars and suns began to glow so brightly that the entire masterpiece of Universe was visible to all of the spirits, and they were proud of their accomplishment and joyous that Universe was again happy.

"Suddenly Universe stared at the empty black void in the cosmic masterpiece and asked why it was not filled with wonder. The great spirits then explained that this special place was for Universe to create a work of brilliance. Universe looked at all the spirits and was so grateful to them that Universe said, 'To honor all of you, my dear friends, I will create the perfect galaxy, and in it there will be a solar system intricately balanced in every way. In this solar system, I will honor you with the perfect planet, and here you can all place images of yourselves that will live in peace and harmony for all time. You will always have enough food, water, and shelter, and life for you all will be everlasting if you take care of your planet and respect each other for eternity.'"

Sparky suddenly sat up and said. "I know! That galaxy was the Milky Way and the special planet is Waipo!"

"That's right, Sparks! How about I tell you what is inside Waipo?"

"Okay, Mom," Sparky said. He snuggled back onto his mom's chest and dreamily looked up at the stars.

"Waipo is a beautiful planet on the surface, but much more of her lies below our paws. Very hot, much more. The inner core of our planet is molten metal about 1,200 kilometers wide. The next layer, the outer core, is 4,700 kilometers thick. It consists of mostly molten iron and nickel. The mantle layer is approximately 3,500 kilometers thick and is composed primarily of peridotite, a coarse granular igneous rock. Igneous rock is produced under intense heat, or rock formed from crystallized molten magma, or volcanic activity. Finally you come out to the surface of the sphere, or the crust, where we live. Waipo's crust varies in depth anywhere from five kilometers under the oceans to fifty kilometers on the continental landmasses."

"Wow! That is not very thick! Are you sure we won't fall through?" Sparky said with great concern.

"Yes, honey," Lucy smiled. "We will be fine. Do you realize that everything on Waipo is always moving and changing? Nothing is ever really static."

Sparky looked at Lucy. "What do you mean, Mom?" he questioned.

"It is believed that convection currents occurring in the mantle layer of Waipo cause the crust layer to continuously move and shift. Apparently at one time, all the landmasses above the sea level on Waipo were joined together to form one huge land area that floated around the planet."

"Really?" Sparky exclaimed with big eyes.

"Yes, honey. One hundred and eighty million years ago, the single landmass on Waipo called Pangaea began to break apart into two huge continents called Laurasia in the northern hemisphere and Gondwanaland in the southern hemisphere. Over millions of years, the land continued to shift to form the present-day continents. But don't forget, honey, the crust layer is under the ocean as well, so there is much more movement and shifting going on than we realize. Waipo's crust is made up of many different plates, or pieces of land. During this constant shifting, Waipo's plates pushed on one another. The weaker plates began to buckle and push upward, and over millions of years, the mountains formed."

"Wow! That is so cool!" Sparky sat up and looked at Lucy. "Do you mean that at one time the tops of the mountains could have been under the ocean?"

"Yes, Sparky. There are things called fossils which prove this fact. Fossils are ancient sea animals that were preserved in the rock as layers of sediment, such as sand, piled up on top of them. Gradually these sea creatures were compressed with the sediment, and the whole thing became the rock that is found on some mountains and other land formations on the continents." Lucy thought for a second and then looked at Sparky. "Honey, with all the movement of the plates on the planet, do you know where grizzly bears originated?"

Sparky looked at her questioningly and guessed. "North America?"

"Good guess, honey, but our ancient ancestors made their way across a land bridge that millions of years ago joined Asia and North America. Grizzlies came across from Asia and gradually spread across North America, as far south as Mexico and out east to the prairies. At one time we ruled much of the land, but the smooth skins killed all the prairie grizzlies and most of the southern grizzlies, and now our habitat in North America is very limited. We are still able to survive in British Columbia, Yukon, Alaska, and a very small part of Alberta, Montana, and Wyoming, but our habitat is still shrinking because of the smooth skins encroaching on our territory. Then they get upset and kill us because we want to find homes and food where they have taken our land."

"That is scary, Mom. I really hope the new smooth skin cubs on Waipo will help all the fur, fin, feather, shell, and light eaters in the future so we can survive and live a long happy and healthy life on Waipo."

Chapter Questions and Research Questions

Chapter 1: Spring Songs and Tickles

1. Why were Lucy and Sparky sleeping?
2. Where were they sleeping?
3. How much does Lucy weigh?
4. When was Sparky born?
5. What sound do bear cubs make when they are drinking bear milk?

Chapter 2: Noni the Giant

1. What is a bear trail?
2. How are bear trails made?
3. Why do bears use bear trails to walk on?
4. How many pounds did Sparky weigh when he came out of the den?
5. What is the name of the valley in British Columbia where Sparky and Lucy live?
6. Research question: what is the significance of this valley? Hint: it's the only one in Canada.
7. What is Noni?
8. How old is Noni?
9. Research question: Three of the many species of trees that grow on the west coast of British Columbia are Sitka spruce,

Western red cedar, and Hemlock. Which one of these trees is the most tolerant of saline water? Which tree has a natural resin that helps prevent rot?

Chapter 3: Flying Fur Balls

1. What kind of animals are Mica and Cliff?
2. What kind of tree was Lucy's favorite scratch tree?
3. Why was Lucy doing the squishy dance?
4. Why do bears rub on trees?

Chapter 4: Weasel-Breath Westy

1. Where was Lucy's summer den?
2. What kind of gulls live at Mouse Creek?
3. What kind of animal is Westy?
4. What was the gull eating and swallowing?

Chapter 5: Swimming Lessons

1. How long are bear cub claws?
2. Do bear cubs like to climb on logs?
3. Do all bear cubs like to swim?
4. What did Sparky do to show us that bears can be sarcastic to their mothers?
5. Why do bears have to learn to swim?
6. If a cub does not know how to swim, how does a mother bear get the cub safely across water?

Chapter 6: Big Beautiful Waipo (see chapter and appendix section for these answers)

1. What continent did grizzly bears originate?
2. How big was the grizzly bears' original North American territory?
3. What is the present size of their territory?
4. How many planets are in our solar system?
5. What is the sun, and what is it made of?

6. How fast does the earth travel around the sun?
7. What holds the planets in place as they rotate around the sun?
8. What is the name of the galaxy the sun is part of?
9. How many stars are in this galaxy?
10. What are light-years?
11. How many light-years is the sun from the center of the Milky Way?
12. How many years does it take the sun to make one rotation around the center of the Milky Way?
13. What is the inner core of Earth made of, and how wide is it?
14. What is the name of the outer surface of the earth, and how thick is it?
15. What was the original landmass on Earth, and how many years ago did it exist?
16. What were the names of the two landmasses that formed when the original split in two? Which hemisphere of the earth did each one shift to?
17. What kind of animal is Skite?
18. Explain how she finds food.
19. What other animal finds food this way?
20. What does nocturnal mean?
21. What other animals are nocturnal?

Chapter 7: Boris the Rat

1. What is meant by the term *circle of life*?
2. Why is it important for all species on the planet to stay well balanced and healthy?
3. What two things could happen if species start becoming extinct?
4. Is it important to respect and take care of all species on earth? Why?
5. Are ants important to our planet's survival?
6. Approximately how many ants are there on the planet?
7. What are three things ants do to help the planet survive?

8. Research question: Are all the oceans around the globe interconnected? If pollution is placed into the Pacific Ocean, could the currents and tides eventually carry it to the Atlantic Ocean? Are the oceans important to our survival and the survival of all life on the planet?
9. Discussion question: Do you think animals have feelings like humans? Do you think they get happy, sad, depressed, lonely, afraid, etc.?
10. Should products we use as humans be tested on animals?

Chapter 8: The Flying Sparky

1. Why do bears float better in saltwater than freshwater?
2. Why is ocean and sea water salty?
3. Which is heavier, saltwater or freshwater? Why?
4. Research question: Is there a higher concentration of salt in the ocean closer to the poles or closer to the equator. Why? Would you float better at the equator? Why?
5. How is it thought that polar bears originated?
6. What are three differences between grizzly and polar bear feet?
7. What is the difference between grizzly bear and polar bear hibernation?
8. What are differences between grizzly bear and polar bear teeth?

Chapter 9: Squiggles in My Mouth

1. What four new foods was Sparky apprehensive to try?
2. What eight-legged land creatures are in the same family as crabs?
3. Why do bears dig day dens?
4. Research question: What are the shells on shellfish and crabs called? What is the equivalent in humans?
5. What is the main predator of grizzly bears cubs?

Chapter 10: The Magic of Feather and Fur

1. What was the smallest bird Sparky saw when he woke up?
2. What kind of bird dove for fish?
3. Name five mammals that eat salmon.
4. What is another name for a salmon egg nest?
5. How much do baby bears weigh when they are born?
6. Do bears have fur when they are born?
7. How long does it take before a baby bear can see?
8. What is the maximum a full-grown dominant male grizzly bear will weigh?

Chapter 11: Cats and Dogs

1. What kind of animal is Calvyn?
2. What was howling?

Chapter 12: Nibbly Bits

1. What makes plants green?
2. What do plants eat?
3. How much sedge grass will a full-grown grizzly bear eat in one day?
4. What are three reasons bears eat sedge grass?
5. What do plants remove from the air, and what do they give off instead?
6. Which plants produce most of the earth's oxygen?
7. Are bears herbivores, carnivores, or omnivores?
8. Name three types of herbivores.
9. Name two types of omnivores.
10. Name one type of carnivore.
11. Explain the difference between the teeth of an herbivore and a carnivore. Explain the difference in the jaw movement of each.
12. What are the five species of salmon that live naturally in the North Pacific Ocean?
13. Approximately how many fish will an adult grizzly bear eat in one day?

14. Approximately how much weight will an adult grizzly bear put on in the fall?

Chapter 13: The Bears and the Bees

1. Why do male bears fight over female bears?
2. Can twins be completely different in appearance? Why?

Chapter 14: Sparky Meets Buffalo and Lefty

1. Why was Buffalo chasing Lefty?
2. Will male bears kill cubs? Why?
3. What are two kinds of sounds bears make?

Chapter 15: Nine-Headed Water Beetle

1. What was Sparky digging for when "the bug" came?
2. What bear skill did Sparky practice to try and chase off the humans?

Chapter 16: Slithery Snakes

1. What family are snakes in?
2. Are snakes cold- or warm-blooded? Explain why.
3. What are the only two areas of the world that snakes do not live?
4. What is the longest snake? How long?
5. What is the smallest snake? How long?
6. How do snakes move along the ground?
7. What shape is the snake's tongue? Why?
8. How do snakes get new clothing?
9. What are the two types of snakes, and how do each variety catch their food?
10. How do snakes eat?
11. How are baby snakes born?

Chapter 17: Hairy the Meddler

1. What kind of bird was making the loud knocking noise, and why didn't it get a headache?
2. Why was Hairy trying to be tough?
3. Why did Lucy stand a certain way?

Chapter 18: Mac and Croaker

1. What are Mac and Croaker?
2. Do some toads freeze solid? Research why and how.

Chapter 19: Swamp Monster

1. What kind of animal is Morse?

Chapter 20: Saved by the Pink Ones

1. What startled Lucy and Sparky to make them run?
2. Why was Sparky afraid to swim?
3. Do all bears know how to swim when they are born?

Chapter 21: Whale Tales

1. What creature did Sparky think were sea monsters?
2. Why was Lucy so excited to see them?
3. How long are humpback whales, and how much do they weigh?
4. How big are humpback whale babies when they are born?
5. Are humpbacks fish or mammals? Why?
6. What family are whales, dolphins, and porpoises in?
7. What are the two types of whales?
8. What is the difference between the two types of whales?
9. What do humpback whales have instead of teeth? What is this made of, and what do humans have that is made of the same thing?
10. What bear sense is the most keen?
11. What is the keenest sense on a whale?
12. How far can a whale voice travel in the ocean?

13. Discuss what echolocation is and how it works.
14. Research questions: what do scientists think the oil located in a sperm whales head is for, and how does this work?
15. What is the world's biggest whale? How long is it, and how much does it weigh? How big is the baby when it is born?
16. How long can the front flippers on a humpback whale grow?
17. What shape are the humpback whale tales? Are they all the same skin patterns?
18. What creatures do whales have growing on their bodies?
19. Do we have creatures growing on us?
20. Research question: what types of creatures grow on human bodies, and what benefit are they to our health and survival?
21. How many humpback whales are there on Earth?
22. Are they an endangered species? Why?
23. Research and/or discussion question: what can humans do to try and protect all species on the planet and the earth itself?

Chapter 22: I'll Starve!

1. What type of rock are the mountains in the Khutzeymateen made of?
2. Research question: What are the five main mountain ranges in British Columbia? Which is the oldest? Which is the newest? What mountain is the highest mountain in British Columbia, and which range is it in?
3. What type of tree loses its leaves in the fall, coniferous or deciduous?
4. What was Lucy looking for?

Chapter 23: Not Just Another Pretty Fish

1. What kind of fish did Lucy catch?
2. On average how big are these fish?
3. What is the biggest species of salmon?

4. How much do they weigh, and how long are they? What is the record weight of a Chinook salmon?
5. Research question: why could farming non-native fish have an effect on natural fish stocks and all animals that feed on natural salmon?
6. What is another name for a salmon nest?
7. During spawning season, what are the physical changes that occur in the salmon's appearance? Why do these changes occur?
8. Do salmon begin to decay when they are still alive? How and why does this happen?
9. How do salmon find their way back to their home river to spawn?
10. Do salmon have a good sense of smell?
11. How do salmon help the trees along the rivers and streams?
12. Research question: how can humans help to keep the oceans healthy and alive?

Chapter 24: Grampy Gimpy

1. What kind of a sound do female bears make to warn their cubs of danger?
2. How old was Grampy Gimpy?
3. Research questions: How long do bears live in the wild? How long in captivity? What would be some of the hazards that would kill a bear? Are grizzly bears at the top of the food chain? Why?

Chapter 25: Salmon Walking

1. Do bears eat grass during salmon season?
2. How many salmon were in Mouse Creek?
3. How many fish can an adult grizzly bear eat in one day?
4. Do bear cubs practice catching fish?

Chapter 26: Tricksters and Steak Bones

1. Does the grizzly's fur change color in the fall? If so, why does it get lighter or darker?
2. Do seagulls eat salmon eggs that are floating loosely in the rivers and creeks?
3. Do eagles mate for life?
4. What is another name for bald eagles and other predatory birds?
5. Are crows intelligent birds?

Chapter 27: Sparky's Big Catch

Discussion question: Grizzly bear cubs on the west coast of British Columbia spend two or three summers with their mothers. During this time, grizzly bear mothers appear to teach their cubs all the bear skills necessary for the cub's survival. The following is a list of some of the skills bears need to survive. Discuss whether you think the skills are taught to the cubs by their mothers or are the skills something the cub would know instinctively. If you like, you can compare how you think the bears might learn to how humans would learn the skill. The skills include:

- catching fish
- swimming
- eating grass
- knowing male bears are dangerous
- finding and eating berries
- eating roots and herbs to eliminate parasites from their systems in the fall
- digging day dens to sleep in for an afternoon nap
- finding the right spot to dig a hibernation den
- knowing when to hibernate
- digging for clams
- eating muscles and barnacles

Chapter 28: The Faces in the Mountain

1. Why were the three men trying to kill a grizzly bear?
2. What lessons can smooth skins learn from all other species on the planet?

Discussion and research questions:

1. What do you think humans (smooth skins) can do to help Earth (Waipo) survive so all species can live healthy lives and no creature is homeless or without food.
2. Research and discuss renewable and nonrenewable resources. How does the human population and/or over population affect both? How can we help to balance everything on the planet?
3. What can each of us do to make the planet healthier, both at home and on a global scale?

Chapter 29: The Long Sleep

1. Why was Sparky so tired?
2. What was hanging in the trees, and why were they there?
3. Why was Sparky so chubby? Was this good? Why?
4. How long do bears hibernate?
5. What part of Sparky's first year was your favorite?

Bibliography

Brockman, Frank. *Trees of North American*. New York. Golden Press, 1968.

Bryson, Bill. *A Short History of Nearly Everything*. Canada. Anchor Canada, a division of Random House, 2003.

Eder, Tamara. *Whales and other Marine Mammals of British Columbia and Alaska*. Edmonton, Alberta, Canada. Lone Pine Publishing, 2001.

Fertl, Reddy, and Stoops. *Bears*. New York, New York. Sterling Publishing Co. Inc., 2000.

Ford, Ellis, Balcomb. *Killer Whales*. Vancouver, British Columbia, Canada. UBC Press, 2000.

Harbo, Rick, M. *Whelks to Whales*. Madeira Park, British Columbia, Canada. Harbour Publishing, 1999.

Hawking, Stephen. *A Brief History of Time*. Broadway, New York. Bantam Books, 1998.

Hoyt, Erich. *Meeting the Whales*. Willowdale, Ontario. Firefly Books, 1991.

Kalman, Bobbie. *The Science of Living Things: What is a Plant*. New York, New York. Crabtree Publishing Company, 2000.

National Audubon Society Field Guide to:

- Mammals. New York. Knopf, 1980.
- North American Wildflowers. New York. Knopf, 2001.
- North American Reptiles and Amphibians. New York. Knopf, 1979.
- North American Trees. New York. Knopf, 1980.
- Western Birds. New York. McGraw-Hill Book Company, 1988.

National Geographic Field Guide to the Birds of North America. Washington, D.C.

National Geographic Society, 2002.

Peterson, Roger Tory. *A Field Guide to Western Birds.* Boston, Massachusetts. Houghton Mifflin Company, 1961.

Pojar and MacKinnon. *Plants of Coastal British Columbia.* Vancouver, B.C. Lone Pine Publishing, 1994.

Sagan, Carl. *Cosmos.* New York, New York. Ballantine Books, 1980.

Sept, J. Duane. *The Beachcomber's Guide to Seashore Life in the Pacific Northwest.* Madeira Park, British Columbia, Canada. Harbour Publishing, 1999.

Stirling, Ian. *Polar Bears.* Ann Arbor, Michigan. University of Michigan Press, 1988.

Weisman, Alan. *The World Without Us.* Toronto, Ontario, Canada. HarperCollins Publishers, 2007.